TIMEBLINK

A Novel

MJ MUMFORD

TIMEBLINK: A Novel

Cover by Elizabeth Mackey

First Printing, 2020

ISBN 978-1-7773362-1-9 (ebook)
ISBN 978-1-7773362-0-2 (paperback)
ISBN 978-1-7773362-2-6 (hardcover)

*In memory of my mother
Lorraine
My loudest cheerleader.*

Author's Note

Welcome to *TimeBlink*, a unique blend of time travel, psychological suspense, and impossible love, all under one cover.

Please note that the narrative explores situations that may trigger uncomfortable responses in some readers. I invite you to consult the **Content Guidance** page at mjmumford.com for more details.

Thank you for venturing into this genre-bending story. May your journey through its pages be as thrilling and unpredictable as time travel itself.

-MJ Mumford

Prologue

SEPTEMBER 27, 1999

A dozen brittle oak leaves tumbled across the field like a pack of angry goblins, scattering in all directions when they reached my feet. I swung one leg over my red Schwinn cruiser and let it clatter to the ground.

"Isla!" I shouted a third time. Only the howling wind answered back. It whistled past my ears, icy, accusatory. *You screwed up, kid*, it said.

My sister's matching blue Schwinn lay in the grass next to mine, the front wheel rotating languidly as if she'd just walked away. I stuck my foot out to stop the motion and glanced over the fence at Janelle's house in the waning afternoon light. Had Isla gone there? Then I remembered it was Monday and Janelle would be at her dad's while her mom worked the night shift at the hospital.

Janelle's wasn't the only darkened house on the block. The whole neighborhood had transformed into a bleak and blustery ghost town in the few minutes I'd been gone. Beyond the chain-link fence bordering the park, there was none of the usual after-work traffic; no cyclists or gangs of yelling kids. No barking dogs. No mothers calling their children home for dinner. At the park, even the graffitied Green Hut behind the

1

ball diamond gave off a deserted air, having been boarded up for the season a month ago. Long chains holding toddler swings clinked in the wind. The only sign of life when I arrived, in fact, had been the blue Volkswagen Beetle disappearing around the corner at the end of Birch Street, which would later become a pivotal detail of the day. One I should've paid more attention to at the time. Instead, I stood, zombielike, next to our bikes, gawking at the empty park, willing Isla to materialize in front of me. When she didn't, I pined for my mom. Or my dad. Anyone. Someone to rub my shoulder and reassure me that the dread building in my gut was unfounded, silly even. That there was a reasonable explanation for Isla's absence. My heart told me otherwise.

When my gaze came around to the rickety fence at the back of the park, I shuddered. Behind the fence was the reason Isla and I had come to Pembina Park in the first place: the Maroon Mansion, looming large in a grove of scraggly oak trees like a cloaked stranger whose face you could not see but whose menace hung heavy in the air. A scruffy crow sitting on the fence squawked twice before twirling off into the wind. I cupped one hand around my mouth calling Isla a final time, shocked by the shrill, panicked noise leaving my mouth.

Again, nothing.

Don't freak out. You've only been gone fifteen minutes.

Or a little longer. Eighteen, tops.

My attention turned to where I'd last seen my sister. Isla would never have abandoned our video camera—or her bike—without good reason. There they were, though, both of them; the camera still attached to the tripod, its lens wedged impossibly in the Schwinn's rear spokes. Isla's backpack sat upright and open on the other side of the park near a break in the fence. I imagined her crouching over it in her neon pink hoodie rummaging for notes from class with her long blond ponytail lashing about in the wind. I chuckled despite myself. We may have been identical on the outside, but even in my imagination, Isla was the neurotic one, making sure our video project followed the outline precisely. In my mind's eye she suddenly turned to me and frowned. Asked me why I'd taken so long at home. I looked down at my twisted, aching, *bulging* wrist curled into my chest and cursed for the first time in my life.

When I looked up, she was gone.

And in the months and years that followed, I'd never stopped wondering if my decision to leave her that day had been the entire reason she'd disappeared.

Not at all, my family had said.

Perhaps, alleged the newspapers.

Probably, whispered the cruel girls at school.

Definitely, said my heart.

Definitely.

Chapter One

Outside The Merryport Pub, sheets of sideways rain and gale-force winds pummelled the 100-year-old building, threatening to flood it or demolish it altogether. Swirling clusters of candy wrappers, twigs, and discarded coffee lids blew in on the heels of the few customers brave—or foolish—enough to be out on a night like this, transforming the pub's foyer into something resembling the Falmouth Landfill. Tumultuous weather systems were by no means unusual for our little west coast city, but it was the abrupt arrival of this one that had blindsided every citizen of Port Raven, especially the outdoorsy set, some of whom had been golfing in starched cotton shirts or enjoying drinks on seaside patios as recently as the previous weekend. Summer was a mere speck in my rearview mirror, and I couldn't have been happier.

I'd just returned from my break halfway through a typical Friday night shift. Normally my work gives me great pleasure, but my bum wrist had been plaguing me all night (as it does when the seasons change), and I wasn't sure how many more bottles of wine I could uncork before it seized up for good. Not only that, but two of my coworkers had conveniently called in "sick", leaving me, Tad and the two cooks out back to hold down the fort by ourselves. A blessing, really. The tips would've been dismal shared amongst the whole team. Just a few more hours and I'd be snuggled up on my sofa with a hot cup of Earl Grey watching my recorded late-night TV shows. Apart from the raging storm outside, it was as close to a normal evening as you could get at the pub, with nothing to suggest something very *ab*normal was about to happen.

Morley pushed through the doors right on cue at 7:30, rosy cheeked and ruffling water out of his hair. He slid into his usual seat at the bar, unwrapping a tartan scarf from his neck. It was the first scarf I'd seen since March; another delightful clue signalling the demise of t-shirt weather.

"Happy Friday the thirteenth, Syd," he said, tugging his thin leather gloves tighter on his hands, blotting them with a napkin from the bar. I smiled. Maybe one day I'd get to see his hands in the flesh.

"What's so happy about it?" I said, grabbing a martini glass in anticipation of his usual order.

"Oh, I don't know. Maybe that I get to visit my favorite bartender?"

"Lucky you."

"Looks like Tad's beaten you to it," Morley said, nodding toward our head bartender, who had been three steps ahead of me all night. I stood back to watch Tad's performance while he prepared Morley's drink. As if sensing my eyes on him, he threw an olive into the air and caught it on the rim of the glass where it balanced for a nanosecond before spiralling down into the drink, nary a drop leaving the glass. He winked at me, twirled around, and placed his creation in front of our customer with the grace of a ballerina.

I shook my head. "Good grief."

"Jealous?" Tad said, flouncing off to his table of chattering clerks from the bank to see if they wanted another round of Merlot. They inevitably would. Tad was also a masterful salesman.

"Hey, he missed an olive," I said to Morley, who, for as long as I could recall, had taken his martinis with *two* pimentoed olives.

Morley looked down at his glass. "Huh. I hadn't noticed."

"I can't wait to tell him," I said, more to myself than him, spearing an olive with a bamboo cocktail pick and plopping it into Morley's glass.

"Come on, the showmanship alone was worth sacrificing an olive," he said.

I looked Morley up and down. "You're going to let him get away with it? Wait. Watch this." I plucked a double old-fashioned glass out of the dishwasher when I spied one of our other regulars, Bart, coming in. His cohorts from the printing company had already been there since five o'clock and were well into their drinks. I knew Bart would want to skip the beer and go straight to the hard stuff.

"Thanks for dropping in during the apocalypse, Bart. Copper Turkey for you today?" I asked, pouring two ounces of his favorite whisky into the glass and sliding it toward him.

"How'd you guess?"

"A good bartender knows what her customer wants," I said, flashing Morley a smile.

Bart knocked back the amber liquid in one gulp and slammed the empty glass onto the bar. "Darlin', you make the best cocktail in the land," he said, peeling off his waterlogged jean jacket.

"Thanks. It's a complicated one," I said, chuckling. "Glad you enjoyed it. I'll send Tad over with a pitcher of Harlequin."

"You rock." He threw some crumpled bills onto the counter and trudged over to his table of colleagues, other crusty press operators, all with a penchant for shouting and swearing and complaining about the calamities of their workday, yet who seemed perfectly content as long as Tad kept the nachos and pitchers of beer coming.

"Impressive," Morley said.

"Eleven years' experience in the making."

"Best Cocktail Artist in the city, if I remember correctly, too."

"Come on, that was two years ago. And only according to that one scrappy rag."

"Still, *some* recognition is better than *no* recognition. Besides, you have some tough competition," he said, nodding toward Tad, who'd taken the prize four out of the last five years.

"Yeah, yeah, now drink up, Dr. Scott. You know how jumpy Tad gets if he thinks someone isn't enjoying his masterpiece."

"*Dr. Scott?* You must mean business," Morley teased, taking a generous swig.

The Merryport attracted all sorts of different characters ranging from bus drivers and press operators to lawyers and doctors and everything in between. Many of those clients were fixtures in the pub, clients whose names the whole staff knew, who visited the pub, say, twice a week for lunch or maybe later in the day for a drink with a friend. Morley—our resident pediatrician—was a zebra of a different stripe; he didn't drop in as often as some of the other habitués, but his visits could've been plotted on a calendar. For the past four years on the second Friday of every month, he would stroll in, settle onto his favorite barstool, and order a classic martini. Not in my whole tenure at The Merryport had I met someone as committed to a routine as Morley. Several months before that, both he and his wife, Collette, had been well on their way to becoming regulars in the pub, popping in once or twice a week for a quick drink or a full meal if time allowed. They'd bustle in holding hands and scooch into a cozy booth in the corner, where they'd chat and giggle and stare into each other's eyes, shutting the rest of the world out. Tad had dubbed them the pub's Most In-Love Couple and had had no qualms about saying it straight to their faces, usually eliciting polite laughter tinged with embarrassment. They were champions, though, and took it all in stride.

After a while, their visits petered off and they eventually stopped coming in altogether. My cohorts were sure it was because they'd shifted their loyalty to the brand-spanking-new Rocky Point Pub down the road, but I wasn't as convinced. And then, that first day Morley showed up at the pub alone, his face told the whole story. Something terrible had happened to Collette. It was then he'd laid claim to the stool at the end of the bar. He'd sit in silence for the most part, occasionally taking up conversation with the customer next to him or the wait staff who should have been delivering trays of beer and greasy pub food rather than stopping to talk. Often there would be a little circle of staff gathered around him while he engaged in their banter, graciously answering medical questions about the children in their lives. The bar's general manager, Daniel, had often needed to shoo away some of the more junior staff members—mostly female, but sometimes Tad as well—to let Morley enjoy his cocktails in peace. My post was exclusively behind the bar, at Morley's end, and a thread of not-so-subtle resentment ran thick among my coworkers for being allowed to chat with him carte blanche.

Today despite his chipper façade he seemed a little off, which I'd put down to the change of weather, not unlike I'd done with my achy wrist. Thinking nothing more of it, I filled a lead crystal tumbler with ginger ale and held it up between us, just like I'd done on many a Friday before. He followed suit with his martini.

"To Collette," I said, clinking my glass against his and hoping, as always, that Collette would have appreciated our little ritual.

"To Isla," he said back.

We both took lingering sips from our glasses, watching each other evenly. Time slowed as an almost tangible energy hung in the air between us until somewhere in the distance a woman shrieked and sent us plummeting back to Earth. I glanced over to the source of the racket—Tad's table of bank tellers—where the shrieker was doubled over with laughter, her coworkers joining in. Morley and I set our drinks down, charged.

"Excuse me, I don't mean to interrupt you two lovebirds, but can I bother you for a pint of pilsner and a gin and tonic?" said a short, round fellow pointing his wife in the direction of an empty table. I hadn't even noticed them come in.

"Wha—? Oh! We were just—Coming right up," I said, fumbling for a glass. Morley was grinning from ear to ear like a schoolboy with a secret.

The gentleman took his drinks and tossed his cash on the counter. "Keep the change. You can spend it on your honeymoon."

My face turned ten shades of red. "Uh, thank you?"

Morley snickered as the man waddled away. "Fooled him, didn't we?"

"No kidding," I said, buffing the counter vigorously with a bar wipe.

Morley raised his empty martini glass. "I think I'll have another."

Thank God. A change of subject. "Really? What's the occasion?"

"No occasion. Just thirsty."

"I can't argue with that. Coming right up," I said, trying to sound nonchalant against a bundle of quivering nerves.

Working in silence, I loaded the mixing glass with ice and opened a bottle of the pub's best gin. I couldn't explain why, but it seemed extra important to get his drink perfect, and not just because I wanted to impress him or even to outdo the masterful Tad. That weird sense of unease was prickling my skin again.

"One killer martini for The Merryport's favorite customer. Complete with two olives," I said, setting it down in front of him. I stood back and crossed my arms, eager for him to test it out.

"Fantastic," he said rubbing his hands together. "You know, I really enjoy your company."

"And I enjoy yours," I said, smiling.

"I always look forward to chatting with you, especially when you're not too busy, like tonight."

I scanned the pub, taking a quick tally. Three tables. It was going to be a sleepy shift unless the cellphone-toting Shawn Mendes fans came to the rescue or the pub was blown apart by the storm, shingle by shingle, brick by brick.

"I haven't seen the pub this dead in months."

Morley stole a furtive glance over his shoulder then leaned in closer to the bar. "Syd, I…well…about our coffee date back in the spring."

My stomach fluttered. The coffee *date*. Just when I thought I'd pushed it out of my mind for good.

He said, "I've been thinking about it a lot lately, especially how you've had a different attitude toward me ever since. More…guarded."

He chewed at his lip, folding and refolding the edges of his damp cocktail napkin. The seasoned bartender in me stayed quiet, letting him continue uninterrupted.

"I know this guy at the hospital, a porter I see every once in a while. His favorite band is the Foo Fighters. When they're on tour in this country, he goes to every one of their concerts. He's fanatical. It takes him until their next tour to pay off his credit card just so he can, in effect, go on the road with them next time. Has it in his head the band will know he's been there, recognizing his financial sacrifice and years of loyalty. He actually admitted to me he gets restless after about the fifth show but wouldn't even *think* of cutting out early or skipping a show altogether. I thought he was crazy until a moment of clarity struck: I was doing the exact same thing, coming to this bar. I'd somehow managed to convince myself that Collette could be kept at peace through my visits to The Merryport that I couldn't bear to stop."

His focus remained on the mess he was making of the napkin under his drink.

"Anyway, I made a deal with myself to stop the madness. It seemed so ridiculous all of a sudden. And you know what? About eight months ago, I did stop," he said, meeting my eyes. "Ah yes, you're looking at me skeptically. You think I'm full of shit because my routine hasn't changed at all."

I nodded, tucking a few wayward hairs behind my ear.

"On the outside, no, nothing would seem different to you, but when that next routine Friday rolled around and I sat in my apartment looking out at the view of the harbor and the twinkling city lights with no one to share it with, I grabbed my coat and jumped in my car. I made a conscious decision to come here, not for a ghost, but for you."

The lights over the bar dimmed a moment, flickered back to life.

"I guess what I'm trying to say is you've been a great friend to me all this time. Thank you."

Is that what this was all about? Friendship? Maybe things *could* be normal between us.

"Furthermore," he said, "I think you are the most beautiful woman I've ever met, inside and out."

An unexpected warmth rose in my belly. Over the years, there'd certainly been no shortage of liquored-up clients proposing to me or proclaiming I was *"amay-zshing"* and *"a gorjush creeshur"* (ah, booze). But this was the illustrious, kind, ruggedly handsome, sometimes awkward Dr. Morley Scott, and he wasn't even two martinis in.

As if reading my thoughts, he raised his glass in my direction, his eyes burning with reckless confidence. Over the chatter of the other guests and the whir of the cocktail blender, I wondered, a little impatiently, what did he want me to say?

Morley finally took a sip of his martini and set it down on the counter without looking away from me. He'd set the glass half on, half off a small pile of loose change. I watched helplessly as it tipped over, its contents splashing onto the counter and dribbling into his lap. Morley jumped off his stool but his foot caught on the rung and he stumbled, slapping the glass off the bar with a flailing hand. It shattered on impact when it hit the tile floor. All this in under three seconds.

Tad materialized out of nowhere with a broom and dustpan shouting, "Oh, kittens!"

The distraction was heaven-sent. The tension between us had been as heavy as cold porridge. On instinct, I reached across the counter intending to pat Morley's hand—or, more precisely, his glove—and say something like, *Don't worry, it happens all the time*," but he snatched his hand away, as if my own was a scorching ball of fire.

I jumped back. His mysophobia was worse than I thought. He was a doctor who was terrified of germs. He'd explained to me years ago that most of his patients and their parents were none the wiser. After all, a doctor wearing surgical gloves at work wasn't exactly a peculiar sight, and even though this quirk was a part of him like my bent wrist was a part of me, I'd completely forgotten.

"No, no, Syd. I should be the one apologizing. Look at this mess. Talk about Friday the thirteenth rearing its ugly head," he said, taking the clean bar wipe I'd finally had the presence of mind to offer him. While he dabbed at the liquid on his gray suit pants, I turned my attention to the empty seats at the bar, willing someone, anyone, to come up and order a drink. It was wishful thinking. When no one came, I set to wiping up the dregs of Morley's drink on the bar while Tad scooted by to dump the broken glass into the bin. As I gathered up the soggy cocktail napkins, I noticed a name written on one of them. *Chris.* I hadn't seen Morley writing it, and there was no other information on it, so I threw it away.

"Syd," Morley said, getting my attention after Tad had disappeared into the kitchen to get a mop. "I meant what I said before. I just wanted to tell you what's been on my mind for a while now. I'm sorry if it makes you uncomfortable, especially…well, because…"

"Because why, Morley? Because I'm married?" It wasn't technically untrue. I'd been with Coop for over twelve years, and we were as good as married. Just never walked down the aisle.

"Yes," he said, folding the bar wipe, setting it neatly on the counter.

"Look, please don't be upset. I don't want this to ruin what we've had all these years."

I crossed my arms and stared at him with a furrowed brow. I never should've agreed to meet with him back in the spring.

He looked at his watch and stepped back from the bar. "I should go. And Syd, I'm really sorry if I've made you uncomfortable."

Just then, five or six drenched twenty-somethings crashed through the doors, jabbering, laughing, shifting the spotlight away from us. The lively bunch made their way to the biggest booth in the back corner while two of them—a couple barely old enough to be in the pub in the first place—stopped right behind Morley and began shoving their tongues down each other's throats in a wild display of passion. Morley turned around when he saw me gaping.

"Hey, get a room why don't you?" he said.

The couple unglued themselves from each other and hustled back outside, ostensibly heeding his request.

"That was effective."

"It's the least I could do for my favorite cocktail artist," he said, winking at me as he adjusted his scarf around his neck and turned to leave. "Until we meet again, Sydney Brixton."

An apology formed on the tip of my tongue then stalled. Why should I apologize? *He'd* been out of line, not me. That's when, as I wiped the counter where he'd been sitting, I saw it. The necklace. *Collette's* special dragonfly necklace he'd inherited four years earlier. It was coiled neatly on the bar as if he'd left there it on purpose. I knew he couldn't have, though, and by the time I opened my mouth to tell him his mistake, he'd already pushed through the doors and into the blustery night. For the last time.

Kendall sat cross-legged on our scruffy leather armchair on the opposite side of the coffee table, cradling a mug of peppermint tea in both hands. Her anticipation was palpable. It was the first time I'd discussed the tragedy at The Merryport with anyone, including the parade of well-intentioned healthcare workers and police officers who'd badgered me incessantly since the whole ugly thing went down more than a week earlier.

On my release from hospital, Coop had been given strict instructions not to leave me home alone, at least in the short term. My sister had insisted on taking shifts to stay with me while Coop worked, and she'd been bringing me toast and cups of tea, magazines, and drawings from her twin eight-year-old boys, Connor and Devin.

"So that's where the necklace came from," she said. "I wondered. It didn't seem like something you'd buy for yourself."

"Thanks for rescuing it," I said from my rainbow nest of blankets on the sofa.

"You're welcome. I'm actually surprised it turned up in all the confusion at the hospital. It looks beautiful on you, by the way. Have you told Coop where it came from?"

"Not yet."

"He hasn't asked? I mean, it's exquisite."

"Sounds like I should be careful, or it might go missing," I said, clutching it protectively between my thumb and forefinger.

"Don't worry about me. I'm not into silver, even high-quality stuff like that."

"Lucky me. To answer your question, no, Coop hasn't asked about it. You know he doesn't pay attention to that kind of stuff. I could bring a baby elephant home and he wouldn't notice."

Kendall laughed.

"Anyway, thanks for looking after me, Kenny, especially with how busy you are."

"Stop it. Remember Marcie Edwards? She almost crapped herself when I asked her to take on my assignments. The poor girl struggled over the summer and this little nugget is keeping her out of bankruptcy. For one more season anyway."

"What about your clients? They won't sue you for ducking out on them? Or hunt you down and kill you? Brides can be vicious."

"That's what contracts are for, my dear. Clause twenty-two: Family Emergencies. Wouldn't you say this constitutes a family emergency? Besides, I could use some time off. My schedule's been insane since May."

As one of the more popular wedding photographers in the city, my sister always seemed to be in meetings with happy-frantic couples or dashing from rehearsal to ceremony to reception. It wasn't that she needed the job. Her and Brett's house had been paid off years ago and they owned three rental properties that never sat empty for more than a few days at a time when tenants moved in or out. They even had a pile of money stashed away for Connor and Devin's university fund. Brett was no slouch when it came to contributing to the family fortune, either; he'd been the city's top-grossing commercial real estate agent for almost a decade. A power duo if ever there was one.

"It's awful. What happened to Morley," Kendall said, shaking her head as if she understood what I'd been through. She couldn't. Not this time.

I picked at some loose yarn on my blanket. She wouldn't be satisfied until I recounted the gruesome part of the story, but I needed a breather for a few minutes and tried a different vein. "I still can't believe he hit on me. He knew full well about Coop," I said.

Kendall gawked at me, blinking, saying nothing.

"What are you staring at?" I said.

"*That's* what you're taking away from all this? That he was flirting with you?"

I sat up, stiff as a board. "Give me a break. The guy died *right in front of me*. Don't you think I've relived that night in my head enough times already? Maybe I want to talk about something less horrible."

Kendall's face softened. "Oh God, I'm sorry. I just——"

"Never mind," I said.

She flipped her chestnut curls over her shoulder and took a small breath. "Okay, I'll agree Morley's behavior toward you was a little…inappropriate. Maybe he thought you were fair game because you're technically not married."

I rolled my eyes. "We're going *there* again? Can't you accept that Coop and I are solid without the damn contract? Have you forgotten we have a mortgage together? Matching tattoos? A goddamned labradoodle?"

"Sorry."

"Stop harping on about stupid shit."

"Fine. I said I was sorry."

Jinx, our eighty-pound bundle of milk-chocolate fluff who'd been asleep on the floor in front of Kendall, rolled onto his back, sighed, and gave me a look of utter disgust through the glass-topped coffee table.

Yeah, Jinx, I know. I suck.

I stared at Kendall, my only blood relative who'll have anything to do with me. We were, on the surface, sisters, complete with that brand of bickering exclusive to siblings, but we were so much more than that. When I'd reached the pinnacle of my teenage indiscretions (angsty mischief like quitting high school, taking up drinking as a full-time job, and, the icing on the cake: scaring my father out of town permanently), Kendall had picked me up, brushed me off, and said that if I didn't get my shit together, I was going to lose the last member of the family I could count on for help: Me.

For some reason, that time it'd stuck. I'd been eighteen, Kendall twenty-five and already married for three years. It would take a lifetime for me to repay her, yet here I was, getting snippy with her again.

Kendall peered at me over her mug of tea, then set it down and came over to the sofa, looking serious, if a bit irritated. She took my gimped hand in one of hers as she settled in next to me.

"I love you, sis. But despite your *alleged* surprise about Morley's move on you, I think we both know what this really was. You keep spewing venom about this guy you describe as a friend, but the way you're handling it? Syd. Do you realize how many times you've mentioned his name in the last few years?"

I pulled my hand out of hers and tucked it under the blanket, keeping an ear out for Coop's car. He was due home soon.

"Morley was a regular. Of course I'm going to talk about him. Would you rather I didn't bore you with stories about work?"

"Listen to yourself," she said, ignoring my question. "You cared about him—maybe more than you're willing to admit. Maybe there was a closeness there you don't want to face out of respect for Coop. And so what if there was? If you're telling me everything, a little innocent flirting never hurt anyone."

She'd always had a good handle on what made me tick, even if I didn't myself. So much so, in fact, that now she had me thinking: Had I really accepted Morley's coffee invitation back in the spring for reasons beyond simple friendship?

"Fine. I'll finish telling you what happened, just so you're clear why I'd rather talk about *anything else*. But then you have to shut up about it. Forever. Got it?"

Kendall nodded.

Morley had departed The Merryport just like countless times before, but in place of his usual tip he'd left the dragonfly necklace. Right off the bat I'd known it was a mistake. No way would he have left that special piece behind intentionally. I snatched it off the counter.

"Tad, cover me a minute?" I shouted to my cohort, flipping up the bar counter and running for the door.

On the way, I stopped. What if he *meant* to give it to me? I studied the pendant in my hand. Although not much bigger than a quarter, the piece was surprisingly heavy, almost unnaturally so, but also delicate. Beguiling. And as the dragonfly's wings twinkled playfully in the warm light of the pub, goosebumps rose over my skin like tiny helmeted soldiers. What if it was meant as peace offering? He *had* been quite apologetic about his behavior toward me.

I turned it over and over in my fingers, fraught with indecision. Should I run after him? Or wait for him to come back for it? I caught sight of the two olives with their bright red centers staring back at me from under Morley's barstool and giggled at the memory of him whacking his martini off the counter like some awkward nerd on a blind date. I was just about to head outside when a woman I recognized from one of the two-seater tables next to the window came charging at me.

"You've run out of paper in the ladies' room," she said, "and my poor cousin is in a bit of a delicate position."

Glancing wistfully at the pub's front doors, I dropped the necklace into my apron and led the woman down the hall toward the supply cabinet. Morley would be back when he'd realized his mistake.

"Thank you so much," she said. "It's Carol's first trip to North America. She arrived yesterday."

"Oh? Where's she from?" I asked, fishing the keys out of my pocket.

"England. She's come for my daughter's wedding. I was so happy when she accepted the invitation."

I smiled. British tourists had always been my favorite. "Well, we can't leave her hanging around in there, can we?" I said, nodding toward the restroom. As I raised my key to the supply cabinet, the ground suddenly rumbled beneath my feet, rattling the building.

Earthquake!

"Hey!" the woman called as I spun and ran down the corridor. She either hadn't felt the earth move or was too focused on her cousin's predicament to care.

"Help yourself," I shouted, tossing her my keys.

When I arrived in the foyer, the few customers we had were clamoring to get outside, and I was last to push out the doors behind the group of bank tellers. We all came to a halt at exactly the same time by what we saw: an older model pickup truck smashed up against the wall with steam spewing from under the hood. The truck's front window was gone; its windshield wipers flipping madly back and forth in mid-air almost comically while rain poured into the cab. But there was nothing funny about the situation. The driver was screaming and rubbing at his forehead while blood spilled down his face. In the crosswalk near the pub's entrance two people lay motionless on the road with bystanders shielding them from the rain using umbrellas or the coats off their backs. I took a few tentative steps closer to see if Morley was one of them. He wasn't. But my relief was short lived when I recognized the victims as the amorous couple who'd left the building moments before Morley.

I had to find him, especially now. I kept thinking *He's a doctor, and these people need help!* I tore down the road to the parking lot next to the pub. His car was there, but he wasn't, which I thought strange since he'd only just left the pub. To be sure, I banged on the window, calling his name, as if it would conjure him up somehow. Had he jumped into a taxi? He hadn't even had two full drinks, but maybe he hadn't wanted to chance it.

Or he might have returned to the pub when he'd heard the commotion. Of course! He was a doctor. They don't walk away from trouble like this. Thinking I must've missed him in the crowd, I made my way back through the throng of onlookers huddled together in the driving rain. Two of the bank clerks were comforting the injured couple in the street while two others directed traffic around the scene. I stopped short of the pub's doors when I noticed another ruckus going on next to the smashed truck. Three men dressed in rain-soaked business suits struggled with the screaming driver, and at first, I thought they were trying to free him from the wreck, but when the man shouted, *"Bitch deserved it!"* I realized that what I'd assumed was an accident was something much more sinister.

The wrestling went on. Once the men had dragged the thrashing driver out of the cab and the crowd parted to let them through, my heart plummeted. There, wedged between the grille of the truck and the pub's stone facade, was Morley. Blood mixed with rain trickled down his face in pinkish streams. His eyes sporadically rolled back in their sockets. Tad was cradling his head with some rolled-up bar wipes, and a woman I recognized as the owner of the consignment shop next door braced Morley's arm on the other side. Things were dire. I should've been rushing to my friend's side, but I couldn't. My feet seemed to be cast in cement and the commotion around me had slowed to half tempo: the rain streaming off the awning syrup-like to the puddles below; the waterlogged bystanders trudging along the sidewalk as if in quicksand; cars cruising by at half speed. In retrospect, the crawling traffic probably wasn't a figment of my imagination. Drivers were slowing down to gawk at the developing chaos or to navigate around the young couple in the street.

When one of the ladies from the bank group yelled, "Back it up! Back it up!" my attention snapped back to full speed, to the horror unfolding in front of me. Morley's eyes found mine, for only a moment, but in that brief look I understood his message: *Don't leave me*.

It was the push I needed. I broke through the crowd and leaned in next to Tad. "Everything's going to be okay," I assured Morley. Was I repeating the cliché now because I'd heard it so many times in the movies or on TV and couldn't think of anything else to say? Given his convulsions, the blood streaming from his nostrils, the way his hand was bent backward at ninety degrees, I believed everything was definitely *not* okay. And those were just the injuries I could see. The internal damage must have been a lot worse considering he was pinned between a truck and a wall.

I leaned in a little closer, intending to say something comforting or at least to hold his unbroken hand, which was curiously missing a glove.

"*Don't touch!*" Morley squawked, shuddering, as if he'd jumped into an Alaskan lake.

I reeled back. It was odd. He'd seemed perfectly unfazed by the others holding him.

One of the businessmen who'd wrestled the driver out of

the truck was now perched behind the wheel with the truck's engine running. "Ready? I'll back it up as slow as I can."

"No!" I yelled. "We should wait for the ambulance!"

"Move it," Morley himself squeaked out. I couldn't argue, especially with a doctor. Maybe he had some insight as to the extent of his own injuries and, accordingly, understood the best course of action.

"Ok, Dan-O, easy does it," one of the suits instructed.

The truck inched back, ever so slightly.

"*Faster!*" Morley cried out, surprisingly loud and clear.

"Are you sure?" Dan-O called back.

"Yes! *Go!*" I yelled.

The guy punched the gas, releasing Morley into Tad's arms like a rag doll. The woman from the consignment store helped Tad lay him down while Morley grimaced in agony. The sirens were loud now. Maybe it would be okay after all.

With heartbreaking effort, Morley moved his head to find me. "Come here," he said, which came out a raspy, gurgled *cubbeer.*

"Ok, people, back off," Tad said, shuffling everyone away. He allowed a woman in the crowd to hand me an umbrella, which was decorated with a giant yellow happy face. It bounced and bobbed in the wind and was a woefully inadequate shelter for my dear friend. I leaned over him, my ear almost touching his mouth, and with all the power he could muster, he croaked out, "Ch-Chapman Falls…eleven o'clock, April twentieth…2019."

"*What?*" I shouted over the thrumming rain, but I'd heard him correctly. Chapman Falls, April twentieth, 2019. Eleven o'clock.

"Morley? *Morley?*"

He opened his eyes and looked straight at me, giving me a huge, joyful smile that penetrated my very soul. I laid my hand over his chest and, surprising myself, told him I loved him. He blinked, and a tear ran down his temple and disappeared into his blood-soaked hair. In his gaze there was no sadness, no fear, no regret; just a beautiful, calm awareness. Moments later, a gray mist rolled over his eyes and snuffed out the final trace of light.

The last thing I saw before I blacked out was the happy-face umbrella tumbling away into the night.

"I'll be back no later than eight," Kendall announced, zipping up her raincoat and grabbing an umbrella off the hook by the front door. Her visit had exhausted me, but at least she was leaving with a better understanding about what'd brought me to the near catatonic state requiring a five-day hospital admission. Too much understanding, in fact. Going into the conversation, I'd flat-out promised myself not to tell her about the underlying weirdness between Morley and me, but there it had gone, spilling out like molten lava once I'd gotten going, right down to the part where I'd professed my love for him. Shit! What was wrong with me? Then again, Kendall always did have an uncanny talent for sucking information out of me when I least wanted to give it. I hoped she'd accepted my explanation that I hadn't really loved Morley, not in the way I loved Coop or even the way I loved her. I'd loved him as a friend.

Kendall brushed past Coop—who was just arriving from his overnight shift at the fire hall—pausing just long enough at the door to give him a rundown of my condition: "Groggy from the pills, but in good spirits. She's started eating more."

I felt like a science experiment with the two of them watching me, scrutinizing my every twitch, reporting their findings, but I smiled in spite of myself; it was nice to see them on the same team for a change.

"There's leftover soup in the fridge. Make sure she eats

when she takes her noon meds," Kendall said before shutting the door behind her.

Coop threw his coat over the back of the sofa and muttered, "*Jayzuss*, you'd think I was one of her kids."

"Now, now. Her heart's in the right place."

"I know, sweetie," he said, rubbing my cheek with the back of his hand. "Sounds like you've been a model patient."

"Anything to make it easy for you guys."

He sat on the sofa next to me, scratching Jinx behind the ear before shooing him away. "Don't worry about us. You need to be good to yourself right now. You've been to hell and back."

"Did you hear the new development about Morley's accident?"

He shook his head wearily.

"It was all over the news last night. Apparently a case of him being in the wrong place at the wrong time. The truck driver's real target was the couple that left the pub just before him. An ex-boyfriend. Mowed them down in a jealous rage, and Morley just happened to get in the way."

"That's awful, babe. I'm so sorry."

"At least the couple are expected to make full recoveries," I said. "How do you do it?"

"Do what?"

"See terrible things every day and carry on with life."

Morley's accident had given me a whole new appreciation for Coop's career choice, and before he had a chance to answer, I said, "I know, I know. You've told me a million times about the counselling, the desensitizing, the numbing repetition." I reached up and patted his chest, right over his heart. "But how about here?"

"Someone has to do it, right? Might as well be a big, strong meathead like me."

I smiled, snuggling into my blanket.

Coop stretched his arms above his head, sighing and

yawning simultaneously. "Anyway, I'm beat. Need anything before I catch a few zees?"

"No thanks, I've had breakfast. Kendall gave me toast with some of that pear butter she canned last month. And I'm fine right here. I've got a good book and the TV for company."

"You do seem in better spirits today. This is the most I've heard you talk in days. And it's great that you're eating more." He leaned over and kissed me, smelling of smoke and soap. He would've showered at the station after his shift, but occasionally a bad fire got under his skin.

"How was your night?" I said, not quite ready for him to leave yet.

"It wasn't the worst, but we definitely had a battle. I'm getting too old for this."

"Aw, hon. I wish I could help," I said, rubbing his arm.

At thirty-eight, Coop was a living, breathing, finely-tuned machine, and his workout regimen would put an Olympic athlete's to shame. When he started fretting about being old, it could only mean he'd had to knock a particularly brutal fire into submission. I leaned back into my pile of pillows to appraise him. Soot-colored circles under his eyes told the story.

"Want to talk about it?"

"You haven't seen the morning news, I take it."

"No time. Kendall's been fussing over me since I woke up."

"Another damned apartment fire. Griefed us from midnight to around four. You know Shipp's Fish on Belleford? It was the building right next door. We got inside and the fire was everywhere. I can't believe it got that bad so fast. I mean, the station's only eight blocks away. We headed up the stairs and on about the seventh floor my oxygen mask started to leak. I was sucking up smoke fast."

"Oh my god," I said, sitting up straighter.

"I pulled an about-face," he continued, "had to crawl over

two other guys to get out. That really got my heart racing. I couldn't get a breath from the time I sprung the leak until I got outside. I got a new mask and went back in there and we fought that son of a bitch back."

"Any casualties?" The answer to this question always helped me decide how much space to give Coop afterwards.

He fastened his fingers at the nape of his neck and let out a breath as long as the day. I rubbed his thigh.

"An eight-year-old boy. He had one of those clip-on reading lights attached to the headboard. Fell asleep with it on. His pillow was touching the bulb."

"Oh, Coop."

"That's what happens in those older buildings when it's up to the tenant to stay on top of the smoke detector batteries."

I could see the whole ugly picture in my mind.

"No happy ending this time," he said, a hitch in his throat.

"A fine pair we are," I said, tugging him over for a hug. I don't know who needed it more. Morley's death was tragic, but an innocent boy whose life was just beginning was something else entirely, even for a seasoned firefighter like Coop who thought the sun rose and set on his own little eight-year-old nephews.

He pulled away from me and stood, wringing his hands. "I really should get some shut-eye. We have that department-wide meeting before my shift tonight, so I'll be at the station for thirteen hours. Kendall's coming back at eight—the twins have a band concert or something, or else she'd be here earlier. You'll be okay on your own for a couple of hours?"

"Of course," I said, meaning it. "She really doesn't have to come at all, you know."

"Maybe. But let's wait and talk about that at your next appointment. For now, just focus on getting better, okay babe?"

I gave him a thumb's up and pulled the knitted blanket to my chin. My heart still ached with the weary knowledge of

Morley's absence, and yes, I was down, but I wasn't about to hurt myself. I was past all that. For years now. I wished they would cut me a bit of slack.

Coop leaned down and pecked me on the forehead. "Shout if you need anything."

"I will. Have a good sleep."

"You should try to get some rest too," he said.

"Whatever you say, Dr. Levin."

"Ha, ha," I heard him say as he plodded up the stairs.

All I'd been doing for days was resting, and I was getting antsy for a walk along the breakwater or—dare I dream?—a good run on the university chip trail. The team at the hospital had said it would be good for me to keep up my exercise routine, but the psych docs stuck their noses in and insisted on rest until I earned a clean bill of mental health. Probably didn't want me running in front of a bus.

Settling into my cozy knitted nest, I closed my eyes and yawned as the wily tentacles of sleep threatened to drag me under. The Merryport swam into focus behind my eyelids, dark and sinister, as if the building itself had killed Morley. The thought was troubling, especially with a trial shift tentatively slated for October fourth, two weeks away. Would I be ready? Daniel had closed the pub for a few days after the tragedy, and apparently everyone else had been back on the job when he'd reopened, Tad included—which was surprising to me given his propensity to turn the smallest problem into a major disaster, often resulting in him putting in a request for days or weeks off work.

Now it was *me* losing my shit. I yawned again, deeply, fighting off sleep while I tried to recall the last time I'd needed a mental health break. Surprisingly, I couldn't.

Chapter Two

SUNDAY, SEPTEMBER 29

On Sunday morning two weeks later, I woke to a steaming cup of tea on my bedside table and Coop looking out into the back yard as he pulled on his tatty gray wool sweater. Beyond his broad silhouette, a soft pink sunrise peeked over our neighbors' rooftops, and something stirred inside me.

"G'morning, Mr. Levin," I said, making him jump.

"Oh good, you're awake. I brought you tea."

"You spoil me," I said, hoisting myself up against the headboard. "Going somewhere?"

"Lucy needs me."

"I need you more," I said, patting the mattress next to me.

He smiled as he adjusted his sweater over his shoulders. "I'll take a rain check on that, babe. I gotta get Lucy running or we'll be screwed when you start work on Friday."

"Boo," I said, sinking into the pillows, annoyed to be taking a back seat to that wretched four-wheeled beast again. I was also thinking about work. My gradual return, one day a week. It's not that I didn't want to go back. I did. But it would be tough without Morley sitting at my bar.

Coop kissed me on the forehead and stalked out of the

bedroom to spend the better part of his day with his "other woman."

Sighing, I grabbed my laptop off of the nightstand. Morley's last words had continued to vex me, and I'd been taking advantage of quieter moments like these to do a little sleuthing.

I pulled up a news article from April 20, 2019, where there had been a story about a woman who'd somehow survived a hundred-foot plunge over Chapman Falls to the disbelieving eyes of numerous witnesses, only to be rescued by an unidenti-fied bystander, then both of them disappearing from the scene without a trace. It was strange indeed but surely unrelated to Morley's message.

It seemed I had one hell of a mystery on my hands, and precious few clues. I knew the *where* (Chapman Falls), and the *when* (April 20, 2019 at eleven o'clock), but not the *why*.

I was beginning to understand the meaning behind that old saying my mother used to quote, "Desperation breeds courage." Take the plan I was currently throwing together from the safety of my cozy, neutral-toned bedroom; the plan where I would visit Morley's family members to see if they knew anything about that date. Surely somebody had to know *something*. It was a bold plan for an anxious homebody like me, but again, I was getting desperate.

I remembered Morley speaking of an aunt and uncle he'd spent time with as a third- or fourth-year medical student. It had been his experience with them that had given rise to his plan of moving to Port Raven as soon as he'd finished med school. His uncle's name was unforgettable: Chuck. It bounced playfully on the tongue when spoken out loud. Chuck Scott. Chuck Scott. There was only one Charles Scott listed in the city, and it would've taken being handcuffed to a pipe in my basement to keep me from going there.

After a quick shower, I settled a ball cap over my still-damp hair and zipped up my down jacket. The air had turned unseasonably chilly overnight, enough to kill the last of my potted geraniums, their leaves blackened and drooped in surrender. I crossed the lawn and poked my head inside the garage door. Coop was hunched over the engine of the baby he never had, the 1970 cherry-red Firewing 426 fastback he'd inherited from his father. The "426 fastback" part held no meaning to me, but Coop never failed to add it in conversation with mechanics or parts managers or mesmerized teenaged boys in parking lots around town. Despite how much it cost us in maintenance and insurance, all the tinkering and cleaning and buffing brought Coop true joy. It was the only thing he had left that reminded him of his father. It wasn't as though I hated it, though. Heads turned when we cruised around town in it, making me secretly giddy.

"I'm off, I said. "Need anything?"

Without looking up from the engine, Coop said, "Yeah, a head gasket."

"Haha. You're funny," I said, but he didn't laugh back. In fact, he was so focused on Lucy he didn't even acknowledge that it was my first foray out into the big bad world alone since the tragedy at The Merryport.

Leaning in for a closer look, I said, "It's bad, isn't it?"

"You could say that. Remember when I found that puddle of coolant last weekend?"

"Uh, sure?" Car talk didn't penetrate my brain much. My face might portray interest, but my head was generally immersed in thoughts of a good book, what to make for dinner, or, right now, Morley.

Coop straightened up and ran his fingers through his precision-cropped hair, completely focused on the enigma that is a car engine with its network of hoses and pistons and doodads I'll never know the names of.

"Turns out there *was* a leak. I should've dealt with it when I first noticed, because it made the engine overheat, and now we've got a blown head gasket and *two* things to fix."

"Oh no. Do you really want me to pick up a gasket?" I said.

"No, just being funny. I ordered one, though. Should be in by Tuesday. Luckily the source of the leak was just a broken hose clamp, which I can fix now."

"That's a relief," I said as if I knew a broken hose clamp was a minor issue. "Can you still drive in the meantime?"

"Not till Tuesday. Don't want to chance causing more damage. Good thing you don't work until Friday and I can use your car, or we'd be up the creek."

"Okay hon," I said, pecking him on the cheek. His face was stubbled and he tasted of salt; it made me want to jump him right there. I filed the thought away for later. "See you in a couple of hours."

✳

A few minutes later, my silver 1997 Civic hatchback sputtered to life and I pulled away from the curb in front of our modest craftsman-style home. It was situated on the border of Port Raven proper and the hoity-toity, well-to-do municipality of Alice Bay where an invisible train track divided *Us* from *Them*. We're on the grotty side. The city planners must have been a less uptight bunch when it came to doling out building permits at the turn of the century, plunking modest 1100-square-foot homes like ours in the shadows of veritable mansions with sprawling grounds and circular driveways. It didn't bother me much though; it was the only home I had ever known, and to me, it was a mansion.

Across the road I spotted "The Nose"—old Mrs. Vanderthorpe—sipping a cup of tea in the comfort of her ugly Edwardian chair appraising me like I was a T-bone steak in a butcher shop. I get it. Your generation was different. You hate my pierced nose. You lose sleep at night thinking about the cursive "Isla" tattoo at the nape of my neck. You would rather eat live spiders than talk to someone with the audacity to plant lowly geraniums in her summer garden and leave them there to wither and rot well into November.

Today I deliberately inched my car past the cranky old bat's house, staring her down as I went. It was petty, I knew, but she had no one else to blame but herself.

Along with The Nose's propensity to sniff out a scandal in the neighborhood, real or imagined, she loved nothing more than to complain to the City about the slightest infraction; a sprinkler left on two minutes past the mandated half-hour limit, or, in our case, the time she'd insisted that Coop had kicked one of her (five?) cats when he'd caught it in our yard. Coop, the selfless firefighter, the guy who'd broken one of her windows last summer to investigate smoke billowing out of the kitchen to find a steadily blackening pot of oatmeal on her stove and the old bat asleep on the sofa in front of the TV. She'd later filed a break-and-enter complaint with the police and sent Coop the bill for the deductible on her broken window.

For that, and for all the other trouble she'd stirred up in the neighborhood dating back to my childhood, I smiled and gave her a cheeky little wave, and she almost hit the floor-boards. I suppressed a laugh and vowed to wave to her more often.

Twenty minutes later I was standing on a stranger's porch on the other side of town, shivering despite bright sunshine and three layers of clothing, half wondering if I should turn around and hop back into my car. Instead, almost unconsciously, I rang the doorbell. Before the thought of abandoning my plan fully surfaced, a delicate looking elderly woman in a dingy flowered housedress and fuzzy blue slippers stood in the open doorway. I swallowed the lump in my throat.

I'd rehearsed the speech a dozen times on the drive over, but I was no more confident for the effort.

"Can I help you?" she said, her forehead scrunching into a dozen creases, making her look even older than her seventy-odd years. I seemed to remember Morley saying her name was Marion or Marnie, if indeed this was the Scotts' house. The idea of telling her I had the wrong address hit me. She didn't know me from spit, and I could march right back to my car and speed off into the horizon. No harm done.

"If you're trying to sell me something, you can forget it." She wasn't the delicate flower I'd imagined. "And I don't believe in God."

"I'm not here to sell you anything," I said. "I'm just trying to find someone."

She eyed me suspiciously. "Are you a movie star? You seem kinda posh for this neighborhood."

I laughed self-consciously feeling rather *un*posh in my ripped jeans and hooded bomber jacket. Maybe it was the sunglasses, which I'd forgotten I was wearing and removed at once, or the ball cap, which was keeping my frizzy, air-dried mop of hair in place and would therefore stay put. "I'm looking for Charles Scott."

Her eyes narrowed and she looked me up and down, probably wondering what the pretty young blonde on her doorstep had to do with her husband. "Chuck's not here."

Bingo. I needed to be sure though. "Does Chuck have a nephew named Morley?"

Silence.

"My name is Syd," I said, holding out my hand. Too formal. She didn't take it. "Are you, uh, Marion?"

"Yes, my name is Marion. What do you want?"

"I knew Morley before…before his accident."

She shook her head regretfully. "Such a terrible waste. How did you know Morley? Did you work with him? Are you a nurse?"

"No," I said, suddenly worried the family didn't know about his visits to the bar. "Just a friend."

"Ah. Well, Chuck's been dead nine years," Marion said, then invited me inside.

"I'm sorry to hear about your husband," I said as we emerged from Marion's kitchen fifteen minutes later carrying cups of tea. I set mine on the coffee table and took a seat on her faded blue velvet sofa. She chose a tattered brown recliner across from me.

"Yeah, well. It was his own damned fault. Quit smoking too late then worked himself to the bone."

"Well, Morley spoke fondly of him. You as well. He told me you and Chuck were the whole reason he decided to move out west." I said, searching for things to talk about that wouldn't set her off. I'd encountered her type at The Merry-port plenty of times—the kind of person that needed breaking in.

"Is that so?" Marion said, raising her brows, suggesting either pride or surprise, I couldn't tell which.

"Very much so. Apparently you and Chuck made a big impression on him when he came to visit. He said his uncle took him to the beaches and the forests and the lakes and everything in between."

She stayed silent, eyeing me like a germ in a petri dish, waiting for me to go on.

"He told me he was so smitten by the city that he brought Collette here not long after they met, hoping she'd fall in love with it too. Of course, she did. You know the rest. You probably already know everything I'm telling you. But it's nice to talk to someone he was close to," I said, a tiny hitch in my voice at the end.

"Yes. Morley was definitely one of a kind," she said. Her

gaze lifted to a spot in the ceiling above my head, as if she were trying to recall a memory. "He and Collette visited me almost every Sunday after Chuck died. Sat in that very spot you are now, drinking tea with me and chatting about their adventures at work and their travels abroad."

"That's lovely," I said when she finally brought her murky brown eyes back to me. I felt sorry for her. She seemed like the kind of person that could have used some extra company, having invited me, a complete stranger, into her home.

"Collette was a physicist," she said brightly, as if to lighten the mood, then laughed. "You already know that, of course, since you were friends with them and all."

"Unfortunately I didn't get to know Collette very well at all. Never got the chance."

"Oh, so you're a *new* friend of Morley's," she said, looking sideways at me. I didn't like the way she insinuated that there might have been something lascivious going on, but I ignored the jab.

"I work at The Merryport. Morley and Collette used to come in together on a fairly regular basis until one day a coworker pointed out he hadn't seen them in a while. It was when Morley started showing up alone that we knew something terrible had happened. He eventually confided in me about Collette's cancer. He said his regular visits to their favorite pub was his way of paying tribute to her memory, but I'm sure you already know *that*."

I couldn't resist the small dig, but I immediately wanted to retract it. She may have been a crabby old thing, but I needed her on my side if I was going to learn anything about Morley's last words. She set her teacup on a TV tray and leaned back in her recliner. A pained, almost disappointed look came over her face, like she'd discovered dog poop on the rug.

I took a nervous sip of tea and commended her on its full-bodied flavor, asking where she'd bought it. She didn't answer. I studied my socks, noticing they were the same shade of pink as the carpet. I lifted my focus to the framed photos scattered about the room on various mismatched cabinets. Amongst a collection of porcelain figurines sat a gold-framed wedding picture where an attractive, young, solemn-faced Marion stood next to a handsome man who was smiling as if he'd just swallowed a rainbow. Morley's Uncle Chuck. Poor guy.

As I reached to put my cup on the table, the old woman finally spoke.

"What did you say your name was again?"

"Syd," I said, a little too quickly. "Short for Sydney."

"Huh. And your last name?"

I considered lying but decided not to risk inflaming her mood further. I still hadn't come around to asking my important questions.

"Brixton."

She let out a deflated groan and stood up, much more nimbly than I would've thought possible for someone her age.

"For Pete's sake, I almost missed it," she said, snatching my coat off the back of the sofa, thrusting it toward me. "Get out."

I leapt up. "What? Was it someth—"

"Take your damned coat and get out of my house."

I accepted the coat as she took me by the shoulder and guided me to the front door.

"Marion—Mrs. Scott—please. I'm sorry, what did I do?"

"Don't pretend you don't know."

"I don't," I said, jamming my feet into my boots, becoming irritated myself.

"Sydney Brixton," she said bitterly, grabbing a stapled bundle of papers from the hall table. She flipped through three or four pages, scanning each one quickly, then suddenly turned the papers around and stabbed at the middle paragraph with her crooked finger. My heartbeat quickened when I saw my name highlighted in bright yellow ink. Before I had the chance to read anything else, she snapped it away and flung it onto the table.

"I have to give you credit, Sydney Brixton, for swooping down on Morley like that, ripping my due share out from under me. Do you know what he left me out of his entire fortune? Some car I've never heard of before. A Tussle? Tulsa? Whatever. First thing I plan to do is sell it. You can bet your bottom dollar on that. And you have plenty of bottom dollars now, missy."

"Please. I...I don't know what you're talking about. Honestly. I just came here to ask you some questions about something Morley said to me the day he died." My eyes flicked to the document on the table. "Maybe those papers can answer my questions."

She rolled her eyes before reaching past me to open the door.

It was now or never. "Do you know the significance of April 20, 2019?"

She nudged me outside. When I turned around for her answer, the door slammed in my face. "...or Chapman Falls?"

I stood there a moment or two before descending the steps, completely baffled. Morley's story was getting stranger by the day. Why was my name on that document? And what fortune was Marion talking about? If there was even the remotest chance that Morley had included me in his will, certainly I would've heard by now, such as Marion had.

Fortunately I still had to stop for groceries on my way home. I took advantage of my time in the aisles reading labels, comparing prices, and assessing the freshness of vegetables to calm my nerves, and by the time I coasted to a stop in front of our house a half hour later, my head was more or less back to normal.

I turned off my engine and sat listening to a group of crows squawking somewhere out of sight. In my peripheral vision, I noticed The Nose at her usual post in the window, and I felt sorry for her just then. What a sad life she led, watching the comings and goings of this sleepy little neighborhood. Marion Scott lived in much the same way and seemed to appreciate my company before our visit had turned sour. Nevertheless, it inspired me. One day soon I would cross the street and invite Mrs. Vanderthorpe over for a cup of tea.

Chapter Three

My all-consuming need to uncover the meaning of Morley's last words had waned little since visiting Marion Scott. The mystery of it was infuriating, and with the possibility that I might be a recipient of Morley's estate added to the mix, the mystery had climbed to a whole new level. How would I even go about finding this information? Contacting the funeral home that handled his final wishes might be a start, but the thought of it made me nauseous. *"Hey, I'm a friend of Morley Scott's. I hear he left me a shitload of money."* I decided to wait for a letter to arrive in the mail.

To give my mind a break, I turned the TV on just before one o'clock. A new episode of *Your Perfect Nest* on the Homestyle Network was about to start and judging by the way Coop had collapsed into bed this morning after his shift, I'd be able to watch it uninterrupted. I was by no means well-traveled or an accomplished cook or even particularly adept at recognizing complementary paint colors and proper scale, but the shows on the Homestyle Network took me places I wanted to go. Escapism in the comfort of my own home.

I cranked up the gas under the kettle for a cup of tea and sunk into the sofa next to Jinx who was lounging wiener up, paws curled as if he were about to break into a full-length piano concerto. He let out a perturbed snort when I pulled my mother's afghan out from under him and settled it over my shoulders.

While the opening credits flashed by, I found myself playing with Morley's dragonfly pendant, turning it over and over in my fingers. Damn. There he was again, bulldozing his way into my thoughts. I wished it would just stop. At the same time, a pang of guilt washed over me. He would never again be able to enjoy the simple pleasure of a mindless TV show. A cup of strong tea. A classic martini with two olives.

I clutched the pendant tighter. "Morley Scott, what the *hell* did you mean by 'Chapman Falls, eleven o'clock, April 20, 2019'?"

For a split second the room went black and my body jerked involuntarily, like a falling-asleep twitch. In fact, for the briefest moment, I believed I *had* fallen asleep—until I was pitched into a roaring cascade of frigid water that shocked me to the bone. It tumbled me over and over, air and water alternately hitting my face. I tried to grab for something to slow me as I gathered momentum, but my arms were pinned down by some unknown entity, my screams obliterated with mouthfuls of water. I caught glimpses of wispy clouds; trees; a dark pool of water. Over and over. Clouds, trees, water. And then came an impact so hard it may as well have been asphalt or brick, but it was more water, dark and turbulent and cold. It pushed me down. Further and further away from the light of day.

My arms were still fixed to my body by what felt like a giant cocoon. All around me, water. I thrashed and kicked and gulped water into my mouth, sucked it in through my nose. Finally the cocoon broke open, and I batted it away, the last of it dangling from my arm. I had to find the surface. I had to get air.

This is it, I thought. *This is how it ends for me.*

At once the bubbling water took on a comforting quality.

Peaceful. Like a womb. And I stopped struggling. From somewhere above, a glowing, undulating form appeared and floated toward me. Shimmering, translucent. Benevolent.

Isla?

I reached out for her.

I'm coming.

And then pain, sharp and violent at my left bicep.

I swallowed another mouthful of water and the fight resumed—not to survive, not to breathe, but to get back to Isla. The force holding my arm tightened. I resisted. But its hold on me was too great.

All at once, a shock of cold air hit my body and I was slammed against some hard and unforgiving surface—cement? rock? In a semi-conscious fugue I saw gray cloud cover. A bird circling. I was aware of sound: water crashing, people shouting, a female voice calling from somewhere far above me. I strained to recognize the voice, but my eyes were heavy, and the world was starting to dim.

"It's okay, she's fine!" came a man's voice. Close, loud, vaguely familiar. And then a blurred face appeared over me, lowering down. Lips meeting mine, warm and gentle. An angel's kiss.

The man drew away and I coughed out a mouthful of water. His face zoomed into focus. "Hello, Sydney," he said, smiling.

It wasn't possible.

Morley Scott was dead. I'd watched him die.

"You sure know how to make an entrance," he said before my world went dark once again.

When I came to, I was nestled under a foil emergency blanket in the passenger seat of an idling car. My head was still foggy, every muscle tightly wound. When I looked out my window, an impressive carved wooden sign welcomed me to "Chapman Falls Municipal Park" and my stomach turned. Had I really just survived a plunge down Chapman Falls and then been pulled from the pool below by my dead friend, Morley Scott? Or had I completely lost touch with reality? I decided to treat it as a dream and let it take me where it wanted.

From the corner of my eye, I focused on the driver. Morley, or at least the man whom I'd assumed was Morley, was at the wheel, whistling, of all things. Curiously, he wasn't wearing his ever-present gloves, making me instantly suspicious, and I vowed that until I learned his true identity, I wouldn't trust him. Two theories seemed plausible: that somehow my old friend from the pub hadn't died after all and had instead managed to fake his own death or—and this concept seemed much more likely to me given my own family makeup—that Morley also had an identical twin. If that proved to be the case, then which twin had actually died, and who was the person driving this car—Morley or his brother?

The car suddenly accelerated, crossing the highway rather than pulling onto it, and we began a slow climb up a narrow, winding road I'd never been on before. Deep potholes rattled the car when we eased over them, and we had to skirt around straggly patches of Scotch broom growing into the road.

The man resembling Morley glanced over when he heard the foil blanket crinkle with my movement. "Oh good, you're with me again. You melted like a blob of honey back there. I have a cabin at Sandalwood Lake, and you can change into some dry clothes there."

I nodded dreamily. Sandalwood Lake. It was an exclusive getaway spot for the more elite members of Port Raven, right across the highway from Chapman Falls. It was so close, in fact, that we could've walked there in five minutes, but I was grateful for the warm car.

After a few seconds the car slowed and we pulled off the

road onto a long gravel driveway lined with white birch trees. The man who looked like Morley had said *cabin* earlier, but the grand log structure that came into view at the top of the driveway could've been featured in an architectural magazine. We pulled up outside the front door. If this was a dream, maybe it wasn't quite time to wake up yet.

"Wow," I said, still fuzzy-headed.

"It's great to have you here, Syd. It really is."

I cocked my head at him.

He chuckled as he turned off the engine then hopped out of the car, circling around front. I clutched at the edges of the foil blanket, wrapping it tighter around me as he opened my door and reached down to collect a plastic grocery bag off the floor near my feet. It looked heavy, as though it contained a bunch of wet clothes, and I was suddenly self-conscious that I might be naked under my foil wrapping. "Your blanket," he said.

The cocoon! My mother's afghan.

"Careful," Morley said, pointing to my wet socks as I swung my legs out of the car. While he supported my arm, I stood, stepping gingerly over a pea-gravel pathway leading to a wide concrete stoop. Morley helped me up the steps and punched in a code at the door.

"Welcome to Sandalwood Reach," he said pushing the massive door ajar.

I shuffled into Morley's living room a half an hour later dressed in a pair of men's yoga pants, an oversized hoodie and woollen lumberjack socks.

"That's a good look on you," Morley said, gesturing toward a chunky leather sofa under a window running perpendicular to the fireplace. He'd built up quite an inferno rivalling any of the fires I'd seen at Kendall and Brett's house, and that was saying a lot. Even with the fire, the room was eerily dark for the middle of the day. It was easy to see why. Outside, heavy gray clouds had begun to gather, threatening a downpour that would likely persist for hours, and all around me, walls of stacked red cedar brought a closeness to the room that felt claustrophobic rather than cozy.

I sunk into my natural position on the sofa with my knees tucked up to my chest then pulled my arms inside the hoodie and wrapped them around my stomach. Two bone-china cups of steaming tea had been set out on the coffee table alongside a matching plate holding a few digestive biscuits. It was a nice touch, but I was too rattled to think about eating or drinking anything.

"What's going on?" I asked before Morley had the chance to settle into one of two matching chairs on the opposite side of the coffee table.

He laughed and picked up his tea.

"I'm sorry," he said taking a sip, setting the cup back down. "I'm just so happy you're in on my secret."

I refused to ask the obvious question.

"You're not going to believe what I'm about to tell you, Syd. I barely did at first either. And I don't know how to explain it gently, because there's absolutely no way to ease a person into it. Just listen to what I have to say and try to wrap your brain around it as best you can, okay?"

He was scaring me. This was probably how he explained a diagnosis to the parents of a child with some terrible disease.

"Oh, where to begin? Ah yes. *Yes*: I am indeed *the* Dr. Morley Scott who's been frequenting your pub for the last four years. And yes, you saw me meet a gruesome demise after a truck rammed me into the wall of The Merryport."

I threaded my arms back through the oversized sleeves and picked up my cup of tea almost without realizing it. I stayed quiet, cradling the cup in both hands in front of my knees, waiting for part two of the story, the part where everything made sense.

"Ah, I'm just going to say it. You've time traveled to April 20, 2019."

I took a sip of tea and held the cup to my lips, a tiny barricade between me and the lunatic sitting across from me.

"Actually," he said, "I've dubbed the phenomenon 'time*blinking*', a more accurate label, wouldn't you say?"

The millisecond of darkness I experienced before plunging into the cold falls flashed in my memory. I shuddered.

"You're crazy," I finally managed, setting my tea back on the table. "*This* is crazy. This…this…dream. The tea is perfect, by the way. Ha, of course it is. Why wouldn't it be? I'm stuck in a dream I can't wake up from!"

As I babbled, Morley's face lost some of its characteristic buoyancy. "It's not a dream, Syd. As a friend and, hell, as an educated professional, I'm telling you that you aren't imagining anything. This is all very much real. You can't deny the blinking sensation, can you?"

I stared at Morley, not knowing what to say, and for a few moments the only sound in the room was the hissing and popping of the burning wood. I focussed all my attention on it, trying to decide whether or not I'd gone mad. If Isla's disappearance and my mother's death hadn't succeeded in pushing me over the edge, this foray into Crazytown certainly had the potential to do just that.

"That silver disc hanging around your neck? It's no coincidence that I'm going to leave it on the bar for you at The Merryport."

I pictured the pendant under the gray hoodie I was wearing. "*Going* to? You already did."

"Aha. Let me explain." He fished inside his shirt and pulled out a dragonfly pendant that looked identical to mine. He kissed it before letting it drop to his chest. "You see, I have a talisman too. Actually, if we want to get technical, it's the same one as yours. Where I am right now, where *we* are, here at Sandalwood, it's April 20, 2019, and I haven't been smucked yet. That's five months away. It's a bit weird, even for me, so your confusion is perfectly understandable."

If I was going to get through this with my mind intact, I had to stop fighting the urge to analyze everything and treat it like a dream. At least for now. I pulled my own pendant (or *talisman*, as Morley had called it) through the neck of the hoodie and held it cautiously in my hand.

"Where did Collette get it?"

"From her grandmother in Peru. Apart from that, she never said much about it."

"What does this have to do with…time winking?"

"Time*blinking*. That little treasure there is the whole reason timeblinking is possible. I discovered it by pure mistake—luck, misfortune, however you want to look at it—and I've seen some pretty amazing things since. I've also experienced a significant consequence, which I'll explain shortly."

"I want to go back now," I said half-heartedly.

"Not before you're properly briefed."

I frowned. "What if I ordered you to take me back right now?"

"I don't advise it. For one thing, you're wearing my clothes. For another, you're too far in to go back now."

I looked down at the droopy pants and hoodie. They *would* be hard to explain to Coop. "Too far into *what*?"

"Can you please hear me out?"

Ten minutes later, I was sitting in the passenger seat of Morley's car, flipping the key fob over and over in my grasp. Not ten sentences into the cockamamie story about the power of his dead wife's dragonfly pendant, I'd had enough of his bullshit. I'd pulled the pendant, or talisman or whatever he was calling it, over my head and thrown it on the coffee table before grabbing the key from a table in the foyer and stomping out to the car. Staccato glances to my right revealed Morley hovering outside his front door, shoulders slumped, waiting, it seemed, for me to change my mind and come back inside. I shook my head at the thought of it.

"Sydney. Please. Be reasonable. If I could send you back right now, I would," he said, his beseeching voice muffled by the car's closed window.

"HA! That's rich. How about *you* be reasonable?" I shouted, turning to glare at him. "I have a kettle on the stove that's probably boiling dry right now. My house could burn down if I don't get back."

Morley paced like a wounded dog between two massive iron planters that flanked the front door. Out of the blue, the memory of his death surged into my head with the force of a tsunami, and I suppressed an urge to run out and throw my arms around him.

"Please come back in, Sydney?" he said, puffs of warm breath blossoming in the air around him. "The kettle won't be a problem. I promise. As God as my witness."

I couldn't help but roll my eyes. "You told me you don't believe in God."

"Come on, Syd. Please? Fifteen minutes, and then you can go."

He obviously wasn't going to budge. I considered walking back to Chapman Falls but thought better of it when I looked at the sky. Thick gunmetal-gray clouds had continued to assemble, the kind that would most certainly unleash a heavy, relentless downpour. I climbed out of the car, slammed the door, and marched past him into the house. I caught him smirking. It's not easy to appear serious in sock feet and yoga gear three sizes too big. When I reached the living room, I stopped next to the fire, glaring at him as he traipsed in after me.

"Ok, spill it," I said marveling at my attitude toward him. Not too long ago I'd stood in utter reverence of this man as a doctor and VIP client at the pub, yet here I was, shouting at him as if he was an unruly toddler.

He padded over to his original chair and sat, waiting for me to do the same, but I was too agitated to sit. I lifted my foot to dig a pebble out of my wet sock. Threw it into the fire without looking at him.

"So as I was saying: One day about eight months ago I happened on a picture of me and Collette in San Francisco while flipping through old photo albums. An emptiness consumed me. You must know the feeling. No more Christmases together. All the birthdays we wouldn't be celebrating. All of it. Gone."

I did know. The loss was paralyzing, especially when those important dates rolled around every year. Even now, twenty years later, the sting was real.

"Right then, I yearned to go back to that moment. Back to sharing laughter and walking on the seawall and eating gelato in the park. To experience those moments that would never be again."

Lines appeared in his forehead exposing a deep and disabling sorrow, and I immediately regretted lashing out at him. He looked past me at the fire, absently fiddling with the talisman in his hand.

"I slid the picture out of the album, remembering that Collette always jotted dates and little notes on the back. Seeing her handwriting again…"

Morley suddenly went quiet. I saw the corners of his mouth quiver. He cleared his throat.

"I read what she'd written on the photo aloud: 'San Francisco, August 28, 2008—'"

And he was gone. Just like that.

I jumped, losing my balance and nearly stumbling into the fire.

"What the *fuck?*" I screamed into the empty room. There had been no sound when he'd vanished, no warning. One moment he'd been sitting on that chair, *right there*, and the next, he was gone. I approached the chair cautiously, placing my hand on the seat. The leather was still warm. To my left, the fire snapped and hissed.

"This isn't funny!" I shouted. My eyes flitted about the room. Burnt orange shadows danced and shimmied over the walls like frisky imps. Any minute, I believed, Morley would spring out from behind his chair or out of the kitchen.

After a few moments, though, when he *hadn't* jumped out of the shadows, I set off to find him, starting upstairs in the master suite where I'd showered and changed earlier. Seeing the bedroom now, it looked completely different; as ominous as the day outside, where previously it had been a soothing refuge for my whirling mind and throbbing muscles.

I scoured every room on the top floor, jerking closets open, lifting bed skirts, repeating Morley's name wherever I went. I repeated the process on the main floor, ending at the door to the basement, hesitant. My head told me I would not find Morley hiding amongst camping gear and jars of pickles. My heart told me I had to rule it out. I shuddered as I reached for the door, scolding myself for having watched so many horror movies over the years. Why had basements been deemed prime hunting grounds for serial killers and monsters?

"Okay, Morley. Joke's over."

As I wrapped my fingers around the doorknob, I heard a thump back in the direction of the living room. "Morley!" I called, sprinting off down the hall.

When I reached the living room, Morley was scrambling to get up from his chair, flushed and wide-eyed, like he'd just walked away from a plane crash.

"*Syd!*" he shouted when he saw me rush into the room.

I wanted to scream. Instead I stood, breathless, staring at him as if he was a ghost. I burst into tears.

"Syd, I'm so sorry," he said, more calmly now, stretching his hands toward me.

Before I could think, I threw myself into his arms, nearly knocking him over. We regained our balance while I wept into his chest, unable to let go as I appraised his *realness*. It was the first time I'd cried since the day Isla had disappeared from my life.

"That was so careless of me," he said as we swayed together in front of the fire. Morley stroked my hair, my face, apparently having overcome his aversion to touching me.

After a few moments I stepped back and wiped my cheeks with the backs of my hands then held them up, regarding them with wonder as they glistened in the firelight. I crammed them into my armpits and cast my eyes to Morley, waiting for an explanation.

"I forgot I was holding this," he said, scooping his talisman off his chest. He dangled it in front of me. The dragonfly's wings pulsed in the flickering light, looking both playful and dangerous at once.

"Come. Sit down. I'll make you more tea."

"I don't want tea. I want to leave."

"Fair enough. I'm just about finished. Please sit," he said gesturing toward the sofa once again. I obliged hesitantly.

"So, did you enjoy your trip to San Francis—" I clapped my hand over my mouth.

Morley smiled. "Don't worry, you're not going anywhere. Two things must take place concurrently for a successful time-blink: you have to be holding your talisman between your thumb and forefinger and you have to recite the location, the time and the date, in that order. The *time* part is actually optional, but we'll get to that eventually. And no, I did not enjoy San Francisco. Not in the least."

"Oh?"

"No, of course not! I can only imagine what it must've looked like on this end. I was worried you would run off in a panic, although you wouldn't have made it very far in four and a half minutes."

"Is that how long you were gone? It seemed like an eternity."

"It was actually four minutes and forty-four seconds."

"You were timing yourself?"

"Back in the beginning, I did. Then I determined that every blink lasted the exact same amount of time, without exception."

I screwed my face up, confused.

"Yes, it's all very strange. Now, where was I?" he said, looking at the fan suspended from the vaulted section of ceiling as if it held the answer.

"Uh, San Francisco? Reading Collette's words?"

"Right! Of course. I recited the place and date, and in the blink of an eye—you know the feeling—I was deposited smack dab in the middle of the San Francisco airport…at midnight. Apart from a few travelers asleep on chairs, it was deserted, so no one had seen me arrive, which was a blessing. How would I explain *that*? I checked my vitals, and apart from a racing heart, all seemed normal. I didn't feel nauseous or drunk or drugged. I wandered through the quiet airport, trying, as you are now, to convince myself I would wake up any moment."

"But you didn't."

"No. No I didn't."

He closed his eyes for a few seconds to gather his thoughts.

"By dawn, with the airport coming to life, panic was starting to set in. I knew I had to get control of the situation. But how? I'd traveled eight hundred miles from home with no idea how I'd gotten there; didn't even have a wallet or phone on me. I contemplated going to the police, but what would I say? They'd have locked me up for sure if I'd told them the truth. And then I worried that I'd died and ended up as some hapless ghost shuffling around the airport for all of eternity.

My confidence bolstered a little when I saw my reflection in a restroom mirror and even more so when a woman on a cellphone bumped into me and apologized."

Morley jumped to his feet suddenly as if he were about to demonstrate the encounter. Instead, he snatched a fluffy chenille blanket from the back of a rocking chair and brought it over to me. "You look chilly."

I accepted the blanket and arranged it over my legs. I had to admit, his story was compelling, and it couldn't hurt to get comfortable while I listened.

"Better?" he said.

I nodded.

"Good. So by that point, several hours had passed. Not only was I exhausted, but my stomach was growling too. I needed food. I pushed my pride aside and started collecting spare change from travelers. It wasn't as hard as you might imagine. People seemed happy to help a polite, well dressed stranger who'd lost his wallet. I'd gathered enough money to order some breakfast in a coffee shop in the departure lounge. No problem at all. Even had enough to buy a newspaper. I gotta say, I was lost without my phone, but it and my pager were both at home on the kitchen counter. I later determined they don't work on timeblinks anyway."

Indulging him, I said, "And that was where you figured out the date? From the newspaper?"

"Aha! See? You get it."

I shrugged, pulling the blanket up to my chin.

"So you believe me."

"I'm keeping an open mind."

"Good, good. There's more."

"No shit. You promised this would only take fifteen minutes. That was a lie, wasn't it?"

He smiled. "I had to fudge the details a little to coax you back inside the house. Don't be angry."

I wasn't. How could I be? Here was Morley, alive and

talking to me after I'd watched him die a terrible, agonizing death, then pull off the most incredible illusion I'd ever seen.

"So, according to what you just told me, can I assume that…that my body isn't still back at home on my sofa?" This was possibly the strangest question I'd ever asked out loud. "I need to know what Coop will find if he wakes up and goes into our living room."

"You—your body, any clothes you were wearing, any jewelry—will disappear from your present during a timeblink, like what happened when I unwittingly traveled to San Francisco moments ago. Should Cooper go into your living room, he will find you missing as well as anything else that had been directly touching your skin, like the knitted blanket you brought along. He will find whatever items you had in your pockets—loose change, a cell phone, your wallet—in a little pile where you'd been sitting. The kettle will be on the stove, perhaps boiling, and the TV will be on, if that's the way you left it."

"What about the sofa? I was touching *that*. How come it didn't travel with me?"

"Nothing bigger than a carry-on suitcase goes. Also, nothing you're standing on: carpeting, hardwood flooring, concrete, asphalt. And no cars, which is unfortunate. It would certainly save you the trouble of taking taxis and busses everywhere. And stealing cars."

"You've stolen cars?"

"You do what y'gotta do."

"So I've been *here* for what, two hours now? You're saying if I go back, it'll be like picking up where I left off, but four and a half minutes later?"

"Yes. Regardless of how long you stay on this side—two hours, two days, two years—you'll in fact have only been missing in your present time for exactly four minutes and forty-four seconds. I don't recommend timeblinking any longer than a week though, unless you can be sure you'll look exactly the same when you get back. Once, after a week-long blink to a beach in Hawaii, I had a hell of a time explaining a fresh sunburn to my secretary. Stay indoors if you slide to a tropical climate for any length of time. Or use sunscreen."

Holy shit.

"You're just going to have to accept this for what it is, Syd. Embrace it."

I eyed the talisman on the coffee table.

"Why such a precise time? Four forty-four?"

He shrugged. "Fluke probably. I haven't been able to figure that out, but it seems irrelevant."

"How did you get back anyway? To your present?"

I had to remind myself that this—right here, right now—*was* his present. *I* was the time traveler.

"I'll come back to that part."

"I thought you'd say that."

He flashed a brief smile. "After that first freak trip to San Francisco, I couldn't timeblink again when I tried. I knew the talisman had had something to do with it because I'd been holding it right before I blinked that first time, so I set about replicating the scene at my apartment. Then I recited exactly the same words, held the same picture in one hand and the talisman in the other. Wore the same clothes. Even drank coffee from the same cup. Nothing worked."

"Well, you obviously figured it out at some point."

"Yes, I'd almost given up. Put it down to one fantastic experience in my life that I could never tell anyone about, and left it at that. Then one day while sitting in my office dictating a progress note, I was struck by the possibility that the missing piece was *order*."

"Order?"

"Remember I said that two things are necessary to timeblink?"

"Yes. You have to be holding the talisman and you have to say the date and destination out loud."

"Correct. But technically there are *three* mechanisms of timeblinking, the third being the *order* in which the details of a timeblink are recited. It must always be the place, the time and the date, otherwise it's a no-go. I'd been reciting it in the wrong order the whole time. That's when I embarked on my first voluntary timeblink."

"Weren't you terrified?"

"Not really. Nervous, yes, but not scared. The first one was terrifying. As I'm sure you understand."

"Tell me about it."

"I took the talisman in my hand and said, 'Jackson Beach, Friday Harbor, July 15, 1995'. You can probably guess what happened next."

I could. I let him continue anyway.

"It was midnight at Friday Harbor, and apart from some noisy teenagers sitting around a fire a little way down the beach, I was alone."

He got up and walked over to the fireplace, grabbed a metal rod and poked at some of the logs, then arranged another on top. He remained by the fire, staring into it as if footage of the night were playing there.

He chuckled. "The kids got all twitchy when I approached them out of the darkness, probably thinking I was there to shut the party down, but I only wanted to know what day it was. They obliged me with an answer then packed up their party and scurried off."

I smiled then gave him a puzzled look. "Why midnight? According to your story, you only recited the location and the date—not the time."

"Great question. If you don't state a time, the blink sends you to your chosen location one second after that date begins, local time."

"So you're saying midnight is the default and choosing a vague location leaves a heck of a lot to chance. That's why you ended up at the airport in San Francisco."

"Correct. And my error not stating a specific location at Chapman Falls is why you ended up in the waterfall itself."

"At eleven o'clock in the morning, no less. Why did you pick that time? Isn't it risky to go when there's a chance you'll be seen…appearing out of thin air?"

"It is. On the fateful night at The Merryport, not only will I fail to give you a specific location at Chapman Falls, but I'll mess up the time, too. I really should add *p.m.* to eleven o'clock or use military time since a blink sends you to the *first* eleven on the clock if you don't state which one. You'll have to excuse my blunder; I'll be in the process of dying when I give you the information."

I stared at him without speaking. He gave me a sheepish shrug and sat back down. "Goodness," he said. "Such a sad face."

"How do you even know about it?"

"What? My death? That story is for another day. I don't want to overwhelm you with too much information all at once."

I only half hoped he would tell me the story about why, now that he knew about the upcoming tragedy, he couldn't stop it from happening.

"So how many times have you, uh, timeblinked?"

His face brightened at my change of focus. "Thirty-six times, well, thirty-seven if you count today's trip to San Fran. I'm sure I'll blink a few more times before I, you know," he said, slicing his neck with his finger, sticking his tongue out to the side.

"Jesus, Morley!"

"What? There's no point in being all serious about it. But enough about me. I need to give you the basics of timeblinking, then I'll send you on your way. Sound good?"

I nodded, snuggling down into the blanket.

He reiterated how the timeblinks occur, hammering the point home that you must always, *always* state the exact place and time unless you want to leave it to chance vis-à-vis plunging over a hundred-foot waterfall in broad daylight.

"Skin is also an important factor in the equation. A huge one. Once you make skin-to-skin contact with someone in present time, they will not be able to see, hear or touch you during a blink. In effect, you're a ghost to anyone you've ever exchanged skin cells with. By some miracle, throughout our entire acquaintanceship, we've never brushed skin."

My mind flew back to earlier tonight when I'd rushed over to hug him. Surely we'd made skin-to-skin contact then?

"However," he said, intuiting my thoughts, "The effect is void if you're in a timeblink. Like you are now."

I nodded. "So that's why you're not wearing your gloves."

He smiled and leaned forward, elbows on his knees, clasping his hands in front of him. "You know, you're lucky."

"Oh?"

"I had to learn all of this on my own. You, on the other hand, have a tutor. Oh the mistakes I could've avoided! Yes, you are indeed very lucky."

I didn't feel lucky. I felt overwhelmed and anxious and tired at once. Morley seemed to pick up on it.

"All right, I'm going to tell you how to get home, but let's meet again soon. At Chapman Falls."

My eyes narrowed. "Can't I come here instead?"

"Regretfully, no. It has to be the falls. Another quirk of timeblinking is that you had to have visited the destination at least once in your life already. Fortunately, I recalled your love of Chapman Falls, and even more fortunately, it's located right across the highway from here."

An idea struck. "Why don't I just come to the cabin in, uh, my real time and touch the door?"

He shook his head. "If only it were that easy. One final nuance of timeblinking is that you can't travel back in time *past* your first contact with a place. Say you went to the Grand

Canyon when you were six years old; you can't blink back to the Grand Canyon when you were five."

It did make sense, and at the risk of compromising my mental health status, I had no choice but to go along with his story, at least for now.

"So when you come back," he paused to wink at me, "you'll be timeblinking to Chapman and walking up."

"What if someone sees me?"

"It will be at night, after the park is closed."

"I'll make damned sure I say a specific location, like *parking lot.*"

He chuckled and nodded toward the stairs. "Anyway, your clothes should be dry now. Go ahead and get changed, then I'll tell you how to get home. I think I've covered all the main points. Any questions?"

God, I had a million.

"Next time," I said. And just like that, I'd made another appointment with Dr. Scott. Five percent of my brain was locked on the idea this was a dream anyway, and it was that five percent that had allowed me to agree to another meeting so freely.

A few minutes later I stepped into the living room wearing my own clothes, finding Morley gazing distantly into the fire.

"That's better," he said when he noticed me in my freshly laundered leggings and t-shirt. My mother's afghan was folded and draped over my forearm, still warm from the dryer.

"I do have one question," I said. "Why me?"

He stood, plucking the talisman off the coffee table and slipping it over my head. Without saying anything, he took me by the shoulders and kissed my forehead—a friendly, almost fatherly gesture that made my heart flutter just the same.

"Because, Sydney, out of everyone I know, you have the most to gain."

"What do you mean by *that?*"

"I guess you'll have to find out the next time we meet."

"Seriously? You're going to leave me hanging like that?"

"You could stay and find out. I told you: whether you stay ten minutes or ten days, upon returning to your living room, only four minutes and forty-four seconds will have elapsed. Fantastic, isn't it?"

That was the understatement of the day. I couldn't possibly stay though. My nerves were shot and I was beyond exhausted. I needed to get home and think in my own space, and *maybe* meet Morley again.

"I'm more than ready to go."

"Okay. Like I said, I had to learn how to return to my present all on my own, and do you know how long it took? Thirty-six hours. It was an absolute fluke, and I'm lucky to have figured it out at all."

"What, like by saying my address and the date and time?"

"Even easier. First, you just hold the talisman in your hand; go on."

I didn't reach for it right away. "I should be honest with you. I haven't decided whether or not I'm coming back."

"You will." His eyes sparkled like emeralds in the firelight. My mind flew back to my real life, my happy life with Coop, and I chased off the butterflies in my stomach.

"You seem very sure of that." I said.

"Yep."

I grasped the talisman. "Okay, I'm ready."

He produced a folded piece of paper from his pocket and tucked it into my other hand.

"Consider this your 'prescription'," he said winking. "For our next visit. Remember: Your skin must be touching anything you want to bring with you or it stays behind."

I looked down at the square of paper in my hand, woozy with guilt. I clamped my eyes shut, suddenly yearning for him to kiss me. Right that minute.

Stop it, Sydney Anne Brixton!

He didn't kiss me. Didn't even touch me, in fact. His voice broke my thoughts. "Syd?"

My eyes flew open.

"Your eyes can't be closed."

"Good grief. Why so many rules?"

"I didn't make them. Just figured them out over time."

"Okay. Let's get this over with," I said, taking the talisman between my fingers.

"All you do next is say *'Return'.*"

"That's it?" I said.

"That's it."

And before I had a chance to change my mind, I said, "Return."

After a split second of darkness—which felt more like a black spark than a blink—I'd been transported to my living room sofa, right where Morley had promised. I ran my hands over my body, taking deep breaths to keep myself from fainting. It seemed I'd survived the return trip unscathed, though there was a ringing in my ears so loud I had to press my hands over them. I hadn't remembered such a piercing noise during my trip to Chapman Falls, though there had been plenty of other sounds.

Amidst the ringing, I made out a brownish blur shooting up the stairs like a missile. Then it hit me: the missile was Jinx, and the incessant, shrill whistling was the kettle on high boil. I threw my mother's afghan aside and ran over to switch off the stove. At the same time, I heard Coop bounding down the stairs, and he flew into the living room in his boxer shorts, wild eyed and out of breath.

"What the fuck's going on?"

I didn't know how much he'd seen. He could've been in the living room once already and discovered me missing only to return moments later to find me standing in the kitchen by the stove. That is, if it all hadn't been a crazy dream. Whatever it had been, I wasn't about to tell Coop about it, not yet anyway.

It was then that my gaze landed on the 'prescription'. Not in my hand, but sitting conspicuously on top of my mother's blanket on the sofa. I tore my eyes away from it and raked my fingers through my hair. "Nothing's going on," I said, trying not to shake.

"Nothing? Jinx just ran past me like he was being chased by a bear, and that damned kettle's been whistling forever. What gives?"

For all I knew, the kettle could've been whistling the whole four and a half minutes I'd been at Morley's cabin.

So there it was. Full acceptance I was bona fide time traveler.

"I, I…I'm so sorry," I said. A tear formed in my lower lid and paused a couple of seconds before slipping down my cheek. "I was in the bathroom."

Coop rushed over and hugged me tight, probably thinking he'd triggered an anxiety attack. Little did he know that the anxiety was in fact guilt, and it had nothing to do with my potentially burning the house down.

"I'm sorry," I sobbed into his chest. My guilt deepened. I'd done this same thing with Morley earlier.

"Shh. Shh. It's okay. It just startled me. Jinx, too, by the look of it."

He kissed me on the top of my head and encouraged me to take deep breaths. He'd never seen me cry. Not once. We stood that way for a good two minutes while we both found a place of calm.

I had to get rid of that note.

"Your hair smells nice," Coop said, taking a step back, trying to lighten the mood. "Are you using something new?"

My heart surged into my throat. Morley's shampoo. The

synapses in my brain went off like fireworks while I searched for an explanation, but none came. "Nope. Same as always."

I felt like screaming.

His eyebrows crunched together, and he chuckled. "Guess I haven't had my nose in your hair lately."

I laughed, nervously I thought, but not enough to give him pause. He looked around the room. "Weird that Jinx hasn't come back."

"The kettle must've really freaked him out," I said, grateful for the change of subject.

"That makes two of us."

"Three."

Coop pulled me in for another quick hug and pecked me on the cheek. "I'm going to get a bit more shuteye. You'll be okay?"

"Yes, yes. Go!" I said thrusting my finger toward the stairs. When I noticed it shaking I snatched it out of air and hugged both arms around my belly. "Get some sleep, mister. I'll be fine."

As he walked away, my phone vibrated on the coffee table.

"That's probably your sister," he said turning around at the bottom of the stairs. His eyes flicked toward the scrap of paper on the sofa but either he didn't see it or he didn't deem it suspicious. "She called my cell while you were trying to burn the place down."

"Why'd she call *you*?" As the words left my mouth, I realized she'd probably tried my phone first, but I'd been on a trip to Crazytown.

"Probably because you were in the bathroom. I didn't have the chance to answer. That's when all hell broke loose down here."

I scooped up my phone and took the call, waving Coop along. "Hey sis. What's up?"

Kendall was frantic on the other end. She said she was just about to jump into her car to come to our place; she'd been worried sick something had happened when both Coop and I neglected to pick up our phones.

"You worry way too much," I sighed, grabbing the folded note. I opened it, only half listening to my sister. Fitting. It was an actual prescription chit from Morley's office bearing a list of three destinations with corresponding dates and times.

Kendall went on ranting about my terrible phone etiquette, but my mind drifted to the dates. *Here I go again, trying to unravel another of Morley's mysteries.*

My thoughts were interrupted by Coop calling me upstairs. I folded the paper hurriedly and tucked it into the novel I'd been reading.

Kendall was still blabbering in my ear. "I gotta go. Coop needs me," I said, switching the phone off and tossing it onto the sofa. I knew I'd get an earful about that later too, but Coop sounded utterly distraught.

I found him on the floor, splayed out on his stomach next to the bed.

"Oh my God, what happened?" I said, swooping down beside him.

"I don't know. He won't come out."

Coop was fine, but Jinx was another story. He'd tucked himself under the bed as far as he could go and was trembling like a leaf.

"Come here, buddy," I said in my gentlest voice.

"The kettle must've really set him off," Coop said, reaching in to stroke the dog's front leg. Jinx whimpered and licked his lips nervously.

"I don't know. Maybe? But it's not like he hasn't heard it before. I'll get him," I said, lying flat. As soon as I started wriggling my way under the bed, Jinx growled and bared his teeth then scurried past me and Coop and out of the room, crashing to the floor repeatedly as his claws skittered across the slick hardwood.

"Jinx!" I called.

Coop went after him and I shimmied out from under the bed, wondering what could've spooked our pup so badly. It was like he'd seen a ghost.

Oh, no.

Jinx had been sitting next to me on the sofa when I disappeared.

This wasn't going to be an easy fix, and I wouldn't blame the poor thing if he were scarred for life. How do you tell your furry kid everything was going to be okay? That there was a perfectly rational explanation for what he'd seen? That his mama was simply a time traveler, and really, she'd only been gone a few minutes?

Just as I'd decided to hang back and give our poor pup some time to calm down, Coop called me from the living room. I didn't want to go down there but couldn't put it off. I had to act as if I didn't know what was wrong with Jinx.

When I arrived, Jinx was in his kennel and Coop was shrugging into his jacket.

"Where are you going?"

"I'm taking him to the vet. He won't stop shaking."

"I—I don't think he needs to go to the vet, hon. He just got spooked."

"Look at him."

Coop was hypersensitive when it came to our dog or any other living being experiencing even a hint of distress. It was a big part of his job, after all, and I considered it one of his sexiest traits. I had to talk him off the ledge. We certainly didn't need to throw hundreds of dollars at this problem.

"I'll take him. You need your rest."

"I won't be able to sleep now," he said, his eyes wide with worry.

I walked past the kennel to give Coop a hug. Jinx let out an anxious whine but didn't bark.

"If you load him into the car, I'll take him. This was my fault anyway."

Coop took a breath, exhaling dramatically. "Okay, fine," he said, grabbing the crate.

It felt a bit sneaky, but then again, I hadn't said *where* I was taking Jinx, and when I opened my hatchback at the park ten minutes later, the big old bundle of fluff was wagging his tail, pawing at the kennel door with his favorite ball in his mouth. It seemed he'd already forgotten about my little indiscretion.

I texted Coop with the good news. He'd seemed relieved but said the bigger test would be when Jinx was back at home where the trauma had occurred. Would he get spooked all over again? I said I didn't think so and felt relatively confident about that. Jinx's problem was with me. Or rather the *lack* of me. And I wasn't about to zap out on him like that again…at least not while he was in the same room.

Chapter Four

Cassandra, my therapist, waited for my answer while she sipped water from an overpriced, over-decorated aluminum bottle that should've been stamped with the words *"the owner of this product is serious about hydration...and you will admire and respect her for it"*. Her hair sat in a messy bun on the top of her head and she was dressed in black leggings with a tailored blazer over a bright green t-shirt. The collar of her blazer was turned under on one side, making me wonder if she'd had to dress hastily after a yoga class that had gone too long before our appointment.

I forced a smile, wishing these sessions didn't make me want to jump out the tenth-floor window. The only thing stopping me was the little movie playing in my head, the one where Coop and Kendall stood behind me like excited parents coaxing a child to ride a bike, cheering me on, encouraging me to keep pedalling.

It's not to say that Cassandra isn't a genuinely lovely person. She is. The loveliness is just a tad overwhelming. She always starts a session with the same question: "How have you been doing?" It's not asked in the way a clerk at the grocery store asks but in a way that penetrates you, pointed in a way,

I'm sure, to dredge up dusty, purposely abandoned memories from the depths of the soul. The emphasis is always on the last word: "How have you been *doing?*" her brows coming together, her mouth held in a sort of pained smile, and it always has the opposite effect on me, forcing my deepest feelings into an airtight bottle. I normally try to appease her with a basic, "Good" or, at the most, "Up and down," partly because I detest talking to strangers about myself and partly because I can't afford to throw the gate wide open. Especially now. I couldn't risk her prodding to the point where I'd be helpless to keep my mouth shut about certain things that *must* be kept under wraps. A shame. All that health coverage wasted on dead air.

Today I didn't give her the benefit of a reply at all. How could I possibly answer? *"Well,"* I might say, *"I time traveled to last April. Saw my old pal who is actually dead. He wants me to come back and see him again, and the crazy thing is, I think I might."*

I tore my eyes away from her inside-out collar to fidget with the strap of my trusty old black purse, a gift from Kendall five Christmases ago, or was it six? The strap was cracked and thinning at the top where it sat on my shoulder and would probably break soon. *Hm. Time for a new purse.*

"At some point I'd like us to talk more about what's going on here and here," Cassandra said, pointing to her head and heart. "Instead of just your activities moving through the day."

Don't be so sure, Cassandra. My activities would blow your freaking mind.

I looked up at her. "You said this was an open, anything-goes discussion."

"It is. But this is what, our fourth session? And I have only a loose idea of who you are inside. Would you like to go over what I *do* know, based on what we've talked about so far? Then build on that, perhaps?"

I glanced at the clock. Fifty-three minutes to go. Somebody kill me *now*.

"Fire away," I said, slumping down in the chair like a moody teenager, suddenly embarrassed for myself.

I'd been quite skilled at introspective stuff once. When I was a kid, before Isla disappeared, I would announce to my family I wanted some "Syd Time" and venture out into the yard on the coldest, blusteriest day to construct a flimsy tent of blankets, bikes, and lawn chairs. I must've been nine or ten. I'd sit, huddled in a sleeping bag, occasionally using shoes or firewood to secure flapping blanket walls, and ponder existential ideas like *Who am I?* and *What's my purpose in the world?* I'd close my eyes, listen to the wind battering the massive oak trees almost to their breaking points and imagine what the universe would be like with no humans, no Earth. No *me*. My brain would almost implode under the weight of the idea. All I could picture was a black void with no beginning and no end, and when Isla went missing and my mother died a year later, I didn't have to imagine it anymore. I stared into that gaping abyss every day.

"Your identical twin was abducted when you were eleven," Cassandra said, settling her glasses on her nose and flipping back a few pages in her notebook.

Talk about starting the session off with a bang.

For a distraction, I looked around the room. The sappy "inspirational" pictures on the walls made me want to scream, so I rested my gaze instead on the floor-to-ceiling window where lazy drizzles of rain streaked down the glass. I yearned to feel them on my face.

"It's okay. We can focus on other things until you're ready," Cassandra said. Out of the corner of my eye, I saw her jot something in her notebook.

I pressed my lips together then blew all the air out of my lungs. "On the day Isla disappeared, my soul went with her." I brought my focus back to Cassandra. She nodded without saying a word.

"We'd been planning out scenes to include in our history video, arguing more than agreeing—you know, like sisters do. Yeah, we argued the last time we were together."

When Cassandra stayed silent, I focused on the metal emblem fastened to one of her patent leather pumps. "We finally settled on a news-style video of the Maroon Mansion, this big, hundred-year-old monstrosity next to Pembina Park. All the neighborhood kids believed it was haunted. Nobody ever saw a light on. None of us had ever seen anyone coming or going, apart from the odd delivery person. We'd had our theories about who lived there, ranging from a child-snatching witch to a family of ghosts and everything in between."

Cassandra licked her lips, like you do when you hear a scary story around a campfire.

"My mother used to get angry with us for being such willing parties to the gossip. I remember her saying, 'Can you imagine how the owner of the house would feel knowing what the neighborhood children were saying? Think about how it feels to be singled out as weird.'"

I adjusted my position on the faux leather sofa to get more comfortable, but the cushion was as hard as granite. I wondered if it was another ploy to get people talking—furniture as a torture tactic.

"That's when my mother suggested we do our history project on the house, proving or disproving the tales circulating among the neighborhood kids. I'd been against it right off the bat. The place creeped me out. The fact it was painted the exact color of dried blood did nothing to ease my fears, either."

"I can imagine," Cassandra said with that pinched, worried look I'd come to despise.

"It was Isla who'd pointed out that the idea was worth considering. Ha. Trust Isla to side with my mother. She'd said it would be fun to learn about the mysterious house while—bonus—looking like heroes in the eyes of our classmates. That point alone convinced me. Surprisingly, the house had quite the colorful history, none of which was the least bit disturbing. The most interesting fact turned out to be the reason there were never any lights on inside the house: the owners at the time, a husband and wife in their fifties, were both blind."

Cassandra placed her hand tenderly over her heart. "That's amazing. You girls faced your fears head on and look what you gained from it."

What about how much had been lost?

"For years after, I was convinced of their involvement in Isla's disappearance, but the police never found any evidence to implicate them. I'd just been so desperate to pin the blame on someone. Anyone that wasn't…"

Me.

With that, the spell was broken. I could feel myself run out of steam, and I collapsed onto the sofa like a deflated balloon. Cassandra nodded. "I'm proud of you for sharing, Sydney. It's a really good start. We can pick up on that thread next time or as soon as you feel ready."

I appreciated her intuition.

"That's a lovely pendant," she said, switching gears completely.

I reached up and clutched the talisman protectively.

"I noticed it at your first appointment," she said. "Do you mind if I ask where you got it? My sister's birthday's coming up, and she's mad for dragonflies. I don't think she has a necklace quite as nice as yours."

"I—I got it from a friend," I said, letting it drop to my chest.

"Your friend has good taste."

I smiled weakly.

Cassandra leaned forward. "Do you know much about dragonflies?"

"Not really."

"I didn't either until my sister became obsessed with them. She says that if you dream about one, change is coming, good or bad."

I raised my brows, hoping this wasn't a trick to get me talking again.

"Interesting, right? She also says that because adult dragonflies have a super short lifespan—four months at the most— in certain cultures they serve as a reminder of the fleeting nature of life and that we should try to live each day to the fullest."

It was like a 500-watt lightbulb went on in the room. I left my appointment a half an hour later knowing exactly what my next move would be.

It was noon when I coasted to a stop at the end of Morley's driveway. From the road, the cabin stood dark and gloomy, looking almost sorry for itself. I cut the engine and cranked my window down breathing deeply as a crisp gust flowed inside. After a soaking rain, the air was heavy with the scents of pine and wet gravel, and the only sounds were the ticking of my engine and water dripping from birch and evergreen branches.

Suddenly I felt self-conscious about sitting outside Morley's grand property in my beat-up Civic like a teenaged girl with a crush. What if I was being watched? Or worse, what if some loudmouthed TV host were about to jump out of the bushes to tell me I'd been had, laughing about what a great sport I'd been through the whole elaborate prank?

Yet that explanation didn't hold much weight, especially with Morley's note sitting on the seat beside me. The cabin's address and three dates were right there in his handwriting, proving not only that time travel was possible, but also that I'd brought back physical evidence of it.

"You win, Morley."

It appeared as though I was going through with it. I had the talisman. I had Morley's 'prescription'. There was nothing to stop me. Especially now, with curiosity pestering me like a hungry dog. Besides, what better way to confirm the power? If nothing happened, if I spoke the date and place and ended up staying right here at the cabin in present time, no harm in it. I'd carry on as normal and chalk it all up to a wild dream I'd once had.

I started the car and eased it down the driveway toward the cabin, parking in the same spot Morley had less than a week ago...*my time.* I climbed out of the car. Granted, this feat could've been performed from the comfort of my own home, like the last time, but it felt safer to do it out here in relative privacy. Without Jinx near me.

I'm really doing this.

I stepped onto the concrete stoop. Lush bunches of winter kale had been planted in the two black urns on either side of the door since I'd been here last. It was well tended, confirming the moderately disquieting impression that someone had been coming here regularly.

No matter. I would only be here—rather, *gone*—a few minutes.

My hand trembled as it met one of the cool, damp logs running horizontally from the door to the right side of the house. As I stepped back, an icy breeze whispered up the driveway and knocked a few strands of hair out of my ponytail. I tucked them behind my ear. Adjusted my collar. Bounced up and down on the balls of my feet a few times. Wrung my hands.

Come on, chickenshit. What are you waiting for?

The destination was ready on my lips. And the time and date. I took the talisman in hand and drew a cleansing breath into my lungs. "Chapman Falls parking lot, 9 p.m., April 28, 2019."

There was a quick black flash behind my eyes—a blink—and then I was somewhere else.

Some*when* else.

In the night sky over Chapman Falls hung scattered, middle-altitude clouds resembling neon cotton balls. Muted light from the last quarter of the moon and clusters of twinkling stars revealed a deserted parking lot, just as Morley had assured me. It seemed I'd arrived at my desired destination intact and at the right time.

As I set off to find Morley's cabin, my foot came down on something sharp, making me jump, and that's when I noticed one of my boots missing. "Great," I muttered. Apparently time travel only allowed for one Chelsea boot at a time. As I bent down to massage my foot, I heard a noise behind me and whirled around.

"Sydney! How unexpected!" came a voice followed by a thin beam of light, and I nearly leapt out of my other boot.

"Shit, Morley! What are you doing here?"

His flashlight found my face. "Sorry about that. Thought I'd be chivalrous and escort you back to the cabin."

He marched up to me and planted a quick peck on my left temple. I felt a warmth rise in my cheeks and was grateful for the dim light.

"You have a knack for scaring the bejeebers out of me."

"I probably should've mentioned I'd meet you here," he said, offering me his arm. "Shall we?"

As I took my first step, I was stabbed again in the foot. "*Damnit!*"

Morley grabbed my arm to steady me, sweeping the beam of his flashlight toward my mismatched feet. "Leave in a hurry?"

"I have no idea what happened. I was wearing two boots

when I left, and then I get here—poof—one boot, lost in the cosmos."

He had a different explanation. "Skin."

"Of course. Skin," I agreed, sarcastically.

"Your left boot wasn't touching your ankle, whereas your right one obviously was."

"Right. *That*," I said. "Come on. Let's get going before I change my mind."

"After you," he said.

Apart from the scant light of the waning moon and Morley's flashlight, the road up to his cabin was unnervingly dark, and I was thankful for his company. When we rounded the last bend a few minutes later, I gasped at the glowing structure at the end of the driveway where elaborate lighting from well-hidden spotlights made the cabin seem bigger than ever. As we made our way up the driveway, I did a double-take: there was Morley's Tesla parked where my old rusted beater had been moments ago, as if it had magically morphed into this sleek white machine *à la* Cinderella's coach. The massive iron planters on each side of the front door were still there, except now they were bare, containing only soil where bushy plumes of purple kale had been growing when I'd left.

Inside the front door, Morley hung my coat on a hook while I took off my remaining boot and socks, rubbing the bottom of my foot.

"How is it? Do you need a bandage?"

"It's fine—just a scrape. No blood."

"Good," he said, gesturing to the living room off the front hall.

The room, of course, had not changed in the interval, except that it felt cozier now that it was dark outside. A healthy fire crackled away in the floor-to-ceiling fireplace generating a warmth I was grateful for on the chilly spring night.

"You look lovely," he said as we walked into the room. "And more relaxed. Much better than the last time you were here." I took a self-conscious swipe at my hair, silently cursing my hastily made ponytail. If I'd admitted to myself earlier that I was coming here, I would've made myself look at least moderately presentable, but today's trip had been quite spontaneous.

"I knew what to expect this time," I said, lowering myself to the sofa. On the coffee table sat a marble charcuterie board brimming with meats, cheeses and spreads along with two champagne glasses filled with fizzy amber liquid. Had he forgotten I didn't drink?

He picked up one of the glasses, urging me to do the same. "I thought a little bubbly would be in order. Sparkling apple juice, to be exact."

I smiled and picked up my glass.

"This is a toast to my travel partner, Sydney Brixton, who decided to come back even when she suggested she might not. Cheers."

It was a bit like old times at the pub as we clinked our glasses together and took sips of the sparkling juice.

"This is bizarre," I said, putting the glass down and reaching for an olive with one of the tiny metal forks Morley had set out.

"It took me a while to wrap my head around it, too, but you'll get used to it."

"Only if I do it again. But you know better than I do on that subject, apparently."

"My lips are sealed," he said, popping a few cashews into his mouth. He was the picture of health: happy, bright. Alive. Obviously excited to have someone else to share his big secret with. He rubbed at the stubble along his jaw when I asked him if he had much more to teach me.

"You've learned the basics: how to blink to a destination and how to get home. I, on the other hand, had to find out all the nuances and limitations on my own. Not that I think you're incapable of figuring it out. You're smart and would be perfectly fine navigating it with or without my help. However—"

He sighed, shifting his focus to a spot above the fireplace where a pair of massive deer antlers hung.

"However, what?"

"However, I do want to warn you about one of the pitfalls."

"That sounds serious."

"It is. And I'd like to get it out of the way now so we can enjoy the rest of our visit."

He stood suddenly and took a position in front of the fireplace like he was about to make a speech to a crowd. From my vantage point, it looked like the antlers were growing out of his head. A minute ago I would've giggled.

"The biggest mistake I've made is using the power to go to the future. It was how I found out when—and how—I'm going to die."

"Oh, Morley, that's awful." Instinct urged me to go to him, to give him a hug or at least a reassuring rub on the shoulder, but I gave him space instead.

He walked over to the window and looked out. Beyond his silhouette, a row of uniformly spaced lights twinkled across the lake, and I realized they were the same low path lights that ran along Morley's beach.

"I tried traveling to dates thirty, forty, a hundred years in the future, to no avail, and I'd all but convinced myself that going to the future wasn't possible. Then on a whim I tried traveling here to the cabin, a week into my future, and nearly had a coronary when it worked.

"At that point," he continued, "I tried timeblinking to a series of dates in the future without success: first three years out, then two, then one year. When the six-month blink worked, I don't know if I was more excited that I'd muscled my way into the future or more concerned about the implications of the timeframe."

"Where did you go?"

"France." He laughed as he turned around, flashing me a nostalgic smile. "I thought, *go big or go home.* Collette and I had gone to Nice for our fifth wedding anniversary, so I blinked to the hotel where we'd stayed up in Chateauneuf Villevieille, where the Alps start—or end, depending on who you talk to. I went at 3 a.m., and at dawn I hitched a ride down with one of the locals going into town. It was beautiful, you know? I stayed the whole day; popped into some of the shops Collette and I had visited then traced the same walk, mostly meandering seaside, to this charming little fishing village about a third of the way to Monaco. Villefranche-sur-Mer. I spent some time on the beach under an umbrella then made my way up to a seaside patio for a baguette and a glass of rosé. Just sat and enjoyed the view, people-watching. Missing my wife."

Morley closed his eyes then, and I didn't want to disturb him. The love he and Collette once shared had obviously been profound, like mine and Coop's. I was suddenly overcome with guilt. *What the heck am I doing here, eating cheese and olives with Morley at his lakeside retreat?* I pushed the guilt down. This man was my friend, and I could visit him if I wanted to.

Morley seemed to sense my unease and clapped his hands together to break the tension. "So, there you have it. Future timeblinking conquered."

It all seemed so lovely and idyllic, yet somehow along the way he'd stumbled upon his death date.

"I had my suspicions about why I couldn't go to the future any further out than six or eight months."

"You can't travel to a date past your death."

He nodded. "Just as you can't visit a date before you were born."

"How did you figure it out?"

He came and sat down next to me. My pulse quickened.

"It was easy. I embarked on a marathon of timeblinks to narrow down the window. Knowing I'd been able to blink to February 1, 2019—when I went to France—and that I'd been *un*successful in blinking to November 1, 2019, I knew it had to be sometime between those dates. I worked my way backward from November 1, one week at a time, until I was finally able to blink to September 13."

I jumped in. "Meaning you were still alive on September 13 but not September 20."

"Bingo. Of course, you already know the rest of the story; further deduction established my means and time of death. Friday the thirteenth, no less. I'm a walking cliché."

"Why don't you just stop it from happening? Now that you know?"

"Believe me, I've experimented a hundred ways from Sunday, and it's just not possible. There's absolutely nothing I can do to stop myself from walking out of The Merryport directly into the path of a speeding lunatic."

I shook my head. It was the curse of September all over again. When the people I cared about disappeared from my life forever. Surely he was missing some key ingredient that would save his own life.

"I know what you're thinking," he said, snapping my focus back. "But we can't change the future. On that note, we can't change the past, either."

"What if there was some way—now that I have the power, too—that we could figure it out together?"

"I was afraid of this. Look, Syd. You're just going to have to drop it. I have to die."

"No. You don't. Don't you think this kind of power landed in our laps for a reason? Maybe you were meant to live. Maybe I'm the key!"

He closed his eyes and sighed. Of *course* he'd thought of all possible angles. Who was I to question him anyway? Me, a recovering alcoholic bartender who hadn't even finished high school.

He leapt to his feet, "This 'change the future' thinking has to stop, Syd. Immediately. I'm the one who's been time traveling, remember? I have many months of experience, and I've learned that you can't"—his voice caught, changing from unease to subtle anger—"you *can't* mess with destiny."

I massaged my forehead with my fingertips so that he couldn't see my eyes, spotting the fancy cheeses and the Capocollo and the fig jam warming on the marble board. Frustrated with his lack of fight, I jumped up to face him. "You're a *doctor*. You change people's destinies all the time."

"Look at it this way," he said. "Since the dawn of time, a person's life has a fixed length. Locked and sealed, the key thrown away. When I save a life, it's *meant* to be, but only because it's happening on a predetermined continuum, not as a result of anyone—you, me, or whoever else might have this power—jumping in from other realms, rearranging events at will."

I suddenly felt lightheaded. "I need some air."

"Perfect," Morley said. "We'll take a walk around the lake."

"In the dark?"

"See those lights along the path? They go all the way around. One of the perks of the community. I'll bring a flashlight, though."

A few minutes later, I emerged from the house in a pair of borrowed boots (Collette's? I didn't ask) shrugging into my raincoat in silence. While Morley locked up, I started toward the beach. In the short time we'd been inside, the clouds from earlier had broken up and all but disappeared, leaving the sky full of glimmering stars. A crisp, light breeze whispered through pine branches, calming me instantly.

When Morley caught up, he guided me down a neatly clipped lawn to a narrow cobblestone path that stretched in both directions. On the other side of the path was a small, sandy beach, in pleasant contrast to the rocky, seaweed-covered shores along the coast. Kendall's boys would love it here.

I'd never been to Sandalwood Lake before, and in fact didn't personally know anyone that had. Observing it now, even in the dark, I saw why it had never been on my radar: it was dotted with about twenty homes, equal to or bigger than Morley's, whose fenced or tree-lined properties prevented the public from getting anywhere near the beach.

"It's magical," I said.

Morley pointed his flashlight to the right and I followed along. "It is, isn't it? I've cut back on my hours and try to get out here as much as possible. With September looming, I'll have to make the most of my summer."

"How can you be so casual about the whole thing?"

"I've known about it for a while now. It's had time to gel."

We walked for a few minutes in easy silence. My brain had some gelling of its own to do, though I didn't believe it would ever come to accept Morley's fate.

As if reading my mind, he broke the silence. "Don't you think there's a reason I've been unable to change anything in the past or future? I mean, I can't blame you for thinking otherwise; I had been of the same mind after my first blink—that a power like this doesn't come along without purpose. In fact, over time, I came to believe the power had fallen into my lap specifically to save my life. How naïve and self-important of me, to think I could interfere with fate or the will of God, or whatever higher power you might believe in.

"It didn't stop me from trying though, from disguising myself and timeblinking to that fateful night at The Merry-port. I went around talking to different people: the group from the bank, the print-shop gang. I gave them simple instructions on the pretense of a surprise party waiting at home for the version of me that was sitting at the bar: I said, '*Tell him his wife needs him at home right away.*' I would have recognized it as a warning from my timeblinking self and high-tailed it out of there. My would-be accomplices always happily obliged, and some even headed over to give me the message, but at the last moment, they'd turn around with a confused look and veer off to the restrooms or back to their table."

My heart felt like it might break into a million pieces, the thought of him having traveled to the future to ward off his own demise.

"Wait a minute. Wouldn't I have been at least moderately alarmed seeing a duplicate of you walking around my pub that night, chatting with other customers?"

"I was in disguise, like I said. You even talked to me."

"I did?"

"You did. I arrived at the pub just after you came back from your break. Knowing the "real-time" version of me would be coming in any minute, I gave you specific instructions to let Morley know I couldn't meet him as planned. You agreed to pass on my message and even got me to write down my name on a napkin. I used a fake one, of course. Then I left. And you promptly forgot the whole conversation." He shrugged as though it hardly mattered, but I felt horrified, and deeply guilty.

"Was the name you wrote down Charles?"

"Chris."

"Right, Chris. I remember finding that napkin and just threw it out, thinking it was someone's garbage. But wait, if all that is true, how come you can remember everything we've talked about here?"

"Have you tried to influence a future or past event in any way since you've been here, other than hypothesizing about it?"

After thinking about it a moment, I shook my head.

"This is a perfect segue into Timeblinking 101: Part 2," he said, grinning. "Or: all the stuff I didn't get around to telling you last time because you had to dash home to turn off your tea kettle."

"Don't laugh. It was pure chaos when I got back—Coop running into the room to find out why the kettle had been whistling for so long and my sister in a panic because Coop and I weren't answering our phones. Not to mention my poor traumatized dog."

"Sorry," Morley said, smirking, one hand over his mouth, "but you have to see the humor in it."

I smiled despite myself.

Our route around the lake was lit with the same low-voltage path lights that ran in front of Morley's cabin, which stayed on all year, according to Morley. Each section of the path seemed to have been created by individual owners rather than any well thought-out engineering, and the surface was uneven in some areas and downright treacherous in others. Morley anticipated these spots and offered his hand to help me cross them. A few stretches between the properties had no formal paths at all. My foot sunk into a patch of mud in one of them, and I wondered if the outline of my borrowed boot would still be there in my present time, six months from now.

Morley's voice cut the silence. "I want to reinforce one of the more important aspects of timeblinking. Remember how I said that if you've had skin-to-skin contact with someone in your natural timeline they will not be able to see, hear or touch you when you've blinked to their time?"

I nodded.

"It includes *you*."

"So you're saying that if I timeblinked to last week when I was at Kendall's house with the whole family, nobody, *including me*, would be able to see me?"

"You got it, you're essentially a ghost. And not one of those floaty, transparent ones, either. You'll be completely invisible."

Silence came again, and again it was pleasant, not

awkward. I was enjoying the freshness of the night air, of spending time with Morley.

We plodded along for maybe fifteen minutes, dodging crumbled stone and overgrown brush. Morley occasionally broke the stillness of the night to tell me about the people that owned the properties along the lake. They all knew each other, most of them acquaintances rather than friends. Most were upscale citizens—doctors, lawyers, CEOs—but one of them, Morley explained, was a window washer who'd hit the big time in the lottery at nineteen, some twenty years previously.

"And this is where he lives," Morley said as we came upon a multilevel concrete and glass structure straight out of a vintage '60s movie. It was gauche and unnecessarily huge and would've been considered ultra-modern when it had been built. "First house on the lake," he said.

"Wow. Must have a big family."

"Actually, he lives alone. His father lived with him for a time, but I haven't seen the old guy in years. Word has it he died, but no one knows for sure. Nobody knows much about him, honestly; and some of us don't even know his real name. We all just call him 'Sparkles' because he comes around and washes our windows from time to time. He also keeps an eye on the neighborhood when the residents are away; checks in on everyone's houses. He doesn't even ask for anything in return."

"The community hero."

"It works both ways. Gives him a sense of purpose."

As I gawked at the giant building with its unwelcoming, bizarre angles, a hefty, beer-bellied man about Morley's age appeared in the bank of twelve-foot windows wearing nothing but bright pink boxer shorts. He stood stock-still for a few awkward moments then raised his hand and gave us a tentative wave.

Morley and I returned the wave then dashed to the next

grouping of trees so the man wouldn't see us doubled over, roaring with laughter.

"Not all heroes wear capes, apparently," I said after we calmed down, setting Morley off all over again.

At about the three-quarter point on the path, we came to a small beach with clumpy damp sand lining the water's edge and a swinging bench suspended between two trees. There was a thick rope with a knot at the end hanging from a massive tree limb over the lake. Two Victorian-style street-lamps at the back of the beach provided just enough light that Morley could put his flashlight away.

We trudged through the sand to the swinging bench where Morley produced two plastic shopping bags from his pocket. We spread them out on the damp wood and sat. My oversized boots dangled in the air while Morley pushed the swing into gentle motion.

"So if the people I'm closest to can't see me during a blink, what's the big deal?" I said, ready to jump back into class.

"The problem is the people that *can* see you. Imagine if I'd gone back to that night at The Merryport to try to change things, to talk to you, undisguised. Tad may have seen you talking to thin air, which would have been rather awkward for you."

"When did you ever touch *Tad's* skin?" I asked, shocked.

"Don't make it out to be as salacious as all that. It only takes a single touch. Once I discovered how all of this worked, I needed to make sure that I'd never be a ghost to *you*; I never gave a rat's ass about Tad or anyone else for that matter."

I was puzzled. Flattered, but puzzled; and it must have shown on my face. He stopped the swing with his foot and cleared his throat before he went on.

"I was drawn to you the first time I came into The Merry-port after Collette died, and it scared me. I didn't understand it. Sure, we'd chatted before—when Collette and I used to come in together—but the energy between us felt different, right away."

He stood up and took a few hesitant steps toward the shore then turned around looking serious, almost tortured. "To be that *connected* emotionally—and physically—to someone in such a brief period of time, well, it's a little mind rattling."

He wasn't kidding. My mind was rattled beyond belief. "Morley, I—"

"It was also the reason I kept my distance from you right from the start, even before I discovered the talisman's power. You see, I've had an unfortunate history of loved ones dying on me, all far too young. My parents in a car accident. My little brother from leukemia. My infant daughter… drowning."

My mouth fell open. He'd had a *daughter*? How did I not know about this? His gaze went to the night sky where the constellation Orion twinkled, forever on guard with bow and arrow.

"Around a week before Collette died, when she could barely breathe and her organs were beginning to shut down, I vowed to myself never to get close to anyone again. I'd felt like some kind of freak, like a modern-day male Medusa, where everyone around me turned to stone."

"Oh, Morley, I'm so sorry."

He brought his focus back to me and let out a long breath.

"When I felt that instant energy with you so soon after I lost Collette, I was disgusted with myself. How could I even think about another woman? And how dare I risk your life— after what I'd just seen Collette go through? Yet it was impossible to stay away. I reasoned that if I only visited you once a month and kept my hands off you, never allowing myself to get too close, the curse would be broken. We could have a long and happy friendship. It was agonizing but look how well it's turned out."

I waited for him to go into more detail about his parents and brother. *His daughter.*

"And when the talisman came along, it sealed the deal. I could never touch you. In our natural time, that is."

I stood and walked down to meet him. "I'm so sorry," I said again, taking his hand. "…about your losses. About your daughter. If you ever want to talk about it, I'm here."

He nodded and squeezed my hand. "Shall we get back?"

Our final leg back to the cabin was spent in silence. My heart was conflicted. One side ached with the knowledge that Morley had suffered losses as great as mine and that he'd taken on the burden of blame for them. The other side was curiously aflutter. Here was Dr. Morley Scott, whom I'd always held in such reverence, confessing feelings for me that went back, what, four years now? He'd certainly hidden it well. Sure, there had been the time we met for coffee, but it hadn't been a romantic tryst by any means. In fact, I seem to recall Kendall accusing *me* of being the smitten one, which was just as preposterous.

Back at the cabin, we pulled off our boots in the mud room and hung our coats on hooks, and a few minutes later as we stood face to face in the living room, I said, "I appreciate your candor about…you know, your feelings toward me, but it's freaking me out."

He sighed under his breath. "I'm sorry, Syd. I'm going about this all wrong. It's just, I know things that you aren't privy to yet."

"Well, that freaks me out even more."

"I shouldn't say anything else. I'll let you figure it out as we go. I think that's best."

"How many more times are we going to meet?"

"I shouldn't say."

"Like, is it once more?"

"Let's wait and see. Let it play out naturally."

"You didn't let it play out naturally when you involved me in this whole crazy"—I made flapping motions in the air with my hands—"timeblinking fiasco."

Morley reached up and stilled my hands. "Let's just enjoy the moment."

"What good is this power if we can't use it to save your life?"

He let out a sound just short of a groan. "Because even if my life can't be saved, the power can be used for other wonderful things. Why do you think I chose to pass the talisman on to you?"

"Because you said I have the most to gain out of anyone you know."

"You *were* listening."

It didn't make sense. "Haven't any of your young patients ever died? Surely there must be some grieving parents out there who'd kill for the chance to see their child again."

"How would I choose? What criteria makes one family more deserving than another?"

And then it struck me. The last date on his prescription.

"Isla," I said, nodding slowly. "You want me to find out what happened to Isla."

He shrugged and flashed me a dimpled smile.

I lowered myself to the sofa. "No," I said. "I can't do it."

He gave me a searching look that suddenly made me feel very selfish. He ran his hand through his hair and sat down next to me without saying a word.

I sighed. "Believe me, no one is more surprised than me. I mean, not a day has passed that I don't think about her. And now, with the power to find out what happened, I just can't bring myself to do it. Oh, Morley. I'm so sorry. You're probably regretting giving me the talisman now."

He took my hand and gave it a tender squeeze. "I don't

regret it for one minute. The power is yours to do with what you wish, even if you never use it again. The thing is…you *will* change your mind one day. About finding the truth."

I smiled dolefully. "Maybe when I'm 95."

The truth was, I simply couldn't fathom an age in my life —35, 65, 105—where watching Isla's fate play out in front of me would help anyone. After months of investigating, the police had informed us that Isla had likely died within hours of her disappearance. What good could possibly come from seeing that? Did I want the perpetrator to pay for what he did? Absolutely. Did I want closure once and for all? Of course I did. But what I wanted more, again quite selfishly, was to protect my current mental well-being. I'd come too far to risk throwing it away now.

"I…just can't."

Morley pulled me over for a hug that I didn't have the energy to resist. Instead, I closed my eyes and allowed myself to appreciate his warmth, his strength. I could've stayed there all day.

Timeblinking—and the myriad possibilities it brought with it —was like a drug, and an hour after returning home from Morley's world, I lay in a tangled mess of sheets, hastily shed clothing, and sweat. My head was nestled on Coop's chest where his heart throbbed rhythmically in my ear.

"Wow. What got into *you*?" Coop said breathlessly. Earlier I'd slipped in next to him, waking him from a deep slumber, running my hands over his body as if discovering it for the first time.

"Whatever do you mean?" I asked, even though I knew. It'd been months since we'd rearranged the sheets so primordially. My own satisfaction had run so deep I'd almost forgotten why I'd given myself up with such abandon in the first place.

Almost.

The memory of my timeblink flew in and smacked me in the face. How close I'd felt to Morley. How dangerously comfortable his world had become, like slipping into an old pair of jeans. And as much as I belonged in *this* realm, as much as I belonged next to Coop, part of me was still at the lake. I caught a tear on the back of my hand before it landed on Coop's chest. What was happening to me? This was the third time in a week I'd cried on a man's chest. I had to get a hold of myself. Couldn't ruin the moment after connecting with Coop on such a visceral level.

"It's just been a while, I guess," I said finally.

"You must be feeling better."

I could've taken his comment as a genuine observation about my improving state of health because it probably was, but instead my brain processed it as a jab suggesting I should get my ass back to work full time. My tears dried up instantly. Yes, times were tight. Yes, we were trying to save for a big trip to Europe. But in no way did I feel ready to face work five days a week. The Friday shifts I'd arranged were enough.

Peeling my cheek off Coop's chest I reached for the glass of water and plastic pill box on the night table.

"You still taking those things?" he said.

"What, the antidepressants?" I said, scooting up to lean against the headboard.

"You know what I mean."

I did. His message was loud and clear.

He said, "Babe, our window is closing. You'll be thirty-two in two days. I'm pushing towards forty."

I'm not in the mood for this.

I threw the pills into my mouth and took a big slug of water, maybe a little too defiantly. "We need to go on our trip before we have little rug rats running around," I said, buying time. Time for what, though? To hash this out again some other day?

Coop trained his eyes on the ceiling. "About our trip," he said after a halting breath.

I sensed a big disappointment coming.

"We're close. But we're going to have to put it off a year."

"What?"

"I'm so sorry. The numbers just aren't there."

"Coop, we've been working like dogs! Not taking holidays, doing overtime, covering co-workers' sick days. When will we have enough?"

He sat up, propping himself against the headboard next to me. Took my hand in his and kissed my knuckles in such a tender way that I nearly forgot to be angry.

"Don't you want our big trip to be the best? Every time I think we have enough and I'm just about ready to book, the hotels and the restaurants and shows we want to go to get more and more expensive. Not to mention the exchange rate. We have to do it up big. Nothing but the best. Live like royalty for a few weeks without worry."

I drew my hand out of his, lodging my fingers in my hair. "I can ask Kendall f—"

His finger flew up to my lips so fast I barely saw it. "It's *our* trip, not Kendall's."

I pushed his hand away and stared straight ahead, focusing on a black and white photo of us at a beach down the coast. An assortment of dust-covered seashells embellished the frame, a few of them missing. "So that's it? End of conversation?"

"I'm sorry, babe."

"Coop. Think about the timeline. What happens to our trip if I ended up getting pregnant today—or even a year from now? Either I'd be pregnant on the trip or we'd have a baby to look after and we'd have to call it off altogether."

"Oh no. We're not calling it off. We adapt. Bring the little guy with us. Lots of people do it, especially in Europe. Kids are part of the culture there."

Damn him. Any maternal urges that might have existed in some dusty corner of my heart scuttled away even further the minute he started asking me to adapt. I mean, it was great that he wanted children. He'd even talked about it on one of our first dates. I really shouldn't have been surprised he was tightening the screws twelve years in.

I got up and shimmied into my rumpled clothes, grabbing my book off the night table. "See you at dinner."

"For fuck's sake, Syd," I heard him say as Jinx skittered out the door with me. I kept going. Maybe after a few more hours of sleep he'd realize the implications of tossing a child into the mix before we celebrated *us*. I hated being the bad guy. It was exhausting. But he had to understand I would have no part in letting some screaming, snotty baby swoop in and ruin our big trip.

The next night, while we ate our dinner amidst a cloud of lingering tension, Coop reached across the table and took the fork out of my hand, laying it on the table next to my plate. He laced his fingers into mine.

"Babe, I love you. So much. I don't want us to end the day before your birthday on a sour note, so I promise to stop badgering you about children. For good," he said. "But before I shut up about it forever, I want you to know one thing: If you ever decide you're ready, you won't be alone. I'm all in, a thousand percent."

I stared at Coop across the table as if I were seeing him for the first time. He wasn't the enemy here. He was my best friend, my lover, and, arguably, my savior. And he wanted nothing more in the world than to become a father. How could I be so damned stubborn?

I picked up my fork. "Thank you."

"Honestly, babe. Not another word."

I nodded and went back to my plate of spaghetti as though nothing had happened.

But something *had* happened. Something big. By the next morning—my birthday of all days—there'd been a huge shift in my thinking, like a tectonic plate heaving and splitting apart, and suddenly, the idea of bringing a baby into our lives looked like a good idea. No, not a good idea. A *great* idea. It was a great, big, beautiful idea I couldn't put out of my mind. I wouldn't dare tell Coop, though, not right now. Or Kendall. *Especially* not Kendall. A shift of this magnitude had to settle in and stick a while before the rest of the world could find out.

I lifted the covers and swung my legs over the edge of the bed being careful not to wake Coop. There it was: my cheery pink pill box waiting patiently for me on the nightstand. I picked it up and glanced over my shoulder at Coop. Even in sleep, he oozed confidence, and if he hadn't been dozing so heavily, I would've jumped him right then and there. Instead, I fished my antidepressant out of the pill box, swallowed it down quickly, leaving the other pill untouched.

A baby.

I suppressed a laugh.

As I stood and slipped into my robe, Jinx bolted out of his bed and ran toward me with his tail wagging so hard it looked like it might fall off. It'd been nearly a week since I'd scared the poor thing to death, but he was back to his chipper old self, maybe even more so, and I wondered if he, too, had sensed the seismic shift inside me.

Chapter Five

Isla

Finn twitches and mumbles something unintelligible from his crib-sized mattress on the floor, dreaming about who knows what? This room? Me? Certainly nothing past these four walls. How do you dream of a place you've never been?

My heart constantly aches for that unobtainable luxury—freedom—not for myself but for Finn. All day long he runs in circles in front of me like a spider in a jar when he should be going to birthday parties and skinning his knees in playgrounds. I've been outside. I've seen the blue of the ocean. Heard a sparrow twittering at dawn. I've wrapped my arms around every member of my family. Cried with them. Laughed with them. For twenty years, I've fantasized about the day we are reunited, from the moment I wake in the morning until I drift into fitful sleep at night. And all the time in between.

My little boy, however, knows no other life outside our prison. Nothing past the hastily installed shower and toilet in one corner, my creaky twin bed in another. The rusted metal patio table pushed against the wall between the toilet and the cabinet that houses our food. The green two-burner hotplate sitting ready to heat a can of soup or a grilled cheese sandwich.

Years ago I'd stopped obsessing about all the things I didn't have and shifted my focus to the things I did have. Basic necessities, for example. Food, water, medication to reduce a fever, all the simple sundries to keep us moderately comfortable. We have a small fridge with a freezer just big enough to keep a carton of ice cream and a tray of ice for our drinks. Three white plastic chairs, one of them holding a molded plastic booster seat secured with duct tape, sit around the patio table. Nothing new, or nice, but enough. We make do. I keep our little ten-by-twelve-foot space tidy—the only thing I can control in a life I have no control over.

My single connection with the world beyond the walls is the weeks' worth of newspapers Viktor mules in, and on the rare occasions he doesn't, I sink into blind panic, terrified he's decided to take the privilege away. If the one small indulgence of the weekly news ever ends, Viktor might as well take away our food and water too. It's the only link to *there* in our tiny world of *here*.

The rule that's always irked me most, though, is Viktor's refusal to get us a television. He knows I'm book-smart, but it's not like I'm about to fashion some elaborate communication device out of dismantled TV parts. He occasionally brings special offerings—books for me and toys for Finn—as a sort of consolation, usually on birthdays or holidays or randomly when I can only assume his guilt gets the best of him.

Finn murmurs again and rolls over. His tattered fleece blanket—the one Viktor brought him when he was born—slips to the floor, and I hop off my bed to settle it back over his shoulders. Earlier, I'd fed and bathed him and read him a story, and as I watch my little trooper now with his mind floating free, hopefully somewhere other than this stuffy, gray box, I can't imagine how my heart had ever survived without him. Had I really made it fifteen years in this airless room without another human being for company? I've never considered Viktor—or his mercifully absent father, Anton—human. They're the lowest of the low.

Cockroaches.

If Viktor knew I thought about him this way, he'd lose his mind. I'm not reckless though. Being completely dependent on someone for every breath affords you little power to speak your mind, especially with a child's safety to think about. There can be no testing of wills, no power trips like back in the old days when it had just been me and Cockroach Senior. There had been plenty of confrontations in my teen years, invariably ending with me on the floor, bruised and bleeding, praying for Anton to just kill me. Viktor hadn't been around much those days. He would've tried to stop his father if he'd been home, he'd said, but someone had to pay the bills to feed this family.

Fortunately for me, Viktor had been marginally more sympathetic to my needs and installed a toilet and a cramped shower stall as soon as his father had stopped coming down. I'd been nineteen. Before that, I'd somehow managed with a medley of plastic buckets and jugs of water, and it had always been Viktor's job to deal with them. I guess he finally got tired of hauling shit out of the basement.

Aside from the necessities for survival, we have just enough mental stimulation to keep us from going completely mad, though I have no baseline on which to gauge my own sanity. I have my books. I'd begged for them endlessly back in the day, and the cockroaches had finally given in to shut me up. By the time Finn came along, I'd had hundreds. Stacks of them lined the walls and filled the space under the bed. I even had some tucked between the mattress and box spring. I'd forbidden the cockroaches to take any away.

Finn's arrival broke my hoarding habit in an instant. I hadn't needed the books anymore, most of which I'd read twenty or thirty times, and it had taken Viktor three weeks to get them all out. It's not to say I don't read now. There are a handful of books in a box under the bed, mostly medical journals and childrearing texts, and while I still take pleasure in reading a new novel whenever Viktor brings me one, I normally give it back as soon as I finish to keep the place as clutter free as possible.

With Finn asleep, I decide to work on a jigsaw puzzle at our kitchen table. On my way over, I catch sight of my reflection in the toaster oven and gasp. *Is that really me?* With no mirrors in the room, it had been a while since I'd assessed my appearance, and I'm mortified by what I see now: cheekbones protruding like thin shelves beneath pale, papery skin, and dusky circles hanging beneath my eyes. The muscles between my neck and shoulders are scooped and lax, accentuating the upward jut of my shoulder joints. I wonder if Finn's noticed his mother wasting away in front of him. I can't waste precious energy worrying about it, though. I've been asking Viktor for extra food for months, and the request has fallen on deaf ears.

As I slip into a chair at the table I hear a faint thump upstairs, followed by a whoosh of air under my door, and I chastise myself—as I do every time—for the small flip my heart does at the promise of fresh supplies. I often have to remind myself not to be so grateful for these small pleasures. They are my right.

While I occupy myself with the puzzle, Viktor stomps around overhead, presumably in the kitchen—I've never made it past the tenth stair without being kicked back down, so I wouldn't know—perhaps making himself something to eat. A few minutes of silence, then the steady flow of urine hitting the toilet bowl. The thunderous rush of water through pipes behind the walls. While these particular sounds reach my dungeon clearly, I've rarely heard voices. Just the heavy thud of feet, the peeing, and the running water. I used to hear

Viktor and his father arguing, but not for a long time now. For all I know Anton moved out or died years ago. Viktor had mentioned once, not long after Anton stopped coming down, that his father wouldn't be bothering me anymore. When I'd asked him what that meant, he'd just shook his head and said, "Not for you to worry about, Princess." I hadn't pushed him on it, and in the twelve years since, he hasn't brought up the subject of his father again.

After several more minutes, I hear his lumbering descent on the stairs leading down to my door. I used to worry about the implications of Viktor falling down those stairs and hurting himself, or even dying, but I've decided that his death —and subsequently mine and Finn's—would be better than living like this forever. Nevertheless, it doesn't stop me from fantasizing about the prospect of a slip-up. One little mistake on Viktor's part, one missed lock, a pizza delivery or a visitor dropping by unannounced when the door is ajar—anything to cause a fumble—and we would be free.

The keys rattle in the lock on the other side of the thick metal door. One click, two slides, one more click.

"Hey, Princess," Viktor says, smiling, as the door swings open. He steps inside, setting two green canvas bags of food on the floor. He has a third bag tonight—it's small and made of brown paper, like a lunch bag. Viktor tosses it onto the table, sending puzzle pieces flying off the edge, then kicks the door shut and locks it behind him. He drops the key into his pocket. That particular habit is ingrained. No chance of a slip-up there.

I flash Viktor an agitated glance, nodding toward Finn who snuffles without waking despite the bang of the door.

"Sorry," he whispers.

"He's getting a cold," I whisper back. "Needs his sleep."

"All right, all right. Cool your jets."

After picking up one of the grocery bags and setting it on a chair, Viktor smacks his forehead with the heel of his hand as if remembering something important. "Damn. Your cake."

I frown.

"Your birthday? Did you forget? I was going to bring you guys a couple pieces."

I hadn't forgotten it was my birthday. I'd written the date in my journal this morning but hadn't given it another thought all day.

"What a jerk I am, forgetting to bring cake. You could certainly use some fattening up. Wait a minute," Viktor says, looking me up and down. "Are you on another hunger strike?"

No, you giant cockroach. I've been telling you for months that Finn's been on an eating rampage and I've been giving him my share.

"Well, don't just sit there, give me a hand," he says when I don't answer him.

After we put the food away, I sit down on my bed, wishing he would just leave. Only he hasn't brought me a birthday cake, and I have no candles to blow out, so my wish probably won't come true. He collects the small brown bag from the table and brings it over to me, smiling from ear to ear.

"Happy birthday," he says, thrusting the bag toward me. I can feel his eyes on me as I take it and peer inside. My heart leaps. It's a dog-eared paperback—the newest Judith Wendles novel, no less—and I can't get it out of the bag fast enough. I'd been asking Viktor for it for months. The book smells of mold, and the bottom third is swollen to double its size, probably from being dropped in a bathtub or a puddle, but it doesn't matter. I hold it in my hands as if it were the rarest diamond on the planet. Where newspapers keep me grounded and in tune with the world, novels are my escape from it.

I stand up and kiss him on the cheek, as is expected of me.

"You're welcome," he says, plopping down on a plastic chair at the table and pulling out another for me. I join him without speaking.

"Look, I'm sorry about what happened last week," Viktor

says, leaning over to rest his elbows on his knees, dodging my gaze. "I mean it. You're just so damned beautiful. I lose control. Can you blame me? Anyway, I thought it would help you feel better."

"I had a migraine."

"Come on, you know I didn't mean to hurt you."

I focus on the bloated paperback in my lap. Maybe it was true. Maybe he really hadn't meant to push me onto the bed and pin me down while I ordered Finn to his safe place under the table with a blanket over his head. Maybe he hadn't meant to ram into me incessantly while I screamed inside so as not to alarm my son. Maybe he really hadn't meant to bash my head against the wall when I struggled under his weight.

Quit making excuses for him! Of course he meant to hurt you!

When I glance back up at him, he looks tortured, like someone who's just drowned his own baby, and I can't help but feel sorry for him. He hurts me because it's the only way he's been able to feel in control since his father pulled me out of the trunk of his car all those years ago.

Chapter Six

Outside my kitchen window, the last of the dead leaves on our peach tree quivered in the breeze with a weary, neglected quality that matched my mood. I sat, drinking tea, surfing social media, dreading the whole lonely day stretched out before me. My shift at The Merryport wasn't due to start until 5 o'clock, and I was bored stiff.

Timeblinking had brought me the kind of adventure I'd been yearning for; so much so, in fact, that I could honestly say our big European trip didn't feel as urgent anymore. I could even argue that timeblinking—and its ability to fulfill my need for excitement at the drop of a hat—was also the reason I'd warmed up to having a baby. The inconveniences of traveling with a child meant nothing when I could zap out anywhere I wanted for four and a half minutes at a time, even with a sleeping baby in the next room. Oh, the possibilities! Maybe I would never tell Coop about timeblinking. We could stay grounded here in our hometown where he's most comfortable, continue our odd week-long excursion to Hawaii, and I could slip away to all the exotic places Coop had no desire to see. He kept citing insufficient funds as the cause for the repeated delays when I knew the real reason: he hated flying. The tiniest wiggle of the plane has always sent him grabbing for his armrests, while lengthy patches of turbulence throw him into a flat-out panic attack. On our last flight he'd started hyperventilating and one of the flight attendants had had to show him how to breathe into a barf bag to keep him from passing out. He'd been mortified. We haven't talked about it since.

I'd been itching to test out timeblinking to somewhere other than Sandalwood, and I decided that going to the day Morley and I met for coffee last spring would be a safe start. The meeting had been on my mind for a while now, thanks to Kendall and her weird theory about me having deeper feelings for Morley. If I went back to our coffee date, I reasoned, I could prove—even if just to myself—that the idea was absurd.

The previous two timeblinks had deposited me in the relative privacy of Morley's world, but this was my first blink to a spot that wasn't on the list, and it felt reckless. If even one of the baristas had brushed skin with me that day, the whole thing could be disastrous. I decided to trust the process…that if there *had* been a scene at the coffee shop, I would have known about it because I'd have already experienced it.

With that reassuring thought in mind, I set my landing site to a secluded corner of the parking lot next to The Bold & Bean, specifically behind a big green garbage bin for extra cover. Morley had always emphasized that no matter how prepared you were, a clean landing was never guaranteed, and I was still holding my breath when I popped into the parking lot a few minutes later. To my relief, a quick scan revealed only a dozen empty cars and a seagull regarding me with suspicion from the roof of an orange Mustang. As I made my way to the café, the gull lifted off, squirting out a big white blob of poop on the windshield as it went. I giggled. Partly because of the mess on the windshield, but mostly because I was in a great mood. It was my first true solo timeblink, and the great and powerful Dr. Scott had had nothing to do with it.

As I reached the door of the café, I caught sight of my reflection in the window and did a double take. Almost didn't recognize myself. It's amazing what a cropped brunette wig and simple horn-rimmed glasses can do to transform someone's appearance. This was going to be easy. With the confidence of a Vegas gambler after a string of wins, I strode into the café, ordered a chai tea latte then turned around to look for a place to sit.

I nearly collapsed by what I saw. There, at a table in the middle of the café was Isla. Sitting with Morley. Deep in conversation as if they'd known each other forever. I'd know her anywhere, even from behind, even in her grown-up body. Maybe, through the miracle of timeblinking, Morley had found her after all and had arranged this reunion for us!

In a matter of seconds, though, the truth hit me. It wasn't Isla. It was *me*. Of course it was me. Yet for one crazy moment, I'd believed it was her. And why not? *She* was over there with Morley. *I* was here, by the counter, glued to the spot, on the verge of fainting.

I was vaguely aware of two baristas staring at me as I swayed on my feet, so I gathered my wits and set off to find a table before my strange behavior caused a commotion. By good fortune, the table behind Syd and Morley was available. I slid into a flimsy wooden chair right behind my past self and glanced at Morley over her shoulder, but he didn't seem to recognize me as a brunette.

While I settled in, I indulged in a little fantasy that the woman sitting with Morley was indeed Isla. It was comforting. I imagined tapping her on the shoulder and the look on her face when she turned around and saw me standing there. How she would fly out of her chair, knocking it over as she threw her arms around me, and we'd hug and hug until someone decided we were making a scene and separated us. Just as I'd immersed myself thoroughly in the fantasy, "Isla" raised her cup of peppermint tea, exposing her wrist. My heart sank. There it was. My ugly, deformed wrist.

There was nothing left to do but sit and listen. I zeroed in on their conversation, where, over coffee, tea, and scones, Syd and Morley chatted about work and the weather and the latest movies they'd seen. Just as my drink arrived, the conversation veered over to the details of Isla's abduction.

Syd explained to Morley that people who'd lived in Port Raven at the time had been privy to the circus sideshow of her family's tragedy as it played out on TV and the newspapers. It seemed the story of an abducted eleven-year-old twin was just as compelling—if not more so—than the impending Y2K debacle.

Morley, lucky him, hadn't been around for any of it, still living in New York at the time. If he *had* been here, he would've seen my father on the evening news pleading for the safe return of his daughter. He'd have heard my mother's tearful victim-impact statement and Kendall's rage as she described Isla's painful shyness and leeriness of strangers. He'd have seen the cameras panning over to my stony face while reporters told their viewers to be on the lookout for a girl who looked exactly like me and that they would be able to tell the difference because Isla wouldn't have a cast on her arm.

Morley told Syd that he'd gotten the general gist of the story from the speculative pieces that were still circulating on the internet to this day, their headlines asking, "*Where is Isla?*" and "*Twin Still Missing, 20 Years Later.*" It was odd being a third party in the conversation. I hadn't owed him my account of the story, but there in the coffee shop, little by little, I watched him tease the rest of it out of Syd.

"It's hard, you know?" Syd said to him. "I'm aware of my obsession, but most of the time it's impossible to think about anything else."

I shuddered in my seat behind them, my heart raw all over again.

"I know the feeling," he said, pulling his chair closer to the table, wearing an expression I hadn't been accustomed to seeing. Sombre. Serious. Even his trademark dimples were missing.

"Do you really?" Syd said. "No offense, but I think what you went through with Collette was quite different. At least you got to say a proper goodbye. She knew she was loved right until the end. Do you know what my last words to Isla were? 'You are so annoying!'"

He winced almost imperceptibly, a reaction I hadn't noticed in the moment. "You had no idea what was about to happen," he said.

Syd slouched in her seat, focussing on her hands in her lap. "But do you know what's worse? What she said as I rode away: 'Love you too!'"

Morley winced again, more pronounced this time. Syd shook her head. "It was said tongue-in-cheek, but damn her for getting the best last word in. She had a knack for that."

They sat in silence for a few beats, then Syd thrust her right hand in front of Morley's face. I could see his puzzled, almost bemused look beyond her splayed fingers.

"Have you ever wondered why my wrist is so deformed?" She asked.

It looked especially ugly floating up there in front of Morley. I wished she'd take it down, but she left it there for God and everyone else to see.

"You mentioned you had a fall when you were a child. A distal radius fracture that didn't heal properly, I presume?"

"Y-yes," she said, obviously taken aback by Morley's deduction. I remembered having temporarily forgotten he was a doctor.

"I broke it the day Isla disappeared." She lowered her

wrist to her lap, massaging it as I tend to do when I'm forced to think about it.

Morley shook his head and folded his arms on the edge of the table.

Syd's shoulders rose then dropped as she expelled a heavy breath. "I'm sure you know most of the details surrounding Isla's abduction already. People can't help googling it when they get a whiff of the story."

"I have a good idea about what happened. And yes, I learned much of it online. Tad filled me in on a few things as well, but he didn't mention that your wrist abnormality had anything to do with that day."

"Tad's a good friend. Great with secrets too."

Morley smiled before his face turned somber. "I understand you and Isla rode your bikes to the park together, that you left for a few minutes, and when you came back, she was gone?"

Syd nodded. "Every detail of that day is stuck in my head like a song on repeat. When I left the park, I was just going home to grab some props for the stupid video project we were working on and get back there right away. My father was at work and my mom was out. I remember racing past Kendall in the living room to sneak her reading glasses out of her bedroom upstairs. Next stop was my parents' closet to get my mom's trench coat, and it took me forever to find it. As an afterthought I stopped in our room to get a wig from our tickle trunk. What an idiot! Stupid decisions like that delayed me getting back to the park.

"Anyway, halfway down the stairs to the living room, my foot slipped and I biffed it. Hard. The coat, the wig, Kendall's glasses, everything went flying."

Syd took a sip of her tea then continued. "Kendall jumped off the sofa to help me. I was writhing in pain on the floor, stupidly thinking, *She's going to kill me when she finds out I wrecked her glasses.*"

"Did you know you'd broken a bone?"

Syd shuddered. "Not on a conscious level. I heard a pop but didn't want to believe it. Isla and I were *never* supposed to leave each other alone, and that's all I could think about. Getting back to the park."

"And that's when you discovered her missing."

Syd nodded slowly. "I felt such a profound sense of loss, like half my body had been ripped off by some wild animal, and in the following days and weeks—and decades—the feeling hasn't waned."

"Oh, Syd," Morley said from his side of the table. I remember wishing that he would reach across the table to touch my hand, a natural reaction that I'd have expected from anyone else. But this had been back when he'd been doing everything he could to avoid touching me.

Syd's shoulders slumped. "*I'm* the reason she's gone, Morley. And why my mom is gone. And my dad. All of it."

"Again, you didn't know. You never could have predicted it; and even if you could've, just imagine what would happen if we could see the future. There would be no spontaneity or the thrill of surprise. There'd be no such word as hope."

"I've *never* lost hope about Isla. I still wake up every day thinking: will today be the day the authorities bring me news that they've found her safe and happy? Or will the other scenario play out? You know, the one where a couple of sad-faced cops stand in my doorway, hats in hands, not having to speak a word. Either way, at least I could stop obsessing about it."

"Have you tried?"

I flinched a little behind them, remembering this subtle turn in the conversation.

"Have I *tried?*" Syd said. "Let's see. Could I stop thinking about what happened to my identical twin when it's all I've thought about for the last twenty years? Hm. Could grass stop being green?"

Morley smiled. "Actually, yes. If you don't water it."

Syd sighed, looked down. Brushed some crumbs off her lap. "I appreciate what you're trying to do, but I've run the gamut of self-help, professional help, medication, you name it. This is the best it gets."

"What if it were the other way around? What if Isla were sitting across from me right now, and you were the one looking down from…wherever," he said, "would you want *her* to be unhappy, not making the most of her chance on this Earth?"

Right there. That's where I remembered feeling as if he'd punched me in the gut.

His eyes darted back and forth before he looked at Syd steadily. "I'm not insinuating, by any means, that I think your life is unfulfilling. It's just. Well, I can relate."

"Oh? I didn't realize you had a sister who was abducted as a child. One that was probably raped, tortured, and murdered."

Over clinking cups and the clamor of the busy café, I felt the sting of regret for snapping at Morley like that all over again. But watching his reaction now, from a distance, he seemed unfazed. He leaned back in his chair and laced his fingers behind his head with a look that said *Get it all out, my dear*.

"What was Isla's favorite animal?" he asked out of the blue.

"What?" Syd said, taking a flustered glance around the café. I remembered feeling suffocated by all the smiling, caffeinated people engaged in easy conversation, feeling I didn't belong in their happy, buzzed world.

"Puppies?" Morley said.

Syd leaned back now too. She folded her arms across her chest.

"Kittens?" His eyes glittered.

That day had been the first time I'd taken a good look at his eyes in the natural light. They were a mesmerizing green, as fresh as a granny smith apple, and I was almost jealous of my past self. Even from behind, I could feel Syd willing herself to look away.

"Okay, we'll go with kittens. What was Isla's favorite color? Wait, wait. Hold that thought; my pager's going off."

He stood, fiddling with the small device that had been sitting on the table since the start. "I'll be right back."

Morley stood and scooted out the door, producing a cell phone from his pocket, punching in some numbers on the way.

Chewing on her thumbnail, Syd watched the unflappable doctor through the window as he talked on his phone. How strange to think that I was living this moment all over again, that Morley was being appraised by two versions of me.

Twins.

My present version saw again how sensually his lips moved and how velvety and pink they were—something else I'd never noticed in the muted light of the pub. He was dressed in what seemed to be an expensive suit like he often was, as if on his way to a job interview or a wedding, though it was a bit rumpled, suggesting no discernible relationship with his local dry cleaner, let alone an iron. Still, the way those clothes hugged his body made me blush even now, imagining what lay beneath. I watched Syd's profile as she gazed out the window. She was puzzling, if I remembered correctly, about why she'd been invited to coffee in the first place. Back then she'd thought she was just his friendly neighborhood drink slinger and had had no idea what he could possibly want with her.

These days, I was all too aware of our connection, and I smiled. *Oh, Sydney Anne Brixton. If you only knew.*

Now Morley was back, settling onto his creaky chair, apologizing to Syd for the interruption. His eyes flicked for a moment to where I sat behind her, and I impulsively looked away. Had he recognized me?

"It was the hospital," he said to Syd. One of his diabetic

patients had just been admitted and another doctor was handling the child's care until his next rounds at 3 o'clock.

"Horses," Syd said after a few moments.

Morley looked confused at first, then nodded, smiling.

"Isla loved horses. And her favorite color was blue. But not just any blue. She spoke often about the time our family piled into a rented motorhome and camped our way down to California. We hit all the usual touristy spots, Laguna Beach being one. Isla was spellbound by the color of the water there. It was nothing like the dark, bottomless ocean we have here. It was light and fresh; the tropical blue of postcards and screen savers. Laguna blue, she used to call it."

"What year was—"

"She loved steamed broccoli," Syd interrupted, "with heaps of butter and salt. Weird, now that I think about it. She liked broccoli more than chocolate chip cookies or ice cream."

Her eyes drifted to the window where a homeless man outside was pushing his life's possessions up Fourth Avenue in a rickety shopping cart.

"Isla hated shopping. Except when it came to books. She was mad for books. Always had her nose buried in one. She wore comfy clothes: leggings and t-shirts; never dresses or anything glitzy. Her hair was long and blonde and pulled back in a permanent ponytail and she used to make fun of me when I grumbled about my hair and experimented with makeup. She would rather read than fuss about fashion. 'Books last forever; looks don't,' she used to say. She was so smart. Super intuitive and curious about how things worked and about biology and chemistry and math. Smart enough to become a doctor."

She brought her focus back to Morley. "Maybe the two of you would've even crossed paths."

He smiled, giving Syd his full attention. She told him about Isla's love of all animals, her dislike of sports, her peculiar quirk of rocking herself to sleep at night. They talked about what Isla looked like, which was easy since she was Syd's identical twin. About how clueless she'd been about her beauty. "And I'm allowed to say that because we were different, not just in personality. The shape of her nose, the position of her eyebrows, even the texture of her hair made her the prettier one. But at a glance we looked like clones. We even fooled our own parents from time to time. We used to roar laughing when they made the mistake."

Morley sat and listened, occasionally shaking his head or nodding with an empathy so genuine I could feel it, even now. After their drinks were long finished and Syd's scone sat hardening on her plate, she was at the point in the story of Isla's disappearance where she'd lost her chance at a happy life for good.

"I assume you know about the baby-blue Bug?" Syd said.

"The one stolen from a house across from the park the day Isla was taken?"

Syd nodded. "On the same afternoon Isla disappeared, a 73-year-old woman—Kitty Salazar—discovered her classic Volkswagen Beetle missing. It was the same one I saw driving away from the park when I got back."

"Did you see who was inside?"

"No. I only got a brief glimpse as it sped away. I should've paid more attention to it, I suppose, but I hadn't even realized Isla was missing yet."

"Wasn't the car found later that night?"

"Yeah. It was the strangest thing. The cops had been keeping an eye out for it when Salazar reported it missing, then they ramped up their search after I reported seeing a blue car matching that description leaving the scene. But they didn't track it down right away, which is weird when you think about how a car like that would've stood out. The thing was like a ghost; absolutely no one had seen it other than me. Anyway, it was returned to Salazar's driveway late that night without a scratch—though the poor old dear's favorite yellow cardigan was missing from the back seat."

"Right, the cardigan. And the DNA? What came of that?"

"You're getting ahead of the story."

"Sorry. Go on."

"Anyway, when I described the stolen Bug as the one I'd seen leaving the area, it'd been impounded and inspected top to bottom, much to Salazar's dismay. She'd driven that car off the lot when it was new in '77 and was devastated, first of all that it had been stolen, and second because it was being considered as evidence in a missing child's case. She'd insisted she'd had nothing to do with Isla's disappearance, even with the discovery of the DNA."

"Ah, yes, Isla's DNA, found in multiple places inside the car. Proving your sister *had* been there."

"Technically. I mean they said it was a ninety-nine percent chance match."

"That's pretty damning evidence. Remind me why it didn't go anywhere again?"

"Salazar's alibi. She'd been visiting a neighbor that afternoon, and when she went home, she noticed her car missing and called the cops right away. The timing of that phone call discounted her as a suspect completely."

"But if in fact the car had been stolen, used for the abduction, and returned to Salazar the same day, wouldn't there have been someone else's DNA found too?"

"That's just it. They didn't find anything. Just Salazar's and Isla's. And that of Salazar's forty-six-year-old son. But he was in Nashville on business that day. Again, with strong alibis."

Morley bit at his thumbnail. "The whole thing is just so odd."

"Tell me about it. I mean, who would've used the car to abduct my sister, steal a little old lady's sweater, then *return* the vehicle later? Have you ever heard anything so bizarre? 'Hey, thanks for lending me your wheels to snatch a kid from the park in broad daylight. Have a great day.'"

Morley shook his head, dumbfounded.

"Everyone following the story knew it would not end well, and we—Dad, Mom, Kendall—we knew it too. When the police finally admitted the leads had dried up and they'd searched every square inch of the city and all routes out of it without a single solid clue to go on, it was over. The Y2K frenzy continued to build while our family's story petered out and died altogether."

And that was when the already tenuous threads holding us together started unravelling.

A barista appeared out of nowhere, collected their cups and napkins, Morley's plate. "You still working on this?" she asked about Syd's half-eaten scone, not too subtly hinting at them to vacate the table.

"No thanks. We're done," Syd said.

"Shall we?" Morley stood and grabbed his coat off the back of the chair.

I followed them out of the café. The drizzle had stopped, and dazzling rays of light peeked through broken clouds. Syd and Morley stopped on the sidewalk to say their goodbyes while I hovered nearby on the pretense of waiting for someone.

"Thanks for listening," Syd said. "You know, having a conversation with someone who was actually interested in *Isla, the Person*, and not strictly *Isla, the Abducted Girl*, was refreshing. I apologize for completely hijacking the conversation, though. Next time we'll have to spend more time chatting about *Collette, the Person*."

There's where Syd had unwittingly made a tentative second date. *Not a date*, I remembered thinking at the time. Coffee with a friend.

"Yes, we'll have to meet again. In the meantime, would

you like a ride home?" Morley asked, gesturing toward his car, parked on the street in front of them.

"I can walk. It's not far."

"Are you sure? Didn't you say you lived near that new Fulcart Foods? I'm going by there on my way to the hospital."

I should've caught it, back then. He shouldn't have known that detail. The only time I'd ever told him where I lived was on my second blink back to his cabin. I must've been distracted by the allure of riding in a brand new Tesla.

"Okay, twist my arm. Can you drop me off at Fulcart's? I need a few things," Syd said. I hadn't really needed groceries that day. I'd needed anonymity. Although nothing untoward was going on, I hadn't wanted to risk Coop seeing me with the dashing gentleman he'd talked to a handful of times when he'd dropped in to visit me at work.

"Absolutely," he said, adjusting his ever-present gloves.

Watching the scene unfold now, I shifted from foot to foot, embarrassed by what happened next. It was where Morley reached over to open the door, so close I could smell the soap he'd used that morning, and I'd foolishly thought, *Holy shit. He's going to kiss me.*

Syd jerked back from him on the sidewalk, breathless.

"You okay?" he said, raising his eyebrows, totally oblivious to whatever delusion Syd had cooked up. She seemed to understand her mistake instantly.

"I—I was about to sneeze," she lied, rubbing at her nose. "It's gone now."

"Don't you hate that?" he said, wrinkling his own nose.

As he helped Syd get situated in the car, I shook my head, disgusted with myself. Imagine thinking he was going to kiss me. Ridiculous.

Morley hurried around the front of the car, pausing at the drivers' side door, casting a look in my direction on the sidewalk. Then he winked at me and hopped into his car.

My eyes darted away as I pretended to look for someone.

It was daft. My cover had obviously been blown, and I wondered how long he'd been playing along. It didn't matter. He was probably happy to see me there. The next time I saw him I would tell him it had all been in fun. Lord knows I'd never tell him the real reason: that I'd been determined to prove Kendall wrong about my feelings for him.

But as I stood outside The Bold & Bean watching Morley's car pull away from the curb, a thought flowed in: *What if?*

What if, in another realm, Morley and I could…

Stop it, Syd! You're playing with fire.

As they turned the corner at the end of the street, I forced myself to remember the guilt that flooded my heart the moment I stepped out of Morley's car that day. When I promised myself to stop approaching lines I shouldn't cross. To stop putting my relationship with Coop in a position it could never recover from. To stop acting like a giddy teenaged girl with a crush.

And I had. It had been so easy. Until Morley went ahead and died, that is.

Chapter Seven

Kendall sat at the wheel of her shiny new metallic green...something or other, idling in front of my house while I slipped hiking boots over scratchy wool socks at the front door. Good grief. That woman changed cars more often than she changed her underwear.

Kendall had been prodding me earnestly to get out of the house for something other than an appointment or groceries or the sporadic Friday night shifts I'd taken at The Merryport, and she'd nearly fallen over when I'd suggested we hit the trail at Chapman Falls. "Are you sure?" she'd said. "It's pretty challenging. And you haven't been very active lately."

If I were going to be coerced to join in with the real world again, Chapman Falls was the only place I wanted to go. I'd reminded Kendall that we hadn't been there together, just the two of us, in years, and she'd agreed it was a great plan. The truth was that I'd been pining to relive some of the raw wonder I'd felt after my first timeblink when Morley plucked me out of the water. Besides, a refreshing hike in the woods was bound to clear some cobwebs out of my head.

"Hi," I said, spreading a tattered Mexican blanket over the back seat and whistling Jinx in.

"Hey you. Hi Jinxy baby!"

"Nice car," I said.

"Thanks, got it on Friday, but I'm already regretting it. It's not the most practical vehicle for a busy mom with eight-year-old boys to taxi around. You still up for this?" she asked as I settled into the passenger seat.

"Of course. It'll be good for me. And Jinx."

As we pulled away from the house, I waved at the Nose and she snapped her head to the side, feigning interest in some unseen thing in her living room or parlour or whatever that fancy room was called. "Ha! Did you see that?"

"What, that you just waved at Mrs. Vanderthorpe? Or that you laughed for the first time in weeks?"

"Very funny. No, I've been giving the old bat the odd wave on the way by, and she always tries to pretend she hasn't seen me."

"Hm. Might it have something to do with your horrible behavior towards her? I mean, really, Squid. She squeals on you for watering your lawn too long. Big deal. Maybe keeping an eye on the neighborhood is how widows fight debilitating loneliness. You're going to be old someday too, you know."

"Oh sure, take her side."

"You're right, I shouldn't be scolding you. I should be happy you're making jokes and getting out of the house. You'd have never agreed to a two weeks ago. What's changed?"

I drew a deep breath, eyeing the familiar patchwork of my neighborhood as it sped by. If she only knew what weight her question held.

"Nothing's changed," I said, shrugging. "The counselling must be helping, I guess."

"Well, well. That's a huge step for you to admit."

I couldn't tell her the counselling had been having absolutely no effect on me whatsoever. Timeblinking was my therapy.

An empty parking lot welcomed us at Chapman Falls. Kendall, Jinx and I jumped out of the car and stretched our stiff legs.

"Looks like we have the whole place to ourselves," Kendall said, pulling on a gray knitted hat and handing me a similar one in teal blue. I took it, grateful. I'd forgotten to bring a hat. Gloves, I'd remembered.

We started off down the trail among a jumble of moss-covered trees while a cool northwest wind slithered down my neck, making me shiver. I wasn't bothered. I was content. For the first time in a long time.

We walked in silence, enjoying the sounds of rainwater dripping off leaves, of birds twittering, of Jinx bounding, unseen, through dense fern beds and rivulets that trickled under boardwalks along the way. Kendall, ten paces ahead, started singing an extremely loud yet melodious version of *John Jacob Jingleheimer Schmidt*.

"Come on, Squid, join in!"

"No thanks." I may have been happy of late, but not *that* happy. Kendall was the singer in the family—another of her myriad talents. I let her go on until she finished the ridiculous song.

"That was a jolly little diddy," I said, meaning it. There was something refreshing about hearing my sister belt out nonsense with such abandon in the middle of a 3,500-acre coastal rainforest.

"Lord knows I hear it enough coming from the back seat. I have to admit, whenever the boys sing it, I get a little goofy myself. Unless they're screaming it at the top of their lungs. Then it's just annoying."

"And Coop wonders why I don't want kids."

"Hey! Watch it, sista!" she shouted without looking back.

"You're not doing a very good job of convincing me otherwise."

"I didn't know you were looking to be convinced."

Her head would pop right off her shoulders if she knew I'd been warming up to the idea of late.

Instead of going straight to the falls, we veered off, taking the cliff-walk trail where we used to picnic when the boys had been younger and Kendall and Brett had had more free time. These days, Kendall complained about the boys' frenzied schedule of hockey practises, piano lessons, homework, and band recitals while she and Brett juggled full-time careers.

Jinx and I were already exploring the headland plateau when Kendall dragged her huffing, puffing butt over the final ridge. I'd forgotten how beautiful it was up there. A craggy, windswept bluff dotted with scruffy native huckleberry and snowbrush gave us a perfect view of the falls as they tumbled into the bay at the opposite end of the trail and flowed out to sea. From this vantage point, the falls looked majestic and enticing, not dangerous at all.

We spread out a couple of dog poop bags on a wooden bench overlooking the sea and sat. Thick clouds hanging almost eye level obscured a normally stunning view of the group of small islands scattered up and down the coast. If the wind hadn't been so brisk, I could've sat there all day.

"I'm going to barbecue the Christmas turkey this year," Kendall said out of nowhere.

"Oh? What made you decide that?"

"I saw a demonstration video a few weeks ago and immediately put my name in for a turkey at that butcher on Twelfth Avenue. It seemed like a no-brainer. You just order the bird essentially flat and deboned—or do it yourself, but who has that kind of time?—then slap on some sausage meat and a ton of herbs and roll it up. I'll probably brine mine first. We'll see if I'm on the ball enough to make that happen."

She would be. In Kendall's house, there wasn't a pillow left unfluffed, a veggie garden not planted, a turkey she couldn't cook to perfection. She seemed to know instinctively how to get it all done. And done well. Likely from the years she'd spent looking after my sorry teenaged butt.

"You and Coop are invited, of course. And uh, I invited Dad this year, too. And Julie and the girls." I could feel her eyes on me. I kept my focus trained on the foggy sea.

"Connor and Dev have been bugging me about seeing their Grandpapa, and I figured, well, no better time than the holidays. Sarah and Lainie are just as excited. They'll be turning fourteen and twelve soon, so this may be the last time they want to spend Christmas with their dad's first family, especially Sarah. She has a boyfriend now, apparently."

Good grief. Who cared? And to use Connor and Dev as scapegoats? They were good boys—they'd always been kind and caring, which is a feat in itself these days with kids—but they had no attachment to their grandfather apart from visiting a week here or there when the family flew out to Buffalo. I was damned sure Kendall hadn't enlightened the boys about how their precious Grandpapa had abandoned me and their mother when we'd needed him the most, and that Sarah and Lainie, who'd come along three and six years later respectively, had been obvious replacements for Kendall and me.

"And we have all those rooms," she went on. "Seems such a waste to never use them. Anyway, it could be fun. All of us together?"

I sighed, pulling my hood over the wool hat Kendall lent me, hiding her from view. "Coop and I were talking about going to Hawaii for Christmas," I lied.

"Oh?"

"It's not set in stone. We've been tossing it around."

"Won't that eat into your Europe fund?"

"We might have to do Maui *instead* of Europe."

"Oh no! You can't settle for Hawaii. You simply can't.

You've been looking forward to Europe forever, Syd. It's not just some whim."

A bitter breeze kicked up and blew my hood against my cheek. What did she know? She had money coming out of her ass.

"Coop insists we don't have enough saved up. Even with all that overtime we've been putting in, we can't get the last few thousand together. And *no*, before you offer, Coop refuses to take anything from you and Brett, and I have to agree with him. This is absolutely our deal. We've been scrimping and saving for four years, and we're not about to quit now."

Kendall's shoulders slumped. She wasn't accustomed to waiting for things she wanted badly.

"It's okay, Kenny. We're good."

Jinx appeared next to me and rested his snout on my lap, snorting once.

"Look, Syd. Even the dog knows it's not right."

"Ha. You're just cold, right Jinxy?" I said, ruffling him behind his ears.

"It *is* a bit chilly up here. Want to head back down? Maybe take a detour along the beach?"

"Nah, not today." I yawned, suddenly eager to get home and snuggle under a blanket with a cup of hot tea.

"Come on. How often do we come here together? And when are we going to get another chance?"

I sighed. She was right, especially with me on the verge of going back to work full time. And it seemed she'd wisely dropped the subjects of Christmas and my doomed Europe trip. At least for now.

"All right. We might as well. Since the rain's held off."

A few minutes later we were leaned up against each other on a weather-beaten log on the beach while Jinx chased seagulls in the surf. The beach, in typical Northwest style, was a rugged stretch of golf-ball sized rocks littered with driftwood, broken shells and patches of brittle seaweed. Like the rest of the park, it remained deserted. The perks of a nature walk on a blustery fall day.

"Just like old times, hey?" Kendall said, snuggling up tighter as the wind lashed at our backs.

I smiled despite my annoyance about our father's impending Christmas visit, which had only confirmed the status of Kendall's relationship with him. I wished she wouldn't sneak around behind my back. At the same time I realized it was a hypocritical thing to think. I'd been sneaking around in a much bigger way lately, and I decided, right on the spot, to come clean.

"So, I have some exciting news," I said.

Kendall smiled as if anticipating something normal, like I were about to tell her I was joining a pottery class.

"Remember how I told you Morley whispered something to me before he died? A date?"

"Sure, yeah."

"It turned out to be...Oh, man."

"What?"

I should've rehearsed this, but she was staring me down. "I can't tell you how, but please believe me when I say that I... oh, God."

"What? *What?*"

"I traveled to that date."

Kendall's forehead wrinkled. I took a huge gulp of fresh sea air, grounding myself. This was my truth.

"Morley gave me the power to time travel. I can't say how, but look, no matter how far-fetched it might sound, you have to believe me. I went back in time to April the twentieth, to this very spot. Well, over there," I said, tipping my head toward the falls. "And I saw Morley. *Talked* to him. I nearly drowned that day, and he rescued me. You can't tell anyone, not even Brett. It's against the rules. And Morley's wishes."

Kendall tried to pull me towards her, but I batted her arms away.

"Stop it, Kenny. I'm not a lunatic. Forget about all that whacko stuff in my past, that's not me anymore."

She leaned away from me, wringing her gloved hands together, chewing at her lip. A half a dozen seagulls took flight at the far end of the beach, screeching at Jinx who'd interrupted their feast on a rotting crab.

Kendall was staring me down. I had to look away. Let her process. Two weeks earlier I'd withstood the same shock and disbelief on my first timeblink. She just needed time to sort it out.

I spotted a wedge of frosted green sea glass poking out of the sand at my feet. I picked it up and brushed it off, wondering how long it had been bouncing around in the ocean, and how it had come to land on this beach. I threw it towards the ocean where it bounced off a rock and disappeared into the foam at the water's edge. After what felt like the lifespan of a blue whale, Kendall said, "Oh, Syd."

They were just two words, but they could've been a hundred.

I vaulted off the log and glowered down at her. "Oh my *God*. You don't believe me."

"Syd. You've been through a lot in the last few weeks. Maybe you need a little extra time, you know...to recover."

"Why do I tell you anything anymore?" I said, tears threatening at the corner of my eyes. "I end up feeling like a complete nutcase with the way you look at me sometimes."

Jinx scrabbled clumsily toward me over the rocks and leaned up against my leg.

"Come on, Syd. Think about how it sounds."

I shook my head at her, slowly, deliberately.

"I want to believe you." She stood, brushing sand off the seat of her jeans, and I took a couple of wobbly steps backward.

"Then why don't you? I've been honest with you my whole life. Why would I lie now, especially with something so big?"

Hearing the words out loud, I realized something. Twins, especially identical ones, lack a filter with each other. We start as one egg split in two, and genetics dictate we share everything. Without Isla around, Kendall had always been my surrogate twin. She'd saved my life more times than I could count, and though we'd had our ups and downs, I trusted her with my life. I couldn't imagine losing her. I needed her to believe me now, to ground me like she always did, not to treat me like some nutcase. She offered her hand to help me over the log, which I declined. She still hadn't responded, and I wasn't going to move until she did.

"I know you wouldn't lie," she said. "Not on purpose. And if you need to talk about it, I'm all ears."

I rolled my eyes. She was pandering but at least she was listening.

"Remember back in April, that story about the woman who plunged down Chapman Falls?"

Kendall frowned. "Sort of?"

"Look it up. She was pulled out of the water by a man who happened to be standing at the bottom, then the two of them disappeared."

"I remember now. Wasn't there a video on the news?"

"Yes. But it was shot from the viewing platform, and the mist from the falls had been so thick that it was impossible to see anything clearly. There was speculation that they'd been swept out to sea."

"But their bodies were never found."

I nodded. "That's because it was me and Morley."

Chapter Eight

Five days later, Coop and I were huddled outside Kendall and Brett's sprawling executive home on the cliffs of Alice Bay with another fall storm raging around us. Jinx was perched resolvedly with his two front paws on the threshold, his nose smushed up against the door. Brett would have built a cozy fire in the great room, and it seemed Jinx was just as eager to get to it as I was.

Dinner at Brett and Kendall's on the third Sunday of every month—or the fourth, if Coop was scheduled to work—had become a tradition. I'd been especially looking forward to it this time. It had been eons since I'd seen Connor and Devin apart from when they'd visited me at the hospital after Morley's accident, but I'd been pretty drugged up and despondent and barely remembered them being there.

The giant maple door flew open thumping against the stopper as a savory mix of caramelized onions, fresh bread and Italian spices hit me in the face. Connor and Devin ran out in socked feet and jumped into our arms on the porch, and Jinx bounded into the house. While we hustled inside, Coop boosted Devin up on his left arm, asking him if he was ready to pig out on his mom's famous homemade pizza. Devin thought it was the funniest thing he'd ever heard and hugged Coop tighter around his neck. Connor, who'd just recently gotten too heavy for me to lift for very long, was already on the ground, walking backwards, chattering to me about his new pet hamster.

"I can't wait to meet him," I said.

"Yay! C'mon, he's in his cage. Mom won't let me take him out of my room."

"Your mom's a smart lady," I said. "You'd never find him again if he got loose in this house."

"Hi guys," Kendall appeared in the hallway and hurried toward us, wiping her hands on her apron. She shooed Connor away to give me a quick hug. I wished she hadn't interrupted. The kids had always made us feel like celebrities whenever we saw them.

"Close that door, will you? We don't need to heat the whole neighborhood. Brett's in the den," she said to Coop over her shoulder, heading back into the kitchen.

I threw my coat on the bench near the door and followed after Kendall. "Duty calls," I said to Coop. "Connor, you can introduce me to your hamster after I help your mom with dinner."

"Awww. Okaaaaay."

"Come grab me if you need any help," Coop said, setting off in the opposite direction with Devin still in his arm and Connor trailing behind. For a millisecond I imagined they were our kids. Parenthood looked good on Coop. I paused to watch the three of them disappear down the hall and my heart swelled, excited for our future.

As I entered Brett and Kendall's restaurant-sized kitchen, it felt like I was seeing it for the first time. *Everything* seemed new and wonderful to me since I'd started timeblinking, even things I hadn't previously appreciated or given a second thought.

"You're looking great," Kendall said as she scooted over to one of the wall ovens to check on the pizza.

"Thanks. Been running lots."

"I didn't necessarily mean your body, although you do make me look like an overfed gorilla."

"Hardly."

It was the first time we'd seen each other since our hike at Chapman Falls, and it seemed like she was going to keep her tongue in check. Good. This wasn't the place for a conversation about timeblinking—not with other people running around.

"Seriously, though. I'm going to start working out again. I've blown the dust off the equipment downstairs and hired Suzanne for three months."

"Your trainer?"

"None other. You're welcome to join me if you like. She'll be coming twice a week."

"Hmm, I just might."

"Really?" she said, turning around to look at me as she kicked the oven door shut.

I nodded. "My core needs work. Will you be doing Pilates again?"

"Oh yeah, lots of core work. Lately I've been feeling my belly jiggle when I run up the stairs, and I told Suzanne to throw as many ab exercises at me as I can handle. And then more on top of that. Can you make Wednesdays and Fridays at 11?"

"Sure. I'll skip my run on those days," I said. "How much is—"

"Don't worry about it. I was doing it anyway. Glad to have a buddy."

After our pizza feast and apple pie for dessert, Kendall and I retreated to living room while the kids helped Coop and Brett clean the kitchen. Outside, the wind still raged, but it had chased the clouds away revealing a bright blue moon that looked close enough to touch. Whitecaps roiled on the ocean's surface and spindly pine trees swayed on the cliff outside the house, looking as though they might snap.

I loved this part of the evening. The part where there was nothing left to do but hunker down and relax in front of the fire. Normally we'd play a board game or dominoes before Connor and Devin headed off to bed, but it had been a long day for them starting with hockey practise at 6 a.m., and they'd probably be ready to put the welcome mat out for the sandman soon.

After drying his last saucepan and asking to be excused from kitchen duty, Connor came over and curled up on the loveseat next to me, leaning his head on my arm. He'd always been the gentler of the two boys, like Isla had been in our duo. I picked up his hand and held it in both of mine and he sighed happily. He was all but solidifying my recent fixation on having children. I still had no intention of breaking the news to anyone—not before I'd lived with the idea a little while longer. It was too new. When I was ready, I would tell Coop and Coop only. I certainly didn't need Kendall going into mother hen mode over it. No. Kendall and Brett would find out when I was past the first trimester, or whenever it is that a pregnancy is deemed viable. And only then.

God, listen to me. Talking like I was already pregnant. *Patience, Syd.*

"Anyone for dominoes?" Coop asked as he and Brett wandered into the living room, bottles of beer in hand. Brett stopped to stoke the fire, and Coop flopped heavily onto the leather sofa where Kendall was sitting, forcing the cushion under her to bounce. I winced. Sometimes Coop could be like a bull in a china shop. Completely oblivious.

"Hey, hey!" Kendall yelled when her wine glass jiggled in her hand.

"Sorry, Kenny. Don't know my own weight," he said, laughing, patting his lap for Devin to come sit.

Devin jumped up on Coop's lap, jiggling Kendall's wine again, and she bolted off the sofa, wavering slightly as she stood. "Brutes," she said, stomping over to the loveseat where Connor and I were sitting and flumped down making us bounce just hard.

"You're the worst," she said to Coop, a slight slur in her voice. I prayed she wasn't drunk enough to open her mouth about my timeblinking. She wouldn't dare.

"Now, now, children, behave," I said lightly.

"Yeah, let's play dominoes," Connor said from his cozy spot between Kendall and me. He yawned and scooched even closer, away from his tipsy mother.

"Borrrringggg," Devin said. "Mom, can I play Chimera Blaster?"

"What? No! No games, especially video games, for anyone tonight. It's bedtime soon."

"Come on, mom. The kids wanna play," Coop said sticking his bottom lip out at Kendall.

My mouth fell open. He was playing with fire teasing Kendall like that. He drained the last of his beer and nudged Devin off his lap to go get him another. I hadn't realized how much he'd had to drink. That devil-may-care attitude right there was why I'd stopped ingesting crazy juice years ago.

Kendall jumped to her feet and tramped into the kitchen where she poured another generous measure of wine. Then she stormed down the hall. I heard the library door slam.

"Uh oh," little Connor said, pulling a faux-fur blanket over his head.

"Way to go, Uncle C! Now she's mad," Devin said.

"Don't worry about her, Dev. She'll get over it."

"Honestly. Will you two ever get over yourselves? Go on, go smooth things out."

His mouth opened in protest, but he stopped himself short when he saw I wasn't joking. He got up and stalked down the hall without saying a word.

Brett, who was standing by the fireplace, said, "Okay boys, time for bed."

They both whined in unison, but I think at least one of them was relieved.

"You, sit," I said to Brett as I jumped to my feet. "I'll tuck them in."

"You sure?"

"I'm sure. Come on boys."

"Yay Aunty Syd! Yay Aunty Syd!" Connor chanted, jumping up and down, suddenly full of life. Devin was a little less excited and plodded behind us as if he were heading for the gallows.

"Good night, boys. Don't give your aunty any guff, okay?" Brett said, happy, I think, to keep his butt planted on the sofa.

After saying my good night to Connor and Marshmallow, his teddy bear hamster, I closed the door behind me. I'd tucked Devin in first, and he was probably already asleep judging by the way he'd mumbled his good night. I leaned against Connor's door, smiling to myself. I could handle this. Kids were a piece of cake compared to the adults in my life. Unbeknownst to them, these boys were sealing the deal in my mind, minute by minute.

On my way back to the living room past the library I heard Coop and Kendall's muffled voices behind the door. They were still talking, civilly by the sound of it, and my heart swelled. They'd made such strides in the past few weeks, playing on the same team for the first time in a long time, and it would be such a waste for them to revert. Brett and I would have to wait them out.

After putting the kettle on for a cup of tea, I joined Brett in the living room. He'd turned off most of the lights and was lounging on the sofa, head tilted towards the ceiling, a cold beer in hand. I took the armchair facing the sofa.

"Pizza coma?" I asked.

"Uggh. Yes. I'm gonna need three hours on the treadmill tomorrow."

I laughed.

"Is it easy? You know, being a dad? Trying to be friends with your kids and an authority figure at the same time?"

He sighed. "Do I make it look easy? If so, good for me. It's the toughest job I've ever had. The time I nearly lost that twenty-million-dollar condo deal was a cakewalk compared to some of the problems I've had at home."

He took a swig of beer. Chuckled. "I'm making it sound terrible. It's not terrible. Not at all. I wouldn't trade being a father for anything. Why do you ask?"

"Just curious. You know the old story. Coop wanting nothing more than to be a dad. The thing is, I can totally picture him in that role. He's so good with Connor and Dev."

"They do love their Uncle Coop."

I nodded toward the library. "It's too bad Kenny isn't as smitten."

"She'll come around. Someday."

"Maybe. But good grief, it sure doesn't take much to set her off, does it? Especially after a few glasses of wine."

"She's a feisty one, for sure. That's one of the reasons I married her. No milquetoasts for this guy."

I laughed. Kendall was lucky. She and Brett fit together like Lego pieces.

"They've been in there an awfully long time. Is there something going on we don't know about?" he mused.

"Ha," I said. "*That* would be the day."

"I know. It's just funny. Kind of like you and me back in the day."

I grimaced. "Oh God. Yes. Sorry about that, especially when you lived with us. I tortured you something fierce."

"I deserved to be tortured. What the hell was I thinking, moving into the only home you'd ever known, invading your private little world with Kendall like that? Thank God it was only temporary. What was it, eight months? Nine?"

"Five," I said. "But I can see how it would've felt longer. I'm so sorry."

He shook his head. "You were young. Trying to find your way in the world."

"I guess I've finally found it."

Just then the kettle started whistling, and I jumped up to turn off the stove. "Want anything? Tea? Coffee? Beer?" I said, dashing by Brett.

"Actually, yeah. Another beer would be fantastic, thanks."

"For you, gladly. At least you can handle your liquor."

I got him his beer and went back into the kitchen, and while I was pouring hot water into the teapot, Coop and Kendall finally emerged from the library. They skulked by me like a couple of feral cats, taking positions at opposite corners of the room. Kendall flicked on the lamp beside her. "Dark enough?" she said to no one.

"I was enjoying the firelight, my dear," Brett said.

Outside, a tree limb smacked against a window. Brett got up and grabbed an iron poker from the hearth. "At least we've got the fire if the power blows."

"Anybody need anything?" I asked, still in the kitchen, praying the newcomers would ask for water. Anything but—

"Can you grab the Bin 17? It's on the counter next to the fridge," Kendall said, an edge to her voice I didn't like. Especially when coupled with a request for more wine. But I wasn't willing to poke the beehive like Coop had, so I hurried the bottle over and poured out a small a splash.

Coop followed me back into the kitchen and filled a glass with water. He gulped the whole thing down, filled the glass again, and wandered back to the living room. Good. He'd had enough booze for one night.

What wasn't good was the stiff silence between him and Kendall. It was unnerving. That's when Brett's comment flew in and struck me out of nowhere: *Is there something going on we don't know about?*

Prickles rose on the back of my neck as I watched Coop and Kendall doing their level best to ignore each other. On one hand, I thought: preposterous. There was no way these inveterate foes could be carrying on behind my back. On the other, I wondered: Should I be worried?

No. Absolutely not.

And then: I could find out.

They wouldn't miss me for four and a half minutes. They were all in their own little worlds out there—one in an agitated fit, another in a happy, beer-induced euphoria, and Coop somewhere in between.

A few minutes later, after excusing myself from the painfully quiet room, I stood in the guest bathroom eyeing myself in the mirror, holding the talisman in a death grip. What had I become? The first whiff of something untoward going on, and I was about to eavesdrop on my sister and my husband?

Damn you, Brett.

It raised ethical questions in my mind. This was the first time I'd be using the power purely for my own gain, whereas the other timeblinks had either been informational meetings with Morley or, in the case of the coffee date, to prove Kendall wrong about my feelings toward my friend.

This was something else entirely.

Spying.

On the two people I trusted most.

Exactly! I trusted them like I trusted the sun to rise the

next day. I trusted them with my life. With my soul. If I'd wanted to know what their conversation was about, I would ask them. And they would tell me. End of story.

But if I *were* going to go, I couldn't afford to waste any more time arguing with myself. Time was of the essence.

I checked the lock on the bathroom door.

"Library, 2800 Seacliff Terrace, 7:45 p.m., October 20, 2019."

I'd made an educated guess about the time, and it seemed I'd arrived ahead of Kendall. Moonlit shadows slithered over the walls like angry snakes, and I shuddered, more from the thought of sneaking around behind my loved ones' backs than the fear of what lurked in the dark.

But here I was, doing it, and even if I wanted to abort the mission right this minute, I couldn't. Morley had proven that phenomenon when he'd accidently timeblinked to San Francisco during my first visit to the cabin and was gone for four minutes and forty-four seconds. That might not sound like a long span of time, but if the 1986 Challenger Shuttle explosion taught the world anything, it was that a mere seventy-three seconds is plenty of time for something to go horribly, irrevocably wrong.

As my pupils adjusted to the low light in the library, I made my way to one of the two armchairs flanking the window. I settled into the chair, studying what little of the room was visible in the patchy, undulating moonlight, trying to stave off the panic building in my heart.

"Fucking asshole," came a voice from the direction of the built-in bookcase that spanned the entire wall behind the desk. I nearly jumped out of my socks.

Kendall was already there, sitting in the shadows behind

Brett's desk. She leaned into the moonlight and picked up a wine glass I hadn't noticed before.

Why was she so angry?

Coop would be coming along shortly. A pang of dread seized my heart and spread through my body like a noxious weed. This was so wrong. Snooping around like this was beneath me.

A brisk knock came at the door.

Kendall said nothing, and for one fleeting, illogical moment, I believed Coop would give up and go away. Despite Kendall's silence he poked his head in anyway, flicking the light on as he stepped in and closed the door behind him. He wandered over to the middle of the room, stopping between the desk and the sofa. "You okay?"

"Leave me alone."

"Come on, Kenny. What's this all about?" He said, leaning on the back of the sofa looking casually impatient, as though he was waiting for a delayed bus.

I was impressed by his use of my sister's nickname, probably hoping to soften her up. I'd always called her Kenny, and Coop used it when he was feeling playful or when he'd had a few drinks, like tonight. He wasn't drunk on the same level as Kendall was, but he'd apparently had enough beer to boost his courage.

He persisted. "Look, I'm sorry I teased you out there. It was all in fun. I thought—"

"Thought what? That the boys could stay up way past their bedtime and be irritable little snots in the morning? You don't have to deal with any of that. You can go home anytime you bloody well please."

Uh oh. The challenges of motherhood were getting to her.

This was a terrible idea. *I shouldn't be here.*

"Oh man. I'm so sorry," he went on.

Kendall hiccupped. "Huh. Of course you're sorry. You

think you can just waltz in here, apologizing like you always do, then expect everything to be fine."

I didn't need to hear how difficult motherhood was—not right now. Not when my current picture of it was all unicorns and rainbows.

I grasped the talisman. "Return."

Nothing.

Great. It hadn't been long enough.

My eyes darted to the door. I could leave the room. But how would that look? The door would swing open and they'd be momentarily spooked but would probably end up blaming the wind. I stood to walk out, then hesitated. They'd both fallen silent, and I decided to wait a few moments. Surely the four and a half minutes were almost up.

Coop stood and took a few tentative steps toward the door. Was he leaving? The timeframe wasn't right. They'd been in this room a lot longer than that. Kendall suddenly lunged off her chair, sending it twirling away behind her. It bumped against the bookcase, knocking over a wedding picture of her and Brett.

"You have *no right* to force your ideals on my sister."

"Pardon me?" he said, his expression incredulous as he turned to face her square on.

She picked up her glass and swallowed the rest of her wine before coming around the front of the desk.

"You know exactly what I'm talking about, mister," she said, bumping her empty wine glass against his chest.

"No, I don't. But I really wish I did," he said evenly.

"She doesn't want fucking kids!"

Oh no. The stress was about *me*. Worse, Kendall was drunk and loose-lipped and seemed primed to blurt out anything that popped into her mind, things I'd told her in strict confidence. Maybe even the stuff about Morley.

"Return!" I said, snatching up the talisman.

Damn it! Still not long enough.

Coop came over to the window right next to me. I followed his gaze out to the sea where he seemed to be searching for answers, trying to understand why Kendall was so opposed to us starting a family.

"She'll figure it out one day," he said, turning around to face Kendall across the room. "I know it. Come on, you've seen her around Connor and Dev."

"Of course she's happy around them. They're good boys. But you guys can go home when you've had enough. When you're a parent, you don't have that luxury." It came out *lushery*.

Coop blew air through his lips.

Kendall went on. "Can you at least wait until her mental status is a *little* more stable? If you could've heard the shit she told me—"

I lunged toward her. *"Shut up!"* I yelled.

"What shit?" Coop said.

"Nothing. She's just not thinking straight, ever since her friend died. You know, her PPSD."

"PTSD."

"Whatever."

"*Not* whatever."

Kendall hiccupped again. "She needs more time with Cassandra."

"Of course she does. What do you think? That I'm going to pull the rug out from under her? You keep forgetting I love your sister."

"Yeah, yeah. I know."

"Look. I'm going to give her all the time she needs to recover from this. But it doesn't change how I feel. I still think she'll make a wonderful mother. It may even help her heal, having a new little life to focus on."

God, I loved this man.

Kendall crossed her arms and stared at him, wavering slightly. "You're an idiot if you think that."

Ouch. Tell me how you really feel, Kenny.

"Hey, hey. That's not cool."

"Think about it. Who's going to look after this fantasy child? You work six days a week, and Syd's a fucking basket case. What happens the next time she has a meltdown? Huh? And Lord only knows how she'd deal with the post-partum stage."

I shook my head. Did she always talk about me—and so mercilessly—behind my back? Maybe she thought she was helping. I snorted out loud. She *was* helping. Helping fuel my resolve about starting a family with the man I loved.

Hearing enough, I took the talisman between my thumb and forefinger. "Return!"

In an instant I was back in the bathroom, and as soon as I stopped shaking, I opened the door and headed back to the living room. It was time to get out of there.

Chapter Nine

The next morning I awoke with my brain racing in a hundred directions. Coop was already at the gym, and I was grateful for the space and time to reflect upon the time-blink to the library. I wanted Coop to tell me about his conversation with Kendall on his own terms, without any prompting from me.

I scooted up in bed to get a better view of the world outside. Rain blasted the window like machine gun fire against a backdrop of rolling gray clouds. A draft from the transom window above our bed blew down my neck, and I pulled the knit blanket up, wrapping it around my shoulders. Normally I loved the dark mystery of fall, but this was getting tedious, and it was still only October.

Listen to me whine.

I had a lot to be grateful for. A loving, doting husband. A great job. A beautiful home. My nephews. Brett and my sister.

My sister. Had she really lost faith in my ability to handle life—particularly to mother a child of my own? Had she forgotten how far I'd come? Before Morley died, I hadn't had a meltdown of that magnitude in such a long time. That had to count for something, didn't it? Or had all this Morley business knocked my mental health-o-meter back to zero in Kendall's eyes?

Why on Earth had I told her about timeblinking? Stupid, stupid move. She'd almost spilled the beans to Coop, too, and he was the last person that needed to know about it. At this point anyway. Now that I'd decided to give motherhood a whirl, telling him I was a time traveler might cast a shadow on his sunny outlook of me. I simply had to keep that kind of information under wraps. No use in two family members worrying that I'd lost my mind.

Unless.

Unless I really *had* lost my mind. Oh God. Maybe it had left years ago, and the people around me were exceptionally skilled at covering it up. Humoring me. Soothing me when I awoke screaming in the night. No, I refused to believe it. I was *not* crazy. I was a person with underlying emotional issues, who also happened to be a time traveler.

Jinx stirred in his bed under the window and let out a guttural sigh.

"Yes, Jinxy, you're going to have to accept it. I'm a time traveler."

I threw back the duvet and shinnied to the edge of the bed. Maybe Kendall was right. Maybe I wasn't mother material. But oh how I wanted to prove her wrong. What I needed was a confidence boost. Maybe get an expert's opinion. A pediatrician, perhaps. Lucky me, I happened to know one. I glanced at the clock. Nine thirty. Coop would be at the gym for another hour.

I yanked open my night table drawer and dug Morley's prescription out of its hiding place at the bottom of a half-full Kleenex box. One date down. This blink would be number two on his list: May 12, 2019, and the destination, no surprise, was Chapman Falls. It also happened to be my mother's birthday, and it remained to be seen if this was a matter of coincidence. What struck me even stranger, though, was the time: 1 o'clock in the afternoon. Morley must have been quite confident I wouldn't run into anyone when I arrived.

As I folded the paper and held it tight, my heart clenched. Because of the loss of Morley. Because of Kendall's comments. Because I was plotting to see Morley, here, on the bed Coop and I shared. I couldn't do it here.

After a shower and a quick hair and makeup job, I hurried into the bedroom Isla and I had once shared. It'd been a while since I'd last visited the room, and it smelled musty, like dust and dead flies. I vowed to vacuum and dust every surface when I got back. I would run Isla's yellowed bedding and tattered stuffed animals through the wash and arrange them, fresh and bright, on her bed. It was an exercise I'd performed heavy heartedly over the years, but today I found I was looking forward to it. My outlook on life was shifting, and suddenly I couldn't wait to get to my 'appointment' with my pediatrician.

My arrival at the falls was met with a small complication when a young boy about the twins' age emerged from the outhouse next to the parking lot the very moment I popped into the scene. I couldn't tell who was more shocked when we locked eyes on each other: me or him. But he appeared to be trying to convince himself that he'd been quite mistaken—that he *hadn't* seen a pretty blonde woman materialize out of thin air. Yet his head shook so vigorously that I thought it might spin right off his shoulders, and when I gave him a small reassuring wave, he turned and hotfooted it down the path toward his family without a scream or even one tiny peep. I scurried off toward the cabin, giving him no opportunity to drag his parents back and thrust an accusatory finger at me.

I let myself into Morley's unlocked cabin ten minutes later, having knocked and gotten no answer. He'd been expecting me and therefore must have left the door open when he knew he couldn't be there for some reason.

"Hello?" I called from the front hallway as I entered the living room warily.

I wondered what he had in mind for this visit. Another Timeblinking 101 class? What more could I learn?

Whatever his plan was, I had my own agenda today. I guess I just wanted to hear from a professional that I was qualified and perhaps even predestined for motherhood.

"Hello?" I said again, stepping through the stone archway leading into the kitchen.

No lights on in there, either.

I fingered the talisman nervously, trying to convince myself to stay, that I was meant to come today because the date and time had been on Morley's list, which was still in my hand. I unfolded it to make sure I'd gotten the details right. May 12, 2019, and if I were to believe the mahogany clock on the mantel beneath the deer antlers, I'd gotten the time right too.

So where was Morley? Had it been a mistake on his part? Had something happened to him so he couldn't be here? Moreover, why had he sent me here in the middle of the day, having told me I would always be zapping to Chapman Falls after the park closed? Fortunately, apart from the little boy exiting the outhouse, no one had been around when I'd arrived at the parking lot, a fact that Morley must have known somehow. Perhaps there *was* something more to learn about timeblinking.

I stuffed the note into my pocket and went about searching the house. It was mildly disconcerting to explore the rooms without his presence or knowledge, but I was sure that he knew me well enough by now that he wouldn't have minded.

On the second floor, I poked my head into each of the rooms, all of them empty, leaving the master bedroom for last.

A shiver went through me as I crossed its threshold. On my first timeblink, Morley had left me alone in here to shower and change into his comfy clothing. My mind had been blown that night, and I smiled thinking about it now. How quickly life changes. Before that, life had been an ordinary and predictable routine of work, dinner and movie nights on the sofa with Coop, and spending time with Kendall and her family; but with timeblinking as a side gig and the potential for a baby on the horizon, my life was turning into anything but predictable. And it didn't scare me at all.

I stayed awhile in Morley's bedroom, stopping to run my fingers over his personal items scattered about. A Stephen King novel about time travel beside the bed. His bathrobe draped over a chair. His hairbrush and cellphone on the dresser. His wallet. My stomach flipped. I'd seen the wallet many times in the years he'd sat at my bar, but this was the first time I'd seen it without him nearby. I swallowed hard and picked it up. The leather was well worn and supple and smelled ever so faintly of his cologne. A ghost of a scent. There, but not there.

Something inside me gave way and I was transported back to The Merryport where I'd watched him walk out the door for the last time. Where he'd drawn his last breath. Where I'd learned the true meaning of the word *final*. And now, here in his room I sought comfort in his possessions. Touching them. Smelling his presence in them.

I slid down the footboard of the bed and sat with my back against it, pressing his wallet to my cheek. I refused to cry. There'd been too much of that lately.

After a few minutes, I gathered myself up off the floor and replaced the wallet on the dresser. As I arranged my t-shirt back down around my hips, a thought occurred to me: Morley's wallet was here, which must've meant he was some-where close. Maybe out for a walk, though that would've been strange since he'd been expecting me.

I went to the window to see if I could spot him. There was no sign of life on the beach apart from two crows strutting around in the sand. The lake's surface was like polished glass, punctuated here and there with reverse images of the homes on the other side, their white or cream facades radiant in the sunlight. A dragonfly flew up and hovered just outside the window then flitted away before I could give it another thought.

Just then, something moved in the trees to the right of Morley's property. Something blue. Was I being watched? Was it Morley? I edged myself out of direct view (if in fact someone other than Morley was watching me), with just my eyes peeping around the corner. A moment later, Morley's neighbor, that weird window-washer fellow—Squeaky? Squeegee?—emerged from the lakeside path and trudged up the beach toward the house. I wondered if I should go down and see what he wanted but thought better of it. Not without Morley there. Surely the guy would leave when he found Morley not at home.

A shiver raced down my spine when he stopped suddenly and looked up at the window where I stood. His eyes locked on mine. Did I see hostility there? Shock? Or was it recognition from the night Morley and I saw him in the window wearing nothing but his bright pink boxer shorts? At any rate, my cover was blown, so I stepped into full view and gave him a friendly wave. He didn't wave back. Just stood there, staring at me with his hands on his hips.

An unnaturally long time passed as we stared each other down, but I wasn't going to be the first to look away. He seemed to sense this and took his gaze to the side of the house, as if something had distracted him, then he stalked toward whatever it was and disappeared from view. It was disconcerting knowing he was down there, like a spider you see in your bedroom one minute only to disappear under the bed the next.

I hurried out of the bedroom and flew down the stairs, reaching the bottom just as Squeaky pushed the front door open. Half of my brain was screaming, *Turn around! Go back up! Lock yourself in the bathroom!* The other half adopted a more assertive position. *Screw that. Find out what the big oaf wants and get rid of him.* I stayed put.

"What are you doing here?" he demanded.

"Visiting Morley." I don't know why I answered when my first instinct had been not to give him any details. Not until I found out what he wanted first.

"*Doctor* Scott left an hour ago."

"I know," I lied. "Can I help you?"

"You're not supposed to be—"

"I was invited."

"You're not supposed to be here when the doctor isn't home."

"Look, uh…what was your name again?"

"Sparkles. I'm the neighborhood watcher. Who are you?"

Sparkles, ridiculous.

"I'm a friend of Morley's, and he invited me here, so everything's good. I'll be sure to let him know you were on guard, though." He seemed like the kind of person that would respond to flattery.

"I think I'll wait for Dr. Scott," the man said.

I walked past him and took hold of the open door. "There's really no need. I can give him a message though."

"Nope. I'll wait. Rules of the lake," he said, advancing further inside the house. He stopped and turned around, folding his arms in front of his thick chest and stared at me down his nose.

He was starting to piss me off now. "Well, my rule is safety first," I said. "And it's definitely not safe to be stuck inside a house with a stranger. I'm not asking you to leave, but it would be better if you waited outside."

The door was still wide open, and when he stayed glued to

the spot, I walked up to him and took his meaty forearm, meaning to guide him outside. He seemed surprised, if not a little amused, that a woman half his size would try to force him out, and he yanked his arm away and twirled me around, locking his arm around my throat. He dragged me over to the sofa and threw me down on my back. I tried to get up, but he pushed me down and put his knee on my chest.

"Fuck! Get off me!"

"Lady. You're the one that's not supposed to be here. And now you've attacked me, so it's looking mighty suspicious. So we'll wait for Dr. Scott together. I'm going to take my leg away, and you're going to sit there and behave yourself. Or else."

What choice did I have but to comply?

"Fine. But you sit over there," I said, pointing to the chair nearest the front door.

"Fine." He took his leg off me and backed away slowly, almost willing me to get up and fight. Then he settled into the chair.

A brief thought to use the talisman crossed my mind as I straightened my clothes and smoothed down my hair, but I couldn't do it with the oaf watching. I'd have to wait for Morley.

Where the hell was he anyway? Maybe he'd mixed up the date; maybe he thought I was coming tomorrow or sometime next week. It seemed unlikely, though. He was a doctor, for goodness sake. Disseminating accurate information was his life. I pulled the prescription out of my pocket and unfolded it.

"Hey!" Sparkles leapt out of his seat.

I waved the prescription in the air, showing him it was just a harmless piece of paper. "Don't get your bun in a knot. I'm keeping myself entertained."

He rolled his eyes and sat back down while I read the note again just to be sure I hadn't mistaken the date: May 12, 2019. That was definitely the date I'd recited when I initiated the blink. I wouldn't have gotten my mother's birthday wrong. But what was this? The time? Now that I scrutinized it closer, I saw it wasn't a *one* at all. It was a *seven*.

That was a doctor's handwriting for you. It seemed I would be waiting a few more hours until Morley returned from wherever he might be. Wherever that was, it couldn't be far since he hadn't locked the door and didn't have his wallet with him. Nobody leaves home without their ID and credit cards. Unless he hadn't left under his own volition.

And what about this goon sitting across from me? Did he have anything to do with Morley's strange absence, if there was anything strange about it at all? Maybe I was reading too much into it.

Almost unconsciously, I reached for the talisman. But it wasn't there. I searched my neckline as inconspicuously as possible so as not to alarm the oaf, but it was truly gone.

It was bound to happen on a timeblink eventually, the failure of the clasp. It'd been faulty right from the start, having come undone at least half a dozen times at home, and I'd been meaning to get it repaired. At one point I'd put the talisman on a different chain but promptly changed it back because I didn't like how it looked. Besides, I had no idea if it was necessary to use the chain and talisman in tandem for a successful timeblink. I'd been meaning to ask Morley about that but kept forgetting. I'd imagined all sorts of disastrous outcomes, the worst of which was finding out I couldn't return to my present time, ever. And now that the talisman was missing, I didn't have to imagine anything. I was about to find out for real.

It had to have fallen off during the tussle with the oaf, and I took advantage of the handful of times he briefly nodded off to search the crevices of the sofa, but it wasn't there. Maybe it was on the floor near the front door where he'd first grabbed me. I'd have to check later.

There was nothing more to do but wait. Five hours to go. At the most.

At some point I myself had nodded off, startling awake by muffled voices outside the cabin. Seeing I was alone in the room, I scrambled around and peered out the window from the back of the sofa, nearly bursting into tears when I spotted Morley on the stoop talking to Sparkles. I hurried over to the door.

Morley was mid-sentence when the door swung open. "—so you must be mistake—Oh! Sydney, what are you doing here?"

"I told ya," the oaf said behind him as I retreated slightly behind the door.

"It's all right, Sparkles. Syd is my guest. I just wasn't expecting her so soon."

"She wasn't on the list," I heard him say defiantly.

"No, and I'm sorry about that. Like I said, she wasn't supposed to be arriving until later. Not until I was home."

"Oh, okay, Doc. Sure thing. Tell her I'm sorry, will ya?" he said, trying to get a look at me over Morley's shoulder.

"You bet. I'll talk to you tomorrow."

"Got it. She wasn't on the list, Doc. Rules of the lake," I heard him say as his voice faded away.

After Morley closed the door, he turned to me with a look of regret. "I'm so sorry," he said. "I wasn't expecting you until seven. Are you okay?"

I flew into his arms.

We didn't speak for the longest time afterward. Morley busied himself building a fire then making a pot of tea while I curled up on the sofa, wrapping myself in his thick chenille blanket. Any other day I would've suggested we go for a walk around the lake, taking advantage of the bright, crisp spring afternoon. Instead I wanted nothing more than to shield myself from the world.

After a few minutes, Morley shuffled into the living room carrying a tray of tea biscuits, a china teapot and cups that might have belonged to his grandmother. I wasn't hungry, but the tea was just what the doctor ordered.

"Feeling any better?" he said taking the chair opposite me.

"Hardly. It's going to take me a while to calm down."

Morley grimaced. "So. Tell me what happened."

"He obviously didn't recognize me from that day we saw him. Must've thought I was trespassing and wasn't about to let me get away with it."

"Did he hurt you?"

"No," I said, rubbing my neck where he'd put me in a chokehold. "I did consider zapping out, but he'd already seen m—" The talisman. I'd forgotten about it.

"I—I was upstairs when I saw him walking toward the house. Probably should've left right then."

Morley raised an eyebrow when I said I'd been upstairs.

I quickly explained. "I was looking for you. When I didn't find you anywhere else, I searched your bedroom."

He scrunched his face up. "Why were you here so early, anyway? Didn't I write 7 o'clock on the prescription?"

"You did," I said, pulling the paper out of my pocket. I got up and handed it to him. Pointed to his chicken scratch, specifically the so-called seven.

"Does that look like a seven to you?" I said.

"Yes." He looked up, scratching his stubbled chin. "Sort of? Could be mistaken for a one, I suppose."

"Well, it *was* mistaken for a one. You doctors and your terrible penmanship."

He flashed me a sheepish grin.

"Don't worry about it. It's over now," I said, knowing I had bigger problems to deal with. "If you'll excuse me a minute, I need to use the ladies' room."

On my way to the stairs, I scanned the front hall, not seeing the talisman anywhere. I had a mildly disconcerting thought that Sparkles had found it and taken it, just for spite. It would do no good to jump to conclusions now; not before I'd searched the house first. Once upstairs, I scoured every room, coming up dry, ending with Morley's bedroom. I looked under the bed, by the window, under the dresser, behind the dresser. I even tore the comforter off the bed and shook it out. Nothing. Maybe Sparkles *had* taken it.

To maintain my cover for going upstairs in the first place, I went into the bathroom and flushed the toilet then ran the tap, studying my worried reflection in the mirror.

How would I get home now?

I started back to the living room with dread my heart. Morley was going to have a fit. As my foot hovered over the top stair, I stopped, steadying myself. What if *Morley* had stumbled on the talisman and was keeping it from me? What if he didn't want me to go back? Ever?

"No way," I said under my breath, wondering just the same.

When I settled back onto the sofa a few moments later, my mind was still whirring.

"Everything okay? You look distracted. Still shaken up about Sparkles?"

"Yes, but not for the reason you think."

"He really is harmless. A bit slow on the uptake but he——"

"I lost the talisman." There, I said it. Come what may.

Morley's brows squeezed together, and he looked at me sideways. It seemed genuine enough, his look of surprise. Maybe he hadn't found it after all.

"What? How?" He scooted to the edge of his seat.

"I—the last time I recall having it was in your bedroom," I

blushed at this, thinking how I'd collapsed to the floor with his wallet clutched to my breast. "At least I *think* that's where I had it last. All I know is that I can't find it now."

He huffed and stood up, planted himself in front of the impressive blaze he'd built in the fireplace. "Well, then, it has to be here somewhere."

"Sparkles and I did have a little scuffle when he found me here. It could have come off then."

"A scuffle?"

I hadn't meant to tell him about that. Sparkles seemed to be his friend, after all. "It was minor. He was just surprised to see me. But now I'm wondering if it came off in the hallway and he picked it up."

Morley shook his head. "He wouldn't keep it. That's not his style. If anything, he put it in his pocket and forgot it. I'll run over there and ask him."

While Morley was gone, I tore all the cushions off the sofa to make extra sure it hadn't slipped off there. It hadn't, and when Morley returned fifteen minutes later, it was to deliver the news I'd been expecting. "No go. Sparkles said he didn't see it."

Not that he would admit, I thought. "Oh Morley, it was that damned clasp. I can't tell you how many times it came apart. I was going to get it fixed. Honestly, I was."

Morley came to sit next to me on the sofa and put his hands on my shoulders. "I think it will all work out. In fact, I'm sure you won't be stuck here with me forever."

I reached up and covered his hands with mine. A crater-sized hole opened in my heart.

"Although it wouldn't be such a terrible thing, would it? You being stuck here?" he said.

It was me who leaned over and kissed him. Once. Square on the lips.

He pulled back, in surprise, it seemed, and his eyes locked on mine. I saw whole universes floating in there. Whole lifetimes. Then he put his hand on the back of my head and drew me close where we surrendered to the longing we'd shared over the years, a longing I'd refused to admit before this moment. And as our lips and our tongues explored each other's, the lines tethering me to reality unravelled and I drifted loose.

Morley felt it too. We pulled back from each other, breathless. He stood and held his hand out to me. I grasped it with a certainty I'd never felt before. We ascended the stairs in silence, slowly, deliberately, perhaps giving each other time to reconsider. But it was too late to turn back. Much too late. This machine had been set in motion the minute he'd walked into the pub all those years ago. He'd known it then, and I must have too.

Hand in hand we crossed into his bedroom and shut out the world behind us.

"See?" Morley said an hour later as we lay entwined in each other's arms, "I'm not mad at you at all."

I smiled into his chest.

My life with Coop had been put on hold, suspended in time, to be picked up when my senses came back. I was prepared for that fall. But I couldn't think about it now. Not with Morley curled around me.

"What on Earth just happened?" I said.

"What happened was fucking epic," he said, sweeping my hair away from my flushed face. "And I cannot wait to do it again."

"You didn't get enough?"

"If we do this every day for the rest of my life—" he made a quick calculation on his fingers, "that's roughly 120 more times—it won't be enough."

I lifted my head off his chest to peer into his bright green eyes. "You're breaking my heart."

"I can fix that. Remember? I'm a doctor."

I smiled again, snuggling back into his chest. "But seriously," I said, bringing us back to Earth. "This can't go on indefinitely."

"Shhh. Not now. I want to carry this moment with me forever."

Forever, he said.

We lay like that for many more minutes, tracing our fingers up and down every surface, every curve—every inch of one another's bodies as though our lives depended on committing them to memory. I could have gone on like that for hours. Morley's body wasn't as broad or as bulky as Coop's, but lean and solid where it needed to be. From the ripples in his abdomen to his taut calf muscles all the way up to his biceps—those biceps!—scrupulously maintained and as hard as baseballs. I'd always wondered if he worked out on a regular basis, and here was irrefutable proof. It seemed he was just as impressed by my body, judging by the way he looked at it, the way his hands moved over it.

I shook my head remembering the reason I'd gone there in the first place: to ask Dr. Scott, the pediatrician, his opinion about me having children. *With Coop*. That discussion was beyond ludicrous now. Besides, I had more urgent concerns. I sat up, pulling the sheet to my chin.

"We have to figure out how I'm going to get back."

He groaned and covered his head with the sheet. I yanked it back, exposing his face and chest. "Come on, mister. This is serious."

"I know, I know," he said sitting up and swinging his legs over the edge of the bed, his back toward me. I hadn't seen his bare back yet, though my hands had explored it extensively, and it took all my willpower not to pull him back under the covers with me.

"What was the purpose of this timeblink anyway? Why my mother's birthday?"

He turned around wide-eyed, "Are you kidding? Today's your mother's birthday?"

I nodded.

"Total coincidence, I swear. As for the purpose of this blink, if you really must know, it was dinner."

"Dinner?"

"Yep," he said, standing, shrugging into his robe. "As you know, you've been on my mind for quite some time, but I was never sure if you felt the same about me. You're an enigma, Syd, but I always knew we were more than just friends. And look at us now," he said, spreading his arms out as if to say destiny had brought us to this room so we could screw each other's brains out.

"What does that have to do with dinner?" I asked.

"Imagine this," he said. "You come to Sandalwood, I charm you with my superb culinary skills and you in turn would be absolutely powerless to resist me. Not that I was going to jump you or anything. By then it would have been all your idea."

"What?" I yelled. "You cook too?"

"Right? Is there no end to my God-given talents?" he said, dramatically drawing the back of his hand to his forehead.

I threw a pillow at him. He caught it and flopped into the armchair behind him.

"Well, I hope you're happy, Dr. Scott. You had your way with me without even turning the stove on," I said, tossing the covers aside, scurrying about the room plucking clothes off the floor.

"Aha! Yes. Though I seem to remember it was all *your* idea!"

My mouth fell open to protest. Until I recalled it *had* been me who'd kissed him first. Ooh, he was good.

He smiled from ear to ear when he realized he had me. Had had me all along, apparently.

"Well, good for you," I said marching into the ensuite to take a shower. "Now you won't have to bother taking a pizza out of the freezer."

I heard him snort.

Towelling off after my shower, I fantasized about living a life here with him if I couldn't find the talisman. A life of quiet nights by the fire. Walks around the lake. Mind-blowing sex. But rationally it could only last 120-odd days, Morley-time. And then what?

As I untangled my twisted bra, a streak of silver hurtled toward the floor and clattered on the tile.

"Hallelujah!" I screamed.

"You've found religion all of a sudden?" I heard Morley say from the bedroom.

I poked my head around the corner, dangling the talisman out for him to see, "I was withholding it all along, just to get you in bed."

"Good grief," he said. "You needn't have devised such an elaborate plan."

I finished getting dressed and came out of the bathroom a few minutes later with the talisman on display in its rightful place. Morley was tapping away on his phone.

"And what about *your* elaborate plan, huh?" I said. "Tricking me into a timeblink to woo me with a romantic dinner?"

He put his phone on a small table next to the chair and stood up, reaching his arms out toward me. His robe fell open, leaving nothing to my imagination, and I scooted over to him, wishing I hadn't gotten dressed so fast.

His embrace was firm yet gentle. "I'm going to take a shower and then cook you a dinner you won't soon forget."

"Oh? You're going through with it? What if I said I'd had

enough of your devious ways and was going home?" I clutched the talisman tauntingly.

"I can't let you leave," he said, wresting the talisman from my hand, pulling it over my head. He slipped it into the pocket of his robe and smiled impishly. "You are ostensibly my hostage now, Ms. Brixton, and you're not leaving until your belly is full."

"You do realize I had no intention of leaving, right? I mean, how often does a lady get treated to dinner *after* sex?"

Chapter Ten

"Um, hi?" Kendall said as I kicked off my boots in her front hall the next morning. I tossed my coat on the bench and headed down the hall toward the kitchen without even looking at her. I must have looked a sight with my hair hanging in a frazzled mop and my face showing the dregs of yesterday's makeup.

I jumped onto one of the white leather stools at the island. "I need a drink."

"I hope you mean a cup of tea," Kendall said, raking a hand through her working-from-home hair.

"Water will do."

"Our workout isn't until tomorrow," she said, taking a glass out of the dishwasher.

I shot her a wistful look. "I can't even think about that right now."

"What's going on?"

"I've been a terrible, *terrible* wife."

Kendall pulled a face.

"Before you say anything," I said, tears pooling in my lower lids, "I *am* a wife. Papers or not."

"Of course."

From the other side of the island, Kendall filled the glass with water and pushed it toward me. She regarded me beseechingly, like she wanted to come and give me a hug but knew better. Instead, she took a sip from her teacup and waited. She could tell there was something heavy on my chest but waited for me to start.

I looked her in the eye. "I've been timeblinking again."

"Oh boy," she said, taking a small breath. We hadn't discussed timeblinking since our hike at Chapman Falls. "Okay. Tell me about it. Something's obviously upsetting you."

"This is between you and me, Kenny. Understand?"

"Yes, of course."

"I mean it. Please don't tell Brett."

"Promise," she said.

"I saw Morley again. At his cabin. I went there for advice, to ask him if I would make a decent mother."

I saw the slightest roll of her eyes, a flutter, toward the ceiling. *Ignore it, Syd.*

"But as soon as I got there, Morley's creepy neighbor attacked me and took me captive."

I was embellishing the story a little to lay the groundwork for what I'd really come to tell her and to justify why I'd done it.

"*What?*"

"Yeah. But it turns out he didn't know he was doing anything wrong."

"Are you going to press charges?"

I looked at my sister as if she were high. "Even if I wanted to, how the hell would I do that?"

"I don't know. Maybe contact the police and file a report?"

"I was in a *timeblink*," I said.

"Right. What was I thinking?"

"Don't patronize me!"

"I'm not. Just trying to figure out why you wouldn't report this guy."

"Never mind about that. Morley showed up and got rid of him. But what's worse is what happened after that."

"Okay," she said slowly, no doubt wondering what could be worse than being assaulted and held against my will.

I took a breath and exhaled. Closed my eyes. "I slept with Morley."

When I looked at Kendall again, it was to see the unfiltered shock in her eyes. We stared at each other a few moments before I said, "And it was awesome."

"Oh," she said, tracing the rim of her teacup with a finger. She waited, apparently letting me revel in my pleasure for a moment. Or maybe she was trying to decide if I was on the brink of another meltdown.

I slid off the stool and paced. My cheeks burned and a headache threatened at my temples. "I don't know what to do."

"Do you need to do *anything*?"

"Yes. I need to figure out my life."

"Are you thinking of leaving Coop?"

"What? No! Of course not!" I fired back, crossing my arms.

"This baby thing is stressing you out again, isn't it?"

I hugged myself tighter. "Yes," I said. "But not how you think."

She cocked her head.

"I've decided I want a baby after all. Well, ninety-nine percent of me wants a baby. I haven't told Coop yet."

"Wow, sis. That's huge."

"No kidding. But now I've gone and screwed it all up! What was I thinking?"

"What happens if you're pregnant? With Morley's baby?"

"You're kidding, right? Do you think I'm sixteen? Of

course we used protection. Besides, I'm still on the pill, or at least I was up until a week ago."

She came around the other side of the island, face to face with me. "Here's my two cents, whether you want them or not," she said. "You could do nothing. Just chalk it up as a one-off *oopsie* and forget about it. Move on. I mean, it's not like you can just drive over to Morley's house and jump into bed with him anytime you like. Besides, sweetie, it can't be good for you, zapping through time and space like that."

"Screw you."

"You think I'm making fun of you? I'm not. I'm simply concerned about your health."

"And by that, you mean my mental health," I said, glaring at her.

She opened her mouth but held her tongue.

"Come," I said, taking Kendall's hand, leading her out of the kitchen and down the hall. We stopped outside the door of the library.

"Here's the deal. I'm going into this room. Alone. And after waiting thirty seconds, I want you to come in."

"This is silly," she said, laughing nervously.

"Pick a place and a date. Any date between my birth and today. A date where I might find out something I don't already know."

"Syd—"

"Come on, humor me."

She rolled her eyes and let out a deflated groan. "Okay. How about September 16, 2000. Our house."

"You're kidding, right?"

"You asked me for a date and a place. I gave them to you."

I shook my head. "All right. September 16, 2000, it is. What time?"

She shrugged, like it was all a big joke. "I don't know, eight in the morning?"

"Fine." I placed my hands on Kendall's shoulders. "Now

listen to me. Wait the full thirty seconds before you come in—"

"You already said that."

"—I'm just making sure you understand the instructions. When you come in, I don't want you to panic. Be calm. Everything will be okay, regardless of how it looks. Understand?"

"Yes, yes," she said impatiently.

"Then, after two minutes, leave the room and close the door behind you. Every fiber of your being will be telling you to stay, but you have to ignore it and do as I've told you. Wait outside the door, and I'll come out when I'm ready. Got it?"

"Yes."

"The timing is important, Kenny. You *must* follow my instructions to the tee."

"Yes, yes," she said again, getting impatient.

I stepped into the library and closed the door.

Kendall could have sent me to a childhood birthday party or our family trip to California or any number of wonderful events in my life, but she picked this date over all others. It was downright cold-hearted, now that I thought about it. To her credit, though, I don't think she would've sent me here had she believed in timeblinking. September 16, 2000, had been another traumatic day in the Brixton family history—the day my mother had died of a heart attack while she napped in her bed.

I arrived just before everyone started gathering for breakfast. In the corner of my childhood kitchen, I lingered invisible, invincible, watching my mother move from counter to sink to stove to table. She was humming. Pancakes and bacon were ready on the table when my twelve-year-old self, Kendall and Dad traipsed into the kitchen, eager to dive into whatever delights their noses had already detected. My dad took his usual seat at the far end of the table. He seemed the most surprised out of any of them by the lavish spread in front of him. And also by my mother's mood. He commented on how lovely she looked in her yellow spaghetti-strap dress. She patted his shoulder and told him he was being silly, then slid into the chair next to him. Syd and Kendall were already hunched over their plates, chewing on bacon, trading sideways glances while their parents flirted.

With everyone seated, a stark awareness jumped out at me: The fifth chair. Empty.

I had to grab for the fridge handle to steady myself. I'd forgotten about our practice of leaving Isla's chair untouched after she'd disappeared. It had been our way of proving we would never give up on her. The sight of it could have sent me swirling down into a pit of despair, but instead, I felt oddly comforted by its presence. It seemed to invite me to sit, and I obliged almost involuntarily.

Across the table, my mother sipped coffee as she watched our family enjoy the meal. Was that pride I saw? Or perhaps a little bit of melancholy? Behind that pleasant smile, I decided, was a wound so deep I was positive it had been what had killed her that day—it would be ruled a heart attack, of course, but had more likely been a broken heart. My sweet, beautiful mom. I wanted to wrap my arms around her slight frame, breathe in the bergamot and lavender scent of her freshly washed hair. I wanted to shake Syd and Kendall by the shoulders. Implore them to give their mother a bit of extra attention this morning. To say, "I love you," and really mean it. I wanted my dad to fake an illness. Play hooky. Anything, so that he would stay home from work. I saw that shit-eating grin on his face as he heaped pancakes onto his plate, engaging Kendall and Syd in light banter, no doubt thinking, *I'm going to enjoy this moment.* Would it have killed him to cancel his meetings to enjoy my mother's good spirits for the rest of the day?

Maybe he'd believed, roughly two weeks before the first anniversary of Isla's disappearance, that my mom had finally kicked her demons aside and decided to start living life again like the rest of us. But how could he have known there would be no more moments like this? In fact, looking at our smiling, happy faces, it broke my heart all over again. None of us had any idea our lives were about to be chucked into a blender and puréed at high speed yet again.

After they finished filling their faces, Kendall pushed her syrup-puddled plate away and reached for a thin paperback book on the counter behind her. "I have to review this one more time," she said, waving it around in front of everyone almost evangelically.

"You'll ace it, kiddo." I liked that Dad still called her kiddo two months past her twentieth birthday. While she'd been a prodigy in the world of photography, Kendall had failed her driver's exam three times, and by this point, she'd been desperate. Later that day, she would pull up in front of the house proudly solo and apply lip gloss in the rear-view mirror after properly angling the wheels towards the curb. She would enter that door, bursting with excitement to drive our mother to the grocery store or the bank, or wherever her heart desired, only to find her cold, lifeless body upstairs in bed. My stomach churned at the thought of it.

One by one we filed out the door, Dad and Kendall on their way to work, Syd to school. Kendall had the afternoon off from her part-time gig at Dad's real estate agency to go for her road test. It was a lovely morning filled with excitement and good cheer.

After kissing us all goodbye simply, without ceremony, my mother leaned with her back against the door for a few moments. Not everyone could pull off wearing such a bright shade of yellow, but she looked radiant in that dress. Her hazel-flecked brown eyes and tinges of auburn in her hair met in perfect harmony with it, giving off a distinct vintage-shampoo-ad vibe. Her skin was faintly sun-kissed—not deeply tanned like the rest of the family's from being outside all summer in a bid to keep things as normal as possible without Isla in the picture.

My mother pushed away from the door, her arms wrapped around her middle like she had a stomach ache, not heart pain. I followed her back into the kitchen where dust particles darted and swooped in the sunny window over the sink like tiny agitated fairies. The dishes from breakfast remained on the table. Two pancakes and a few bacon crumbs on Mom's favorite Petit Point china platter. Half-finished glasses of orange juice. My dad's unread newspaper. A dirty napkin on the floor. I was disgusted with my family for having left such a mess.

My mother walked over to the sink and vomited. It was at this point that the heart attack seemed to manifest itself. Oh boy. Did I really want to see this? I would be with her when it happened, and maybe by the small miracle of these time-blinks, she wouldn't feel alone. So the answer was yes. Yes, I would stay with her.

Seemingly unfazed by having just thrown up, she rinsed the sink, filled a glass with water and set it on the table, then changed course suddenly and walked right through me. It was the oddest sensation. There, but not there at the same time, like she was the ghost, not me. She fished out some paper, a pen, and an envelope from the junk drawer next to the fridge and brought them to the table. Pulled out Isla's chair. Ran her fingers over the curve of the rail. Sat.

I slid into the chair across from my mother, strangely free of anxiety or sadness; it helped to keep reminding myself that this event had already occurred, that I would be powerless to change anything now. Lucky for me, I'd inherited a bit of my mother's unflappable nature, and the fear of the unknown had rarely vexed me like it did my sisters. I remembered how expertly my mother used to calm Kendall's and Isla's nerves when they were going on about some perceived calamity they had no control over, like air travel. Isla in particular loathed flying, but we'd done a lot of it back when we were a whole family—mostly to England to visit Dad's parents when they'd still been alive. Isla would be in the throes of a full-blown panic attack at forty thousand feet, and my mother would hold her close, rub her back, and repeat some combination of reassuring words over and over: "There's no use in being upset about something that hasn't happened. Take deep breaths. In....and out. In....and out. Good. Now pretend the turbulence is a bumpy road and you're already at the farm riding Fleesha in the meadow. There, isn't that better?" On and on it would go, sometimes for hours, while I read or napped or watched the Earth stretch out below me like a giant patchwork welcome mat.

My mother had that calmness about her now, sitting at the kitchen table, taking unhurried sips of water now and then. She waited for a full three minutes, staring at the blank page before picking up the pen.

My Dear Cyril, she started. My father had never told me about a note she'd written to him that day.

She continued, gathering momentum as she wrote.

I've tried to be happy. I've tried to be there for all of you.

"What the—?"

The despair is too heavy. It's too much to carry around every day. Please know that it has nothing to do with you or Kendall or Sydney.

"Mom! Stop!" I screeched, bolting out of my chair, the legs scraping the floor. Her pen froze; her eyes darted around the room. Maybe I *could* change destiny. A power like time-blinking didn't fall into your lap for no reason. I reached for the chair, meaning to heave it across the room to give my mother a sign. Within the span of three seconds, I saw all that could be gained by saving her: Syd doesn't go off the rails, Dad doesn't run away, Kendall doesn't have to be her sister's keeper. Syd goes to university.

Syd doesn't meet Coop.

Deflated, I unwrapped my fingers from the chair. Morley had warned me about this. The acute desire to restore order, to right wrongs. Choosing between saving your mother's life and meeting your soulmate might seem like a no-brainer for most people, but this was no ordinary life choice. This was timeblink reality, which bears no resemblance to normal reality, and Morley had been adamant that we couldn't do one damned thing to change it.

My mother resumed her message undeterred while I begrudgingly made my way to a spot behind her left shoulder. I'd come too far to run away now.

Isla has been gone for almost a year, and the thought of going through life without her has broken me. Any outcome is unbearable. My mind goes places it can't help going. Has someone violated my baby girl? Has she suffered? Is she dead? If she's not, the alternative might actually be worse. Is she being tortured? Does she think about us? Does she blame us for not protecting her? Where is she?

WHERE IS SHE?

I can't stand it. Please accept my decision. I love you and the girls so much. But I can't live like this anymore.

Maggie xxx

Heart attack, *bullshit!* I paced the kitchen floor with my own heart racing, and I wanted to rip it out of my chest and throw it at her. How could she do this to me? It was like watching a horror movie through the gaps of your fingers; the horrors would continue whether you saw them or not.

My mother wrote *Cyril* on the envelope, slipped the note inside, licked it shut. She pressed the letter next to her heart, and her features softened, as if she were reconsidering. Thinking about all there was to lose if she followed through with her plan.

Before Isla's disappearance, my mother had been staunchly protective of us girls, sometimes to the point of my complete embarrassment. Once, when I'd been pushed down on the soccer field by another player then run over by two girls from the opposing team, my mom had come charging onto the field, screaming at the linesman to pay attention. She'd rushed in to help me, but the only injury I'd suffered was the one to my ego. I remembered being furious with her for making a spectacle. I'd stomped off the field and run home and hadn't talked to her for two days.

After Isla disappeared, so did my mother's fighting spirit. She'd lost any semblance of the bubbly, confident woman I'd known before the tragedy. I'd have given anything to experience some of the old feisty protectiveness that had once embarrassed me. Instead, she'd sit in a recliner in her bedroom staring at the wall vacantly for hours that often stretched into days, and it had been up to my father and Kendall to take charge of things. At the time, I'd been wallowing in my own sorrow and was of no help at all.

Still, I think if my mother had simply *looked* at me occasionally rather than avoided me after Isla's disappearance, I'd have weathered that period of my life better myself.

But all *that*? The love and the loss and the fairy-tale picture in my mind of who my mother had been and what she had represented? That was gone. Oh my God, and my father! He'd known! How could he have lied to me and Kendall like that? He'd told me in no uncertain terms that my mother's death had been due to heart failure. Not this. She'd actually *chosen* to relinquish her duties as my mother. As my advocate. As my friend. Permanently.

As she set off up the stairs, I let out a scream from the depths of my soul that scared even me. Her steps were slow and deliberate. When she reached the top, she turned around, tears streaming down her face, and I swore she looked straight into my eyes as she yelled, "I'm sorry! Please forgive me!"

I knew she couldn't see me, but that brief connection went right through me. I collapsed on the last stair. My throat closed around what felt like a boulder-sized rock lodged halfway down my esophagus, and no air could enter my lungs. I was aware of my mouth opening and closing. There was no sound. Only the lonely silence of grief and guilt and fear swirling around me, surging, building.

I raced up the stairs before I was even aware of it. *"HOW COULD YOU?"* I screamed.

Oh, I was definitely going to see this through now. The fairy tale I'd believed for nineteen years would end today.

When I arrived at her bedroom door, she was tucking the letter into my father's night table drawer. She touched his pillow tenderly. Oh, Dad. It was hard to hate him right now. He should've stayed home. But then what? Would she have put it off for a day? A week? Ten years? Isla had never been found. The inner torment might've destroyed what little was left of my mother's spirit. Maybe Dad would've still been bringing meals to the recliner where she sat staring off into space. Or she'd be in a psychiatric hospital now.

But at least she'd be alive. At least she wouldn't have deserted me.

She came around to her side of the bed and sat down gingerly. Kicked off her fuzzy pink slippers. Tears dripped off her chin, making dark yellow spots on that pretty dress. She was quiet, not distraught.

I left my post in the doorway to sit next to her, as much as it stung to be that close. She pulled her night table drawer open and produced two bottles of pills.

"Why, Mom? You had Dad to help you through it, and Kendall. And me! Well, maybe not me," I said, wiping tears from my cheek, "I know it must've been hard to look at me. To be constantly reminded. I saw the blame all over your face. Every day. What do you think that does to a twelve-year-old girl? Huh? What do you think that does to someone who felt responsible for her sister's disappearance? Hey? You *coward! What do you think it does?!"*

She popped the lid off one of the bottles and spilled the

contents into her hand. A tear dripped onto the mound of little green discs, and she appeared to take this as a sign. She poured them all into her mouth and swallowed them down with water. Angrily, it seemed, she threw the empty bottle across the room where it bounced on the hardwood floor and rolled out into the hall. She downed the second handful of pills quickly, as if she didn't want to change her mind, and again launched the empty bottle into the hallway where it broke in half. She screamed from the depths of her soul, and in that moment, I ceased to recognize her. She was so angry. Maybe at the world. Or herself. Or me.

"Return!"

On arriving back in Kendall's library, I heard a shrill squealing noise. Someone screaming. *Damn it! Kendall!* She wasn't supposed to be here.

Seeing the room was empty, however, a harsher reality hit: the screams were coming from me. I clapped both hands over my mouth, forcing myself to calm down, realizing that Kendall had respected my wishes after all.

How was I going to tell her about this—that our mother hadn't died from natural causes, but chose instead to end her own life? For me, my mother's memory was now forever tainted. I couldn't *unsee* her suicide. But I could spare Kendall that pain. After all, she'd had twenty years with my mother, and she'd always talked about how they'd become more like friends than a mother and daughter in the years before Isla had disappeared.

It was settled, then. I would not tell Kendall that our mother had chosen death over us. I swallowed the lump in my throat and got up to let Kendall into the room. But she wasn't on the other side of the door.

"Kenny?" I said, sticking my head out, looking both ways down the hall. No sign of her. That's when I heard a weak moan from behind the desk, near the bookshelves.

I found Kendall lying on the floor on her back, disoriented, blinking rapidly. She must've fainted when she'd come in and discovered me missing.

"What happened?" I said, diving down next to her.

"You…you," she couldn't get the words out.

"Disappeared?"

"Yeah, that," she said, wincing as I helped her sit up.

"What hurts? Your head?"

"No. It's my hand. My wrist," she said lifting her right hand to assess the damage, leaning against me.

"Let me see," I said.

I glanced at my own right hand. I'd know a broken wrist if I saw one. Kendall's wrist was swollen but there was no obvious displacement of bone, yet when I touched it, she jumped.

"I'm taking you to emergency."

"No way," she said, cradling her hand. "You…aggh, fuckitty fuck, that hurts. You gonna tell me how you did that?"

"Did what?" I said.

"Ha, ha."

"Have you not been listening to me at all?"

After helping her to the sofa, I went to the kitchen to fetch a bag of frozen peas to wrap around her wrist.

"That was a great trick, sis," she said as I sat down next to her. "Now tell me how you did it. Are you and Brett in cahoots? Did he install a secret room behind the bookshelf without my knowledge?"

"I can't tell you—"

"The hell you can't."

"—I can't tell you how I did it but can say that I legitimately left this room for roughly four and a half minutes."

"So why'd you tell me to wait outside?"

"I told you—a number of times already—I'm not supposed to reveal *how* I did it. It would be against Morley's wishes."

"You do realize Morley's dead?" she said indelicately.

I looked her straight in the eye, suddenly wanting to hurt her. "No shit. I watched it happen. And now I've seen Mom die, too."

She stared at me blankly.

"Why did you pick that date?" I asked.

She threw her focus to the floor and adjusted the peas on her wrist. Without looking at me she said, "How much do you know about that day?"

Her tension was evident in the way she was holding herself, not from the pain in her wrist, but from something deeper. And it was at that moment I understood.

"You *knew*."

Her eyes shot up to meet mine. "Knew what?"

"Kenny. I *saw* what happened."

"I don't know what you're talking about."

I jumped off the sofa and planted my feet right in front of her. "I was there when she did it! Don't lie to me!"

Kendall looked toward the door, maybe thinking of making a run for it.

"Did you see the letter, too?" I asked.

"No."

"Don't lie."

She brought her focus around to me again. "I'm not lying. Dad said there was a letter but he only gave me a brief idea about what it said."

"Holy, shit, you knew all along. You knew she killed herself, and you chose not to tell me."

"It wasn't my place."

"It wasn't your place? Kendall! I've been merrily skipping through all these years idolizing our mother! Thinking she was this flawless angel whose time was cut short because of a defective heart! She chose death, Kenny! Over us!"

"Calm down."

"*Calm down?* You stood by and watched me worship that bitch!"

"Syd! You don't mean that. You're just upset."

"Of course I'm upset! She was my hero!"

"That doesn't have to change. She was my hero too, you know. And I still remember her with love."

I paced in front of her, seething.

"She was hurting beyond anything you or I could fathom. We have no idea what it's like to lose a child. God, I can't even imagine it."

"But we know what it's like to lose a mother to suicide. What could be worse than that?" I said. "With Isla, we had no control over what happened. At least that's what the shrinks have been peddling all these years. Our mother made a choice."

Kendall stared at me. Bit her bottom lip.

"And you conveniently kept it from me."

"I'm sorry, okay? I'm sorry I didn't tell you that Mom couldn't handle the pain of losing her child."

"I lost my identical twin! And *I'm* still here!"

"You seem to have forgotten the times in your teens when you—" Kendall said, cutting herself off. "Look, people deal with grief in their own ways. Everyone's different, and Mom was no exception."

"I get it. Okay? I get it. It's just hard to understand why you kept it from me."

"Dad didn't tell you either," she said.

I blew air through my lips. "So, you're both a couple of lying dirtbags."

"That's not fair."

"Fuck," I said, stalking over to the window. Angry waves crashed on the beach below, their force traveling through the rocky bluff all the way up to me.

I turned around. "Do you believe me now? About time-blinking?"

"I—I..."

"Even after all this?" I said, spreading my arms around the

room.

"I want to, sweetie. In the worst way," she said, tears pooling in her eyes.

"So how do I know about Mom? About the letter?"

"Maybe you found it. At the house somewhere."

I shook my head, disgusted.

"Maybe you came home early that day and saw her writing it. I don't know."

"Seriously? Do you really think I'm lying? Or, worse, that I'm delusional? Completely fucking crazy?"

"I want to believe you."

"The pills were teal green. Oblong. Embossed with the number 200. She took two full bottles of them."

Kendall's eyebrows shot up. She'd been the one to find our mother that day, after her drivers' test. The first person on the scene.

I continued. "She threw the empty pill bottles into the hallway. One of them broke in half."

She stared at me for a good fifteen seconds, trying to process how I would know that detail when I'd come home hours after my mother's body had been taken away and the house restored to its original order.

Kendall stood up, cradling her sore wrist against her stomach. "So you're a time traveler, are you?" she said.

This time my tears did flow. In a torrent. Kendall had never seen me cry, and I think it scared her a little. She threw her good arm around my shoulder and drew me close.

My tears flowed even harder. "All I ever wanted was for you to accept me."

"I do, sweetie," she said, rubbing my back. "I do. And I promise not to doubt you again."

I smiled. With my face and with my whole heart.

Her face suddenly brightened. "Does this mean we can find out what happened to Isla?"

I sniffed and wiped a tear from my cheek. "I've thought about it."

"And?"

"I can't."

"What? Why not?" Kendall said, lowering herself to the sofa. I helped her reposition the bag of peas on her wrist as I sat down next to her.

"First of all, Morley says it's impossible to change anything that's already happened."

"I didn't suggest we should. But we can find out what happened to her, right?"

I took a big breath. "Really? You think I should go back and watch Isla being raped, tortured and killed? If you think my mental health is shaky now, can you imagine how it would be after that?"

"Why are you assuming she's dead all of a sudden? You've always insisted she was still alive."

"I just can't take the chance, Kenny."

"Send me, then!"

Oh, she was persistent. "Look, I wish you could, but it's not possible."

Maybe it was possible, I didn't know. But I wasn't willing to jeopardize my ability to timeblink quite so quickly.

"Have you gone back? To see Isla, you know, before she was taken?"

"No. I've only ever visited Morley. And now the day Mom died. I'll get there eventually…back to see Isla. But it's too soon. The idea has to sit in my heart a little while first."

"Okay, fine, I'm not going to argue with you. But if you change your mind about sending me, I'm in. That son of a bitch won't even know what hit him."

Which was precisely the reason I could never allow her to go.

She rubbed my shoulder with her good hand, smiling

tenderly. "In the meantime, let's figure out this Morley dilemma, shall we?"

Chapter Eleven

The next day, I laced up my running shoes, plugged in my earbuds, and bounced down the front steps toward the university chip trail. As my feet found their rhythm on the sidewalk, as my favorite Pixies album blasted in my ears, my brain whirled in several directions, invariably circling back to the effects of yesterday's emotional timeblink. Learning of my mother's suicide had had the potential to plunge me into a bottomless hole of self-pity, but Kendall had cleverly steered me toward the more pressing issue of the day: how I was going to handle the whole sleeping-with-Morley fiasco.

She'd been right, though. My last timeblink to his cabin had been a huge mistake, one I'd regretted instantly and wanted to erase from memory. But what Kendall didn't know was that the memory of the encounter—Morley's embrace, his gentle touches, the slow, steady mingling of body and heart leading to frenzied sex—had not waned in the meantime. In fact, it had become more vivid, more urgent. Intoxicating. To the point where it was all I could think about.

This morning when Coop had gotten home from work and crawled into bed, he'd kissed me behind the ear and whispered that he loved me. He'd traced his hand down my back and circled around to the front, drawing his fingers over my stomach in a meandering line up to my breasts where he'd caressed them for a moment. When I didn't respond, he drew his hand away and flipped over. I'd heard him sigh.

A week ago, I wouldn't have pretended to be asleep. I'd have given in to his touch, his soft breath in my ear. I may've even told him my heart was warming to the idea of a baby.

How could I even think about that now, given what I'd done?

As I started across the intersection at Smithson Road and University Avenue, a horn blasted. Tires screeched. Cold metal struck my left leg, sending me tumbling onto a car hood. I rolled off, landing on my feet, winded, looking around, hoping nobody had seen what'd happened.

I'd been so involved in my thoughts, so deep into my music that I hadn't even heard the car coming, which I noticed was a silver Civic not much newer than mine, and as I was getting my bearings, the driver sped past me with his fist out the window yelling, "What the fuck, bitch?!"

I shut my music off and pulled my earbuds out. Wiggled my arms and legs, surprised to find they didn't hurt. Fortunately, the bump from the car had been low impact, and my roll onto the hood had been more to get out of the way than the result of a damaging blow. A cyclist skidded to a stop beside me.

"Are you okay?" the fresh, freckle-faced woman said, her eyes wide.

"Yeah, I think so."

"What a creep," she said, whipping her phone out, snapping a picture of the car as it sped off. "I'll send you this pic. What's your number?"

"That's okay, I—"

"Oh, Sydney! I didn't recognize you at first! Hang on," she said, scrolling through her contact list on her phone while I tried to place her face. I heard the email swoosh off.

"It's me, Candace," she said, pulling off her bike helmet when she saw my confusion. "Mike's wife. Mike Winton, from the fire hall?"

"Oh! Yeah, yeah, it must've been the helmet," I said. Candace was the sprightly little redhead that was forever trying to get me and Coop out to the bowling nights and the family picnics and God only knows what other lame activities the fire hall's social committee lined up. We'd attended a couple of the barbeques, mostly to appease Candace, but work shindigs aren't our style. Both Coop and I detest small talk, and these gatherings notoriously crawled with seasoned small talkers.

Right on cue she said, "Did you get my email about the Halloween potluck? I don't remember getting your RSVP yet."

I had seen it, but I'd sent it right to the trash unread. Halloween parties ranked number one on our most-despised social gathering list.

"I think I do remember seeing it. I'll take another look. We've been pretty busy with my sister's family lately," I lied, unable to think of a good excuse.

"Oh, I hope you can come. It's going to be *amaaay*-zing," she said. "There'll be prizes for best costumes...three categories this year! Oh, and I'm making my famous chicken witch's fingers."

I had to get away from this imp. She was making me more anxious by the second. "When is it?"

"The Friday after Halloween. I know, a bit weird having it after the fact, but that's the only date we could get Henderson Center."

"Oh, darn," I said sounding less sincere than I'd hoped. "I work Fridays. And I'm not sure what Coop's schedule is yet." I wasn't lying. That Friday might very well be one of the few I'd been scheduled for. As for Coop's calendar, he was likely working that night too, so at least that gave us a partial excuse not to go.

"Surely you can take one night off? You know how these things work at the fire hall…there are always a few party poopers who don't *do* these functions. Maybe Cooper could switch with one of them."

"I'll see what I can do."

She smiled, then her face lit up as if remembering something. "Hey, was Cooper working when that…you know…*thing* went down just as the guys were starting their shift?"

"What thing?"

"He didn't tell you? About…you know…that certain celebrity?"

I wished she'd stop saying "*you know*." I didn't know. And I was getting impatient.

"It was…now let me see, a couple of Thursdays ago. October ninth or tenth…whatever the Thursday was. Come on, certainly he told you about….you-know-who," she said, winking at me.

I shook my head. October tenth was a Thursday, I knew that much, because it was my birthday. Coop *did* work that night, much to his regret, but Kendall had more than made up for it by treating me to a pedicure then dinner at Giordano's Bistro.

"Oh, come on. Husbands don't keep those kinds of things secret!"

"Honestly, I don't know. Unless the celebrity turned out to be the woman they rescued from the clothing donation bin."

She shook her head rigorously. "Goodness, no. You've *got* to ask him about it. I know, I know, the confidentiality thing, but Mike always tells me the juicy stuff. I would *never* tell anyone else, of course. Well, my mom maybe. And my best friend. And, Doug, my hairdresser. But that's it."

"Coop takes the confidentiality oath to the extreme," I said, making an excuse. But he trusts me inherently, and it would have been out of character for him not to share something big. Like the time he had to cut our mayor out of handcuffs after his so-called *girlfriend* had locked him to the bed and lost the key.

"Ask him for sure. Huge Hollywood celebrity. I'm actually surprised it's been kept from the paparazzi, but maybe that's why she's in town—gave them the slip and came here for some anonymity."

"Maybe." I said.

"Anyway, think about the party. I should get pedalling. Yoga class," she said, hitching her thumb toward the purple mat sticking out of her backpack.

"I will."

"Oh, and if you need a witness statement, let me know. I'd be happy to stick it to that jerk."

"Thanks. Enjoy your yoga class," I said, plugging my music back in and sprinting off toward the chip trail. I could feel her eyes on my back, probably waiting for proof that all my bones were still intact, and by God, I would give it to her even if my ankle had been fractured in a dozen places. Fortunately, the only injury I'd sustained was the giant bruise to my dignity.

When my feet finally hit the chip trail a minute later, I was already out of breath, but I was far away from Candace and that was what mattered. I wasn't fond of people like her; super friendly and approachable but absolutely oblivious to social cues. They goaded and pushed and bullied until you gave into their wishes, which often had nothing to do with your own. People like that were generally completely blind to the fact that not everyone needed to surround themselves with a hundred superficial friendships rather than two or three solid ones.

Tad, my illustrious cohort at The Merryport, was one of those people. He'd always found my relationship with Kendall a bit of a cop out and had even called it unhealthy. He'd never understood why I would choose to spend time exclusively with my sister when the world was brimming with fun and interesting people. To prove this fact, he'd coaxed me out to a smattering of parties over the years, all of which had exhausted and overwhelmed me, and after the last one about two years ago, I'd asked him to stop inviting me along. He'd obliged, begrudgingly, though still occasionally got his jabs in: *"Ooh, Syd! What exciting hijinks did you and your saucy sissy get up to on your days off? Knitting circle? Did you bake bread together?"* he would say. I'd given up trying to explain it to him. The Tads and Candaces of the world would always criticize relationships they didn't understand.

Kendall's friendship was crucial to me now more than ever with the complications of timeblinking and Morley thrown into the mix. She, the super devoted wife and mother had decided to look the other way when I told her I'd slept with Morley, actually encouraging me to embrace the encounter and learn from it, then move on. It had surprised me a little, to the point where I'd wondered if she'd ever been in the same position. I'd been prepared for a full-out verbal assault—her typical practice whenever, in her eyes, I was about to ruin my life. She'd had a point, though. I'd taken the wrong fork in the road, and now it was a simple matter of backing up and setting myself on the right one. Toward Coop. Toward my living, breathing, faithful partner who yearned to create a tiny new version of us. As much as it hurt to imagine what that meant for my friendship with Morley, there could be no more timeblinking to see him.

A fresh layer of cedar chips had recently been spread on the trail and a burst of energy shot through my body, giving me a lightness I hadn't felt in years. Coop was going to lose his mind when I told him I was open to having a baby and that it wasn't a knee-jerk reaction to the current stresses in my life but an idea that'd been brewing under my skin for a while.

I was ready.

An hour later I lay in a warm bath with my hair piled in a knot on top of my head, thinking about the logistics of bringing a new life into the world, and my body went rigid with panic. The idea of waiting for my birth control to run its course, of sorting out the timing of a maternity leave, of figuring out how to get childcare after I went back to work and of traveling to Europe with a baby sounded like so much work. Was I *really* ready for it?

And what if, months or years from now Coop somehow found out I'd been unfaithful? What then? What would become of us? Would he be able to forgive me? I didn't plan on telling him. Ever. But what if the weight of my guilt manifested during the postpartum stage and I blurted out that I'd slept with Morley? *It had only been once, babe,* I would explain. Only once. And it had been after Morley's death, so in effect, did it even count?

Would that make a difference in Coop's eyes? In mine?

I toweled off after my bath and pulled on my jeans, the pink cashmere sweater Coop had given me last Christmas and my suede slippers. As I sat on the edge of the tub listening to the water gurgle down the drain, I fingered the talisman, turning it over and over, imploring it to set me free from the guilt.

And then I said, "Chapman Falls, parking lot, 6 a.m., May 13, 2019."

As the sun began its gentle rise in the eastern sky, I made a graceless trek up to Morley's cabin in my slippers. When I reached the driveway, I was relieved to find his car parked in its normal spot out front. Behind it, the house exuded a lonely, deserted air. None of the grand exterior lights were on apart from two recessed pot lights over the front stoop, making the door glow like a magic portal. As I loitered at the bottom of the steps in the dewy spring morning, I realized it was the first time I'd dropped in completely unexpected, and I hoped I hadn't made a mistake. I hoped Sparkles wasn't lurking about, and after a quick glance around the property, I saw no sign of him, only a squirrel bouncing across the damp lawn.

Before I had the chance to change my mind and go home, Morley's front door opened and he stepped out onto the stoop. He didn't notice me at first while he turned and fiddled with the lock, but when he spun around, he stopped dead in his tracks.

"Syd," he said as a smile brightened his face. "This is a nice surprise. And so early in the day."

"I figured an early morning blink was just as safe as a night blink."

"Is everything okay?"

I looked down at my slippered feet and sighed. "Definitely not."

He turned back around to unlock his front door. "I was worried about this. Come in."

"Weren't you going somewhere?"

"Just to the gas station for milk. It can wait," he said, guiding me into the house.

In the living room, I kicked off my slippers and curled myself into a ball on the sofa next to Morley, saying nothing for a few tense minutes. When I finally spoke, my voice cracked. "I messed up. Big time."

"If you mean what happened between us, you were just following your heart."

"No. I was following a fantasy. And now I can't take it back."

"You'll go on. Your life will unfold the way it's supposed to, regardless of what happened yesterday."

It *had* just been yesterday in his world. In mine it had been two days—but it had felt like an absolute eternity of rationalizing, worrying, and guilt-tripping. Hating myself and everything I stood for. Yearning for Morley's touch like a heroin addict looking for her next hit.

"How? Every time I look at Coop now, I think of what happened between us."

"You'll find your way, love. Please. Trust that it will sort itself out."

"Easy for you to say. You didn't sleep with a dead man." I slapped a hand over my mouth the moment the words escaped. "Oh God. I'm so sorry."

"Hah. Don't worry about it. My flippancy must be rubbing off on you. Look, we need to focus on what's happening *here*," he said, placing his hand over my heart. Cassandra had said much the same thing at our last session.

I pushed his hand away without looking at him. "An hour ago I vowed it was over. That I would never come here again. And here I am. Apparently so eager to get here I didn't even bother with shoes."

He chuckled. "So why did you come?"

I couldn't answer him. Not out loud. Not when I wanted to say: *Because I'm in love with you. Because I can't stand the thought of going through life without you. Because I need you. In bed. Right fucking now.*

Heat rose in my cheeks. I bolted off the sofa and went to the darkened fireplace where I stood chewing my thumbnail. "I don't know."

He smiled and leaned back, spreading his arms across the back of the sofa. I looked away. Damn. Once you've had a drink from that bottle, just try cutting yourself off.

"I'm telling you, Syd, you have nothing to worry about."

"Am I going to have a baby someday?"

He cocked his head. "You're asking *me*?"

"You seem to know everything about my life and how it's

going to pan out. It's creepy," I laughed. "But in a good way, I guess."

"Come. Sit," he said, patting the sofa. I skulked over and flopped down next to him, just far enough away that we wouldn't accidentally touch.

"Do you think it's possible to love two people equally but for different reasons?" I said.

"What, like how you love Coop and your sister?"

"Stop fishing. You know what I'm talking about."

He reached over, took my defective hand in both of his, and kissed my knuckles. When he looked up to meet my gaze, I felt a crackle of energy between us. I'd just professed my love for him, and it scared the shit out of me.

"I am one hundred percent in love with you too, Sydney Brixton."

He leaned over and kissed my forehead. My nose. When he got to my lips it was over. The waiting and the yearning and the self-doubt and self-loathing. Every cell in my body needed him and we ended up exactly where we'd been two days ago, my time.

If my life continued along this trajectory, his fantasy would be fulfilled; he would be making love to me every day for the rest of his life.

I eventually returned to the dull, cramped bathroom of the house Coop and I shared while the last of the water from my pre-blink bath trickled down the drain. My heart was torn in two. On one side was all my love for Coop; a tender kind of love that, if I had my way, would last until 'death do us part'. On the other side was Morley where an urgent, passionate love resided; a love that couldn't last forever by virtue of what we understood about timeblinking. Didn't it stand to reason that I help him make the most of his remaining days, especially since Collette was gone and he was alone?

Who was I kidding? This arrangement was just as much for me as it was for him, and it had absolutely nothing to do with simply offering him comfort.

I stormed down the two flights of stairs to the basement, depositing my wet towel and my running clothes from earlier into the washing machine. I started it up and leaned against it, my mind whirring in time with the machine.

My eyes landed on the door of "The Cave," the small cold-room my father had constructed around a naturally hollowed out rock roughly the size of a minivan. Exposed bedrock was common in basements in this part of the city where homebuilders had once worked around the terrain instead of excavating it, during a time when basements had been considered places to store canned goods, extra furniture and off-season clothing rather than proper living spaces. Fully one-third of our main floor upstairs had been built on top of the "roof" of The Cave, serving effectively as an insulator from both heat and noise. As kids we would spend hours down here camping out and holding tea parties in it, tripping on the rough floor, ending up with bruises and skinned knees. It used to drive my mother nuts, but it hadn't stopped us from coming back for more, even when she'd tried to forbid us from using the room as a play space.

My phone buzzed in my pocket. An email.

I was surprised to see Candace's name in the inbox, considering she'd already sent me the picture of the car that hit me.

Hey Syd,

Hope you're still okay with no ill effects from that jerk running you down.

Just wondering about the Halloween Potluck. Mike told me Coop isn't scheduled to work that Friday, so I'm hoping you can convince your boss you need a day off!

Anyway, crossing my fingers.

Talk to you soon.

Candace

PS: Have you asked Coop about Miss Movie Star's embarrassing situation yet?

I slid the phone into my pocket and didn't think about it again until later that night when Coop joined me on the sofa where I was watching a documentary on emperor penguins.

"So what was the big deal about October tenth?" I said.

He looked at me puzzlingly then chuckled. "Is this a trick question? It was your birthday."

"Besides that. I heard there was a bit of a kerfuffle. Right when you started your shift."

"'Kerfuffle'?" he echoed, smiling at my word choice.

"Something big apparently."

"Oh, *that*," he said. "It was nothing. Who's making something out of it?"

"Candace. She said some big movie star got herself into trouble, and she couldn't believe you hadn't told me."

Coop rolled his eyes. "*Jayzuss*. Some people. It must be tiring worrying about petty shit all the time."

"I know. It's like she was happy to hear a celebrity was having real-life problems. I myself couldn't care less."

"Right? That's why I didn't tell you. I knew you wouldn't have given a crap."

Now that we were talking about it, I figured he would go ahead and tell me, but he kept his focus on the TV. "So, what happened anyway?" I laughed, feigning indifference.

"*Jayzuss!*" he said again. "What's your deal?"

I recoiled, startled.

He sighed. "Sorry, but look, now you're one of '*those people*.'"

"Hey, don't worry about it if you're going to get all pissy."

"I'm not *pissy*. Like I said, it's just not important."

He was right, it wasn't important, and I didn't want to

start a fight over nothing. I tried a lighter subject. "Feel like going to the Halloween potluck?"

"Which potluck?" he said, as if we'd been invited to several.

"The one the hall is arranging. At Henderson Center. It's coming up fast, next Friday."

He cocked his head at me. "Really? Since when did you start going to Halloween parties?"

"Since Candace practically begged me to come. And Cassandra *did* mention a little social activity couldn't hurt my recovery. Besides, we're due for an appearance."

He blew an agitated breath through his lips.

I carried on, undaunted. "There's not much time to figure out costumes. What could we go as?"

"A firefighter and a bartender?" he said, humoring me.

I put my arms around him and drew him close, suddenly desperate to break the tension in the room. God, he smelled good, fresh out of the shower with a splash of his signature cologne. Fuck Candace. Coop wasn't keeping secrets, he knew me well enough to know what mattered to me, and I put his defensive, snippy mood down to sheer exhaustion. He'd been working so hard lately. "I'll come up with something," I said.

"Sure, babe. Were you into this show?" he said picking up the remote.

"Not really. I've seen it before anyway."

He flipped to the Red Wings-Senators game.

"I'm actually kind of excited about the party," I admitted. "Could be fun pretending to be someone else. Maybe we could go as a seventies couple. Ooh, how about Sid and Nancy? But in a twist, I go as Sid and you be Nancy. Wouldn't that rock Candace's little witch fingers?"

He smiled weakly then winced when Borowiecki tied the game 2-2.

"You should've seen her face when she told me about the

food she's bringing to the potluck. So excited. Like she'd just won the frickin' lottery."

Coop frowned. "Wait, you actually *saw* her?"

"Oh my God, I didn't tell you! I was hit by a car on my run today."

"*What?*" he said, turning his attention wholly on me.

"It was nothing serious. I was crossing the street at the university, totally oblivious to everything around me."

"And?" he said.

"I crossed the road without even thinking, and boom, I was on the hood of a silver Civic just like mine. But I jumped onto it more or less to get out of the way."

"Shit, babe. I can't believe you didn't tell me."

"It wasn't a big deal. Candace witnessed the whole thing, but she'll probably make it sound worse than it was if we go to that party."

"You were running with her?" he said, surprised.

"No, no. She happened to be riding by on her bike. We got to talking and she reminded me about the Halloween thing."

"Did you exchange phone numbers with the driver?"

"He didn't stop. Too busy yelling at me for getting in his way, and I don't blame him. I would've been pissed too. Anyway, Candace sent me a picture of his license plate. But I'm totally fine."

"You should report it as a hit and run," he said.

"Coop, I'm *fine*."

He wrapped his bulky arms around my shoulders, holding me close, and all the earlier tension floated away. Where was my mind, cheating on this man? I had to make it up to him.

"Goddamn coward. He shouldn't get away with it."

"You're not listening to me," I said into his neck, but he persisted.

"He might hit someone else. *Worse* next time."

"I'm ready," I said.

"Good. Make sure you tell them there was a witness."

"Coop. I'm ready…for a baby." I said, pulling away from him and taking his hands into mine.

"What?" he said, eyes widening.

I nodded. "I've had an epiphany, I guess."

He pulled me in for a hug so tight it almost took my breath away. His body jerked as he held me, and I realized he was crying. I should have been happy too, but now that my epiphany was out there, put into actual words, I was terrified. I would have to find peace with my decision.

Soon, not today and not tomorrow, but soon, I would take one final trip to Morley's cabin and tell him the news. Tell him I had a good man by my side, a *living* man who I intended to grow old with.

Then I would look Morley in the eye and say goodbye.

Chapter Twelve

There are perks to having a partner with no living relatives. No trying to figure out where to spend Thanksgiving and Christmas. No birthdays to remember. No family arguments. No aging relatives to take care of. No obligations whatsoever. But there *is* one huge disadvantage: my lone wolf has no one to share wonderful news with, so I inevitably end up being his sounding board.

Most of the time I didn't mind, but Coop had been nattering on for hours about all the plans he'd obviously been making in the background in anticipation of the day I finally told him I wanted a baby, and by five-fifteen I was ready to slap him. How could he have not noticed the weariness in my eyes? My clenched jaw? My hand rubbing at the back of my neck? And I thought Candace was bad at social cues.

"Shit, princess, I gotta go," he said after rattling off a list of home improvements he suddenly felt compelled to complete.

"*Princess?*"

He shook his head almost apologetically. "Well, naturally! I can't call you *Queen*. That sounds too old."

He leaned down to kiss me on the nose then dashed up the stairs to get ready for his shift.

I suppose I should've been grateful for his joy but instead I was excited for his departure. That I wouldn't have to hear another word about what shade of green we were going to paint Kendall's old room. The *nursery*. Good Lord. What had I done? I would find my way around this new idea eventually; I just needed a bit more time.

Coop left the house half an hour later with a light heart and a promise not to keep prattling on about babies, but why would he make a promise he could never keep? This was his dream come true. He needed to talk about it, excessively, and I would do everything in my power not to shut him out.

After he left, I tried watching TV. Reading a book. Napping. Perusing social media—purposely scrolling past anything to do with other people's children. But I was too agitated to sit and concentrate on anything. My mind kept circling back to Candace and her email. I pulled it up again and re-read it. Her final sentence stood out just as annoyingly as it had the first time I'd read it.

PS: Have you asked Coop about Miss Movie Star's embarrassing situation yet?

Maybe I could fish the information out of Candace. It wasn't that I really cared about the identity of this star or the terrible thing that'd happened to her, it was more a question of why Coop was withholding it from me. As my fingers hovered over the keys, I had a thought: Forget Candace. I didn't need her when I could timeblink to the Thursday night in question myself and find out who this mystery celebrity was. Ooh, this power had its merits.

Ten minutes later—or two weeks earlier…however you want to look at it—I was standing with my back against our garage waiting for Coop's Firewing to emerge. It was mildly unnerving, spying on him like this, but it was the easiest way of finding out who this movie star had been without asking him to break his confidentiality oath. Yes, it was devious, but no one would be the wiser.

I didn't have to wait long. The garage door rolled up and Coop pulled out. The drivers' side window was down and I heard John Mayer blasting from the speakers. Coop was singing along to *Say*, and I had to laugh. God, he loved his John Mayer, and it always made my heart smile, seeing my big, burly fireman cranking out those corny ballads from his manly muscle car.

By good fortune, my own car was free for use. It'd been my birthday, and Kendall had already picked me up for a surprise pedicure followed by a carb-packed dinner at Giordano's Bistro. I ran around the front of the house and jumped into my car, throwing a glance toward The Nose's house to see if she was keeping tabs on me, but by some small miracle, she wasn't in the window.

When I reached the end of our street, another car came along, and I let it slip into place between Coop's car and mine. At the main road, Coop turned right instead of left to go to the station. The other car followed. Odd. Maybe he'd decided to stop for something along the way. A coffee or some gas. But he kept going, eventually pulling into Fulcart Foods. While he parked in the short-term spot out front, I nestled my car between two SUVs.

A few minutes later, Coop emerged from the store carrying two canvas shopping bags full of groceries. There was a bouquet of yellow flowers sticking out of one, and I smiled. He'd bought me flowers! But in the next moment I realized that he'd never given me the flowers—not on this day or any day since. He popped the bags into the trunk, climbed into the car and headed back out onto the main road, still going east, in the opposite direction of the fire hall. This was getting weird. I started my car and followed, this time with two cars between us, gripping the steering wheel so tightly my fingers started to cramp.

After a couple of turns down major streets, Coop pulled onto North Glenora Road, which led out of the city into more rural territory. The two cars separating us kept going straight when Coop turned off, so I had to keep a reasonable distance to avoid being spotted, which wasn't too hard with the dark of night on my side. After passing two or three acreages, a beat-up green farm truck pulled out of a driveway in front of me, so now it was Coop's muscle car, the truck, and my Civic bumping down the neglected rural road.

"Where are you going, Coop?" I asked, my heart thumping faster in my chest. No wonder he hadn't told me about the mystery celebrity's problems; he hadn't even been working.

We traveled along the dark road for about fifteen minutes until Coop's car slowed and turned down a short gravel driveway leading to a dilapidated garage next to an equally dilapidated house. The truck carried on, and I maintained my speed behind it to avoid bringing attention to my car, which I was afraid Coop would recognize. As I blew past the house, the garage door rolled up and Coop's Firewing coasted inside.

"What the fuck?!" I yelled, accelerating to the point where I nearly slammed into the back of the farm truck. A small distance down the road, I pulled over and parked next to a low white fence bordering an immaculate cream and white two-storey home. Warm light glowed in the windows, and a little boy who looked a couple of years younger than Connor and Devin, was playing a piano in the living room.

By then I didn't care who could or couldn't see me. I stumbled out of the car and nearly fell, regaining my balance as I slammed the door with a tinny bang. My brain was numb and my legs were as stiff as tree trunks as I started toward the house. Coop had kissed me on the lips an hour earlier, wished me a fun birthday dinner with Kendall, and walked out the door to what I'd thought would be a ten-hour shift at the station.

Instead, he'd bought groceries *and flowers* and driven straight here. And he had his own remote to open the garage door.

I was out of breath when I got to the house, arriving in time to see Coop lugging the grocery bags up a set of crumbling concrete steps to the front door. He set the bags down, and while he fiddled with his keys, I took a good look at the house.

It was a tumbledown mishmash of mossed-over shingles, broken shutters, and layers of old paint that had bubbled and peeled like scalded skin. Plywood panels had been nailed to the basement windows, and the surrounding land was littered with junk. The front door was painted half turquoise, half chalk-yellow, as if someone had been called to dinner in the middle of the job and never returned. It had probably been a lovely family home years ago, like the others scattered along this road, but now it looked like something out of a horror movie. I shifted my focus to the bags sitting at Coop's feet, and I noted the flowers were roses. Yellow roses, which practically glowed against the backdrop of the lifeless house. At least they weren't red.

Really Syd? You're commending him on his choice of flower color?

As the door swung open to a darkened room I raced toward the house and flew up the stairs, reaching the top just in time for Coop to slam the door in my face. I heard two deadbolts click into place. Great. I leaned over both of the precariously attached iron railings on either side of the front steps to get a look inside, but the windows were covered with grungy drapes that looked like they hadn't been cleaned since the house was built in the '40s.

Every neuron in my brain was firing. What was he up to? I flew back down the steps and picked my way through scattered trash to the rear of the property where I thought I might be able to get a peek inside, maybe through a back door or window. Wishful thinking. The only access to the house was through a second-floor door, but the porch leading to it no longer existed; only the posts remained, piercing the sky like giant sabres.

"What the fuck, Coop?" I said, sidestepping the garbage on my way back to the road.

In retrospect, not being able to confront him right away had been a blessing; a showdown of that scale needed a boatload of preparation first.

Kendall opened her door to me half an hour later, present time. I was quivering with rage. I'd driven past the fire hall on the way over and spotted Coop's car in the parking lot, and it had taken every ounce of willpower not to charge in there and confront him. The lying bastard was probably bragging to his buddies that I'd finally agreed to have a baby. I almost vomited at the thought.

"What's wrong? Come on, sit down," Kendall said as she led me into the living room where a cozy fire crackled and a nearly empty glass of red wine sat on the coffee table. Kendall flopped down on the sofa while I veered into the kitchen and grabbed a glass from the rack, filling it with the remaining wine from the bottle.

"Syd!"

Kendall jumped to her feet when I brought the rim of the glass to my lips. I pulled it away and looked at it. Swirled the liquid around a couple of times.

"Fuck," I said, slamming the glass down on the counter. I was surprised it didn't break.

"Oh my God, are you okay?" she said, fixing her hair into a bun on top of her head.

"No. I'm not."

"What? *What happened?*" she said. "Is this about Morley?"

"Coop's cheating on me."

"What?" she said again. "No way. Come here. Sit."

I stalked into the living room and parked myself beside her on the sofa. "While he was supposed to be working on *my fucking birthday*, he took flowers and groceries to a house out in North Glenora."

"And you're just telling me *now*? That was two weeks ago!"

I shook my head. "No, no. I only found out tonight—during a timeblink. Coop's at work tonight. At least his car is."

"Good grief, this confusing. You went back in time and saw him with another woman?"

"No, I didn't see anyone else. The house was dark. Boarded up like Fort Knox. Couldn't get a decent look anywhere. So I left. I barely remember the drive, but I had to get the car home before zapping back to present time."

"Oh, sweetie," Kendall said looking pained. "Maybe it's not what you think."

"I know what I saw."

"Yeah, but before you jump to any wild conclusions, think about it first. Maybe he's helping someone. You know, taking groceries to an elderly shut-in before work."

"Wouldn't he have told me?"

She shrugged. "Some do-gooders like to do good anonymously."

I really hadn't considered that possibility, even though it would've been just like Coop to do such a thing. The fact that Kendall was defending him was a good sign, too.

"Damn, Kenny. I almost had a drink over this."

"It's okay. You didn't," she said, rubbing my shoulder. "You got through it without a drop."

I sighed, not quite convinced by the shut-in angle, but my heart felt a little lighter. Thank God I hadn't stormed the fire hall and confronted him like I'd wanted to. I'd need to dig a little more before doing anything so rash.

"And what if he *is* cheating on you?" Kendall said.

I glared at her.

"Oh. *I* see," she said, nodding carefully.

"What's that supposed to mean?"

"What it means is, you haven't exactly been an angel yourself. What's that old saying about pots and black kettles?"

I leapt to my feet. "Why do I tell you anything?"

"The question should be: Why do you tell me *everything*?" She picked up her glass, took the last mouthful, and set it down.

"Because I trust you. And because you don't judge me. Well, most of the time."

"Look, all I'm saying is that you can hardly complain about Coop's behavior considering what you've been up to with Morley at his lakeside cabin." She shrugged expressively. "In fact, I would venture to say that if Coop *has* been cheating on you, he may actually be doing you a favor."

I shot her a look.

"Think about it. You've been racked with guilt over sleeping with Morley. What better way to minimize it?"

I spun on my heels. "Gotta go."

"Home?"

"Yes, *home*. Not running off to Morley, if that's what you're thinking."

"Are you going to ask Coop about it?"

"When I have evidence."

Kendall got up and followed me to the door, giving me a quick hug before I stepped outside. Her face showed a network of worry lines.

"I got this," I said. "Thanks for the talk."

A few minutes later, after another cruise by the fire hall to make sure Coop's car was still there, I pulled into my driveway and sat, staring at my house. So much had changed in the two hours since I'd been home. I glanced at my rear-view mirror in time to see Vanderthorpe's light go out in her living room.

Once inside my house, I headed straight for Kendall's old bedroom, now our makeshift office. I wasn't sure what I thought I might find there. Receipts from jewellery stores and restaurants I'd never been to? Phone bills showing unfamiliar numbers? It was a futile exercise, I knew, when the best way to expose a cheating spouse was to get access to their cell phone. It would be easy to find out his password, too, with the power of timeblinking and invisibility working for me. Still, it was worth a quick look in Coop's files.

The heavy oak desk was a relic from my father's real estate company that had been left behind when he'd fled east. My important papers were stored in the left bank of drawers, Coop's in the right. I found old ticket stubs, packs of stale gum, and a dozen or so ballpoint pens in the top drawer on his side. Nothing damning. From the second drawer I pulled out a disorganized stack of utility bills. It was a wonder he was able to keep track of it all, but it probably made sense to him. Almost immediately I came across an electric bill—in his name—to an address I didn't recognize, and my heart sank when I realized it belonged to the house out in North Glenora. He was paying the old lady's bills, too? I stuffed it back in the pile and kept digging.

His cell phone statements listed the standard charges, nothing out of the ordinary. Unfortunately, they didn't include a list of numbers called or received, so that was a dead end.

By now a mountain of papers littered the desk, and with nothing but the electric bill as evidence, I began gathering up all the papers to put them away. As I picked up one of the piles, an envelope slipped out and tumbled to the floor. It was addressed to me. The top edge was ripped and ragged, as if it had been opened hastily. The return address in the top left corner didn't ring any bells—a barrister and solicitor somewhere downtown, a lawyer I'd never heard of, nor had the occasion to contact. My mind suddenly flew back to the day at Morley's aunt Marion's house when she'd hustled me out the door after accusing me of stealing her fortune, and I snatched the letter out of the envelope. The thick, watermarked paper quivered in my hands as I read it.

Dear Ms. Brixton:
I'm sure you are aware that a close acquaintance of yours, Dr. Morley Christopher Scott, has passed away. Please accept my condolences for your loss. Dr. Scott appointed me to represent his estate, and I would like to meet with you to discuss the details of said estate as you have been named as a beneficiary.
Please contact me at your earliest convenience to arrange an appointment.
I look forward to meeting with you.
Sincerely,
John P. McKenzie, PLC
McKenzie Law Group, Barristers & Solicitors

Holy shit. Marion had been right. I'd been named in Morley's will. But why? I'd only been his friendly neighborhood bartend—Oh God. That wasn't true anymore. He and I had been meeting at his cabin a while already. This was a huge find. Something that Coop, for whatever reason, had decided to keep from me. And it begged two questions: Why? And what else was he hiding?

Chapter Thirteen

Coop

S he was onto me.

There was only one 1997 silver Civic hatchback in the city with a 23-inch rust spot in the shape of Austria. We'd joked about it often, that crusty brown spot, considering Austria was one of the countries Syd wanted to visit on our grand European vacation. The vacation I would never go on, not even if that meddling bitch Kendall paid for the whole thing. I hate planes. I hate spending money on things I can't touch. I especially hate listening to foreign languages. And nothing irks me more than when she goes on and on about all the places she wants us to visit.

Syd followed me here a couple of weeks ago, but I haven't let on that I know. Been playing it cool ever since. Been making plans. Big plans. I'm almost finished, and I can't wait to roll them out, but for now, I gotta keep it cool.

I hadn't noticed her tailing me until I'd already pulled into the driveway. Saw her cruising by in my rear-view mirror. Well, I hadn't actually *seen* her; I saw the car. The road is pretty dark way out here, but that rust spot sticks out against the silver paint like a birthmark on an Irish baby. By the time I'd noticed her it was too late to change course.

I had to assume she'd been following me since I'd left the house. Of all the days I'd decided to buy roses. Fucking roses. They were sticking out of one of my bags, and assuming she'd seen me come out of Fulcart's, there was no way she could have missed them. A simple bag of groceries might've been easy to explain. But the roses? Only a fool would've missed the neon letters painted on that particular wall.

How much did she know, though, really? I'd studied the video surveillance on the little cracked screen on my phone, and she'd kept driving when I'd pulled into the garage. The camera is pretty sensitive, even in the dark, and when I reviewed the recording later, I'd confirmed that she definitely hadn't pulled over and stuck her nose where it didn't belong. From every angle, the property was quiet apart from a raccoon sniffing around for scraps. She must have decided to keep going. Wise decision. Things would've turned ugly if she'd come knocking.

Really ugly.

Tonight I was going to enjoy a couple beers before visiting Princess and Finn downstairs. Relax a little. I was still so stressed about Syd having followed me here last week that I needed a little extra numbing of my senses. The whole mess had been bugging the shit out of me. I kept waiting for her to say something, anything, about it. But she still hadn't. She was carrying on like normal, like she hadn't seen me pulling into a strange garage on a dark country road when I should have been at work. Ha. That was rich. She herself was supposed to be having dinner with that bitch, Kendall, that night. Apparently Syd had been just as deceptive.

I'd been thinking about why she hadn't confronted me yet. It was possible she hadn't actually seen me pull into the driveway. That she'd lost sight of me and driven the entire stretch of North Glenora Road before giving up and leaving.

That was a long shot, I knew. It was more likely she'd kept driving because she *had* seen me, and now, despite acting completely normal, she was quietly freaking out. Plotting her next move. Maybe searching for a rental apartment to run away to.

Relax, dude. You're too paranoid.

I sat down at the table and cracked a beer, enjoying the sound of the can opening. I'd never really fancied the taste, truth be told, but it was refreshing.

I looked around at my little dump of a kitchen. I really should've fixed this place up when that asshole father of mine died twelve years ago, but it wasn't easy keeping two houses in good shape. The ravages of neglect and time showed everywhere in this house; the light fixture hanging over my head, for instance, only had one working bulb out of four. Someday the last one would burn out and I'd be forced to do something about it.

Beer number two. It didn't impart the same thrill as the first, but it was still pretty damned fine, and after my third beer, I went downstairs carrying this week's groceries and the rest of my twelve-pack. When I kicked the door open, Princess and the boy were on the bed, hurriedly folding up a checkers board, pouring the red and black plastic pieces into the box.

I loved my little family. My sweet little Finn and my beautiful secret Princess. If it hadn't been for Syd talking about her occasionally, I would've forgotten her real name altogether. The old man had forbidden me to speak it out loud the moment she'd arrived here; too risky, he'd said. The one smart decision he'd made in his entire shitty life.

"You didn't have to stop your game on my account," I said, plopping the bags on the floor as Princess scurried off the bed. One of the bags contained a bouquet of flowers. Huge white lilies. I'd asked the florist for the most fragrant flower in stock, and she hadn't disappointed.

"We were finished our game, right Finn?"

The boy nodded, jumped off the bed and hooked his arms around his mother's leg.

"I brought you something special tonight." I said, pulling a beer out of the box, cracking it open and holding it out to her. Some foam spilled out over the top and dribbled onto the floor. "Go on, it won't bite."

She took the can, wiped the side with her hand and held it without taking a drink. Her eyes darted over to the lilies in the grocery bag then back to me. A wave of pity swept through my gut. She was so excited at the thought of getting another bouquet of flowers. I noticed the roses from two weeks ago hanging limply over the sides of a plastic jug in the middle of the table. My heart lifted. I'd done good, bringing her fresh flowers, and I vowed to buy them for her more often. And with the plan I was working on in the background, she was about to get much more than just flowers. Much, much more.

I pulled the bouquet out of the bag and presented it to her as she set her beer on the table and accepted the lilies. She closed her eyes and buried her nose in the blooms. Took a big whiff. Ah, that was what I liked to see. Her senses on over-drive. Yeah, I needed to start buying her flowers more often.

Finn pulled on her arm and she lowered the bouquet to his nose so he could breathe in the powerful scent. My heart swelled with joy when his eyes lit up.

"Yum!" he said, poking one of the fuzzy stamens with his tiny, lean fingers. "Can we eat them, mama?"

"No sweetie. We don't eat flowers. But can you do something for me? Can you throw those old flowers into the garbage then fill the jug with fresh water? The new flowers are very thirsty."

"Okay mama!" he said dashing over to the table.

I loved how helpful the boy was to his mother. My mind flashed forward to his teen years, knowing this arrangement couldn't go on for much longer. Maybe after I loosened up Princess' surly attitude with a couple of beers, I would tell her about the plan I'd been working on, the one that was going to change her whole life. If she cooperated, that was. If she didn't, well, her life would suddenly get very dark.

After Syd followed me here, I'd panicked. Not a crazy, do-something-stupid type of panic but more of a *shit-this-sucks* kind of panic. I really should have been preparing myself better for the day Syd discovered my second life. Not that I'd been deluding myself all this time, believing it would never happen; the possibility had always lurked just beneath the surface, like the potential of an earthquake to strike any moment. And here it was, *that* moment. Right off the fucking Richer scale.

Over the past two weeks I'd been doing aftershock management. Figuring out logistics. Going over the plan again and again. Getting Plan B and even Plan C set up in the background, preparing myself for all the ways my original plan might fail. Yeah, I had the element of preparation on my side, leaving nothing to chance, leaving no loose ends. If only Syd knew that her lying and cheating and snooping around had been the kick in the ass I'd needed to finally put my brilliant plan in motion. The one I'd been fantasizing about for years.

And really, did she think I was stupid? That I'd fall for the baby bomb she'd dropped on me yesterday? I knew what she was up to, oh yes, I did. She was using the one thing I'd ever wanted—the one thing I'd ever asked her for—to throw me off track. To distract me while she snuck around. What a bitch. Too bad her devious ways had only fast-tracked my plan. Oh, she was gonna lose her mind when she found out what I've been up to!

I grabbed another beer and downed it in five gulps.

Finn was busy at the sink filling the flower jug with water when suddenly he gasped and spun around. His eyes were wide and questioning and he was making pathetic little squeaking noises and clawing at his throat. I noticed reddish-yellow smears on his nose.

Princess rushed over and scooped Finn up, and when she came rushing toward me I saw the same marks on her nose. Pollen. Finn was allergic.

"He needs to go to the hospital!" Princess shouted as she brushed past me toward the door. It was locked, of course, and I made no attempt to open it.

"Viktor! Please! *Now!*"

"You know we can't do that," I said, walking over to the sink to turn off the tap.

"We *have* to get him to the hospital!"

"Babe, we can't."

She thrust Finn in front of me. "Then *you* take him. Please, Viktor. He's your *son!*"

Finn's lips were now vaguely blue and he was struggling to breathe.

"Viktor! *Please!*" Princess yelled.

I knew in that moment what had to be done. I unlocked the door and swung it open. Princess immediately tried to skirt past me in the doorway with Finn in her arms. What was she thinking?

I shoved her away. She came at me again, throwing all her weight into me. For such a scrawny thing, she was surprisingly strong, especially with Finn's weight behind her. I body-checked her back into the room, slamming the door behind me, sliding one of the deadbolts into place, then shot up the stairs like my feet were on fire. The seriousness of the situation hadn't escaped me. I simply hadn't wanted to alarm Princess; she needed to be calm. She needed to keep her shit together and look after our boy while I worked out a way to save him. It was my duty.

I raced out the front door, down the steps, across the driveway. Shoved my key into the garage door, trembling. I'd never felt so helpless. Not once on the job had I encountered such blind panic. It was the wrong key.

"Shit, shit, shit."

I grappled with the mess of keys looking for the square gold one, but I couldn't see it. *Come on! It's the biggest key on the ring!*

Finally after going through the other ten keys, I found the right one. Rammed it in the lock. The door sprung open. I rushed over to the trunk of the locked car. *Fuck! Why do I have so many keys?* I fiddled for what seemed an eternity, all the time thinking about how I would never be so fumble-fingered on the job. It's different when its one of your own. At last I found the right key and wiggled it into the trunk. "Come on, come on, open goddammit!"

As if the car understood the gravity of the situation, the trunk sprung open, bouncing a couple of times when it hit the top. I began chucking all the contents onto the garage floor. Plastic grocery bags, empty pop cans, a hockey stick, a spare helmet from the station. No goddamn medical kit! It was neon yellow! How could I not see it? Fuck. Syd must've taken it.

In a rage, I grabbed the last item in the trunk, Jinx's beach towel, and whipped it behind me. And there it was: the medical kit. I snatched it up and spun around to get back to the house. In my haste, I tripped over a rusted muffler and crashed down on top of a pile of old tires.

The kit went flying, popping open on impact, its contents scattering over the floor of the garage. I scrambled on my hands and knees over to the scattered supplies.

Shouldn't have had that last beer.

Bandages, tape, scissors, a bottle of nitroglycerin.

Where the fuck was that epinephrine pen?

I laid down to get a look under the car. It was there, but out of reach. I jumped to my feet to look for a rake or something to pull it out. *The hockey stick!* I grabbed it and extracted the epinephrine in one pass, stuffing it and whatever else was within arm's reach back into the medical kit.

I was back at the basement door in under ten seconds. Princess was screaming her damned head off. I'd rarely heard sound coming from that room in the whole twenty years apart from the night Finn was born, but that had been a different kind of screaming. I burst back into the room.

"Put him on the bed," I commanded, pulling the epinephrine out of the kit.

"He stopped breathing!"

Finn had only been wearing a t-shirt and underwear, so his tiny leg looked vulnerable and exposed. I pulled the cap off the device, and just before I was about to jam it into his thigh, I stopped.

"What are you waiting for?"

I held the device up in front of her face. "It's for an adult."

"Do it!"

"It could be too much!" I shouted back.

"*Do it! We have no choice!*"

She was right. Couldn't take him to the hospital. No time, even if that were an option, and without any further thought, I rammed the pen into Finn's leg until I heard a click. Then counted to five.

Chapter Fourteen

Coop's work schedule had always been more or less predictable. Rotating day and night shifts: two ten-hour day shifts, followed by two fourteen-hour night shifts. After each of these, he generally had three days off. But I'd been doing some sleuthing on the firefighters' union website, and I'd learned they're mandated to get four days off between shifts. The fact that Coop had only ever taken three was worrying, to say the least.

At eight thirty on Friday morning, I heard the garage door rattle up as I lay in bed listening to robins chirping incessantly about the wonders of the new day. Jinx, hearing it too, scrambled out the bedroom door and down the stairs to wait for Coop at the back door. Of course he would. Jinx had no idea what a jerk his master was. I climbed out of bed to watch Coop cross the lawn and tramp up the back steps to the house. Had he been at work or had he been with *her*? I'd waited long enough. Today was the day I would call him on it.

"Syd?" Coop called up the stairs about two minutes later. "Babe! Are you home?"

When I didn't answer back, he yelled again.

"It's Jinx!"

I groaned. I wasn't in the mood for Jinx's problems right now, but I had to keep things normal. For now. I jumped into some clean clothes from the laundry hamper—jeans and a black long-sleeved tee, baby pink ankle socks—and headed downstairs.

When I got to the living room, it was empty. No Coop. No Jinx.

"Coop?"

His muffled voiced came from the basement. "Come quick! Something's wrong with Jinx!"

I certainly did not need dog problems, but Coop was obviously distressed. When I turned the corner at the bottom of the stairs, Coop was propped against the washing machine holding Jinx in his arms. The dog was licking Coop's face, like he does when we clip his nails or have to pull burrs out of his coat. The old *shower-them-with-love-and-they'll-stop* ploy. Jinx looked fine, apart from the nervous licking. Coop, on the other hand, didn't look fine. Purplish bags hung beneath his eyes like velvet swag curtains. His face was pale. He looked like he'd been awake for three days. Maybe he *had* been at work.

"What's wrong?" I said.

Coop bent over and allowed Jinx to jump out of his arms. The dog came running over to me, tail wagging, and I crouched down to scratch him behind the ears. "You okay, buddy?"

"The dog's fine," Coop finally said, taking a few steps toward me. I stood, bristling a little, though I couldn't say why.

Coop edged closer so that all I could see was the expanse of his chest, and when I stepped back, he grabbed my forearm. I tried to snatch it away, but he held firm.

"Hey!" I said.

"Damn, Syd. You've been up to no good."

Jinx whined at my feet. I tugged at my arm to no avail.

Before I knew what was happening, Coop jerked me

around and wrenched my hand behind my back then pushed me toward The Cave at the back of the basement.

"What are you doing?" I said, trying to wrestle out of his grip.

He pushed me into the room without letting go and I stumbled slightly over the exposed bedrock of the floor.

"What are you doing?" I repeated as shoved me to the floor just inside the door. I scrambled to get up. Halfway to my feet, a searing pain ripped through the back of my head and then everything went dark.

Chapter Fifteen

Isla

The walls seem closer, the ceiling lower. In all my twenty years of captivity, I've never felt so trapped and helpless: not during my beatings, not when I was being raped. Not even when Finn made his way down the birth canal into this screwed-up world.

Viktor left when he couldn't handle Finn's condition any longer. He'd just walked out that door and locked it behind him as if it had been any other day, not a day where his young son was teetering on the brink of death. It shouldn't have surprised me. Why would I expect him to suddenly grow a conscience? With him gone, though, there's no one to scream at. No one to comfort me if my son dies.

I prop Finn up higher in my lap, rocking him back and forth. His breaths are shallow and ragged, his skin clammy. I unfold the medication leaflet and read it for probably the eighth time. It indicates seeking immediate medical attention, even if the anaphylactic symptoms go away. It also states a second dose should be administered if the first one doesn't help. The pamphlet offers no protocol to follow if a second dose isn't available, nor does it mention what to do if you're being held captive in a psycho's basement and unable to go to a hospital. The instructions really should be updated.

"You're going to be okay, baby."

But will he? His breathing and state of consciousness haven't changed perceptibly in the fourteen hours since Viktor jabbed the medication into his leg. He hasn't opened his swollen little eyes or tried to talk. My only solace is that he's still breathing. I have to hold onto that tiny shred of hope. If only Viktor cared as much.

Where the hell is the coward, anyway? What if he never comes back? What if he can't stand the idea of opening the door to a dead toddler and his enraged mother and bought himself a one-way ticket to Aruba? I shiver at the thought and shift Finn off my lap. His breathing quickens. "Shh, shh, sweetie. Mama's getting a cold cloth for your head."

On the way back from the sink, I'm distracted by a yellow pop of color beneath my bed. The medical kit! I curse under my breath for not noticing it earlier. Another dose of epinephrine may have been right under my nose the whole time.

After getting Finn settled, I spill the contents of the kit out onto the table: gauze, bandages, antibiotic ointment, scissors, the usual stuff. No epinephrine. That would've been too easy. But what's this? A brown plastic bottle full of pills. I push down on the cap and twist it off, shaking a few light gray tablets into my hand. One side is engraved with an *M*, the other shows the number *300*. I have to assume they're painkillers, probably strong ones. I pour them all out onto the table and, for lack of something better to do, start counting them. "Five, ten, fifteen…"

When I'm finished, I scoop all 148 tablets back into the bottle and stand it on the table in front of me. I glance at Finn. His lips are blue, his breaths shallower than ever.

I look back at the bottle and an idea settles in.

Chapter Sixteen

My body jerked and the room zoomed into focus. Apart from Jinx standing over me licking his chops, I was alone. The only thing in my stomach—tea with honey from this morning (was it even still the same day?)—threatened to gush out, either from the effects of the throbbing at the back of my head or from the horror of seeing my wrists and one of my legs fastened to the shelves by plastic zip ties.

I scanned the dim room, lit only by a 40-watt bulb hanging from the middle of the ceiling. I lifted my head toward the door. It was closed, probably locked.

"Hey buddy," I said to Jinx, rearranging myself so that I was sitting against an empty microwave box under the shelving. He gave me a lick on the cheek then planted his butt on the floor, resting his head on my lap.

"Coop!" I yelled, recoiling from the pain at the back of my head, wondering how long I'd been out. Wondering, since it was impossible to reach the back of my head, if there was blood at the site of my pain. Trying to deny the knowledge that Coop had actually hit me on the head—with what? His fist? A baseball bat?—knocking me out cold. How had it come to this?

Possible explanations surfaced, and number one on the list was that the man who'd struck me on the head and locked me down here simply could *not* have been my Coop. I remembered thinking the same thing when Morley rescued me from Chapman Falls on my first timeblink. If Coop didn't have an evil twin, he most certainly had to be on some kind of hallucinogenic drugs. Or hypnotized. Or had had his brain taken over by aliens. Whatever the reason, the crazed person that had tied me up in here couldn't have been the man I'd shared my life with for the last twelve years.

Not one to sit around and wait, I began sawing the zip-tie around my wrist against the sharp edge of the post, but after about five minutes I stopped, recognizing the futility in it. The tie was fastened too tightly for me to get any decent leverage, and the vigorous sawing had only forged bright pink bracelets in my skin.

"Fuck!"

Spooked by my outburst, Jinx got up from my lap and padded over to the door. He curled into a ball and promptly fell asleep. I immediately felt alone. If only I could zap right out of here and—

"What an idiot!" I yelled. If ever there had ever been an appropriate time to use the power of timeblinking, it was right now. I leaned toward my hands and snagged my forefinger under the chain, pulling it out of my shirt. I took hold of the talisman between my finger and thumb, ready to blink my way out of this disaster. But where would I go? And what would happen when I came back? I had no idea where Coop was, and if he came downstairs during the four and a half minutes I was gone, there was no telling what the consequences would be on my return. And what about Jinx? No, I couldn't use it. Not until I was sure my captor was occupied for at least five minutes and Jinx wasn't in the room. I could be waiting for a while.

A couple of hours passed before Coop let himself back

into the room. Jinx jumped to life and skirted around him, taking a position just outside the door looking in, whimpering intermittently, licking his lips.

"What the fuck, Coop? Is this a joke?" I said, scrabbling to get comfortable.

"Shit, you're feisty, babe," he said, standing over me with his hands on his hips. "You put up quite the fuss earlier. Which is why you're in restraints now."

Jinx, finding courage, scurried past him to sit next to me.

"It's okay, buddy," I said, leaning my head against his scruff. Even as I said it, my heart told me things were definitely not okay. Had Isla gone through something like this? Damn it! This was my husband, not some stranger who'd snatched me from a park.

Coop grabbed a folded-up camping chair from a hook in the wall, set it up about five feet away from me and flopped into it.

"It seems you've been busy behind my back."

Morley's face flashed in my mind, and I felt my cheeks redden. "Oh?" I said. "I could say the same about you."

"We're not talking about me. We're talking about you—specifically about your spying and your lying, and worst of all, your *cheating*—and you're going to tell me all about it," he said, leaning his elbows on his knees and clasping his hands together. Maybe it was his uniform and his interrogatory disposition, but he reminded me of a cop just then.

"Oh come on, Syd, don't look so surprised."

I bit my lower lip involuntarily. He had me on all three counts, though the lying part was more a withholding of the truth than outright deception.

"Babe. Why so sneaky? Following me to my house in Glenora?"

I felt my brows bunch together. "So it really is your house?"

"Yeah. So?"

"So…This is the first I've heard about it."

He stuck his bottom lip out and shrugged his shoulders.

"How long have you had it?"

"Well, if there's any hope of getting you to 'fess up about your doctor friend, I might as well go first."

He leaned back in the camping chair and sighed. "The house belonged to my asshole father. I've been maintaining it since he died."

"Not very well," I muttered under my breath, recalling the run-down state of the house.

"Pardon me?" he said.

"Nothing. Why didn't you tell me about it before? And why were you stocking it with groceries? And roses?" Ha. I had him.

He glanced around the basement. "To get away from *this* depressing hell-hole."

When he looked back at me, he saw the sting and his demeanor softened.

"It didn't start that way. When old pops kicked the bucket, I thought I might fix the house up for us. You know, restore it to its original condition. I was so excited about our little family moving out there to the country to take advantage of the fresh air, the wide-open space. The peace and quiet. But the dream lost its charm. I didn't see worth in just the two of us living way out there. Alone."

Was he seriously dredging up that old argument, even after I'd told him I wanted a baby?

"Tell me about your dad," I said, steering him toward a less volatile subject. "I know your mother died when you were a baby, but you've never talked about your father, even after all these years, apart from the fact that he left you his Firewing when he died. Beyond that…nothing. I don't even know his name or when he died."

"Anton. Twelve years ago." Coop took his ball cap off and repositioned it back on his head, and as an afterthought added, "You actually met him once, when we bumped into him at Gaynor's Hardware on Derry Road. I introduced him as my former boss. In fact, you might recall the meeting. He was quite rude. Next question."

I did remember that day, and remembered it well. The greasy old guy had looked me up and down as if I were a stripper on a dance floor and tried to hug me. He'd reeked of booze and cigarette smoke. "Oh, son. You dirty dog!" he'd said. I remembered wriggling out of his grasp, shaken.

That had been Coop's dad? I'd thought his use of the word *son* had been unusual at the time but put it down to a friendly gesture between old colleagues. In turn, I'd left it alone, praying we wouldn't cross paths with the slimy jerk again.

"Wait. Back up," I said, doing the calculations. "I've only known you for thirteen years. You're saying he died shortly thereafter?"

"He sure did," Coop said, smiling.

It was mindboggling. To find out that Coop's father had died in the early years—early *days*—of our relationship and that he'd gone through the loss without confiding in me.

"Why didn't you tell me? You knew I'd experienced loss too. I could've helped."

"It was no loss, believe me. It was a blessing. But let's get back to *you*. You know, your cheating ways."

I wanted more information about Coop's dad and the house in Glenora but knew better than to push. Besides, my back was starting to ache, and when I shifted my weight to get more comfortable, Coop somehow took it as an admission of guilt.

"Fuck, Syd. How long were you shagging the baby doc before he croaked?"

Good God, who was this insensitive brute? I wanted my sweet, loving Cooper back.

"What makes you think I was sleeping with him?" I said.

"Well, for starters, your work situation. If he'd been your

friend, like you say, you'd have been back full time when the pub reopened, like everyone else."

"Coop, I saw a man get flattened between a truck and a wall. How would *you* react?" It was a terrible argument. Events like that were part of his job.

"I have proof!" he shouted.

"Proof of *what*?"

"That your precious doctor was more than just a friend."

"I call bullshit," I said, sitting up straighter.

He suddenly bolted out of his chair, knocking it to the floor, then stormed out of the room. If I was reading the situation right, he was going upstairs to fetch the letter that named me as one of Morley's beneficiaries. Too bad for him, though, he wasn't going to find it unless he looked under the lining of my lingerie drawer.

Less than two minutes later, I heard Coop barrelling back down the stairs. His rage sucked all the air out of the room when he burst through the door.

"*Where the fuck is it?*" he screamed, spittle flying from his mouth.

"Where is what?" I said smugly.

"You know what I'm talking about!" he screamed. "Not only have you been cheating on me and following me all around the goddamned city, but now it seems you've been digging through my private stuff."

"That's rich, considering the letter was addressed to *me*."

He pointed a finger at me, his eyes wild. Veins I'd never seen before popped out on his forehead. "So you admit it! Where is it? *Where are you hiding it?*"

I looked up at the ceiling and laughed. "You're kidding me, right?"

"I'm dead serious."

"Don't be an ass."

"This isn't a joke, Syd. Treat it like one and you'll be sorry."

"What did you just say?"

"Look, just tell me, and I'll let you go. I don't even care about the letter. Just tell me. Were you fucking that doctor before he died?"

Technically—and honestly—I could say, *"No. I was not fucking that doctor before he died,"* and leave it at that. But no. Coop could keep me tied up for a decade and I wouldn't give him the satisfaction of an answer, the truth or otherwise. Not with the way he was treating me. Let him imagine all sorts of wild things—like I'd been doing since I'd followed him to North Glenora. I'd tell him about Morley when he confessed to what was going on behind *my* back first. Not a moment before.

We sat facing each other for a good two minutes, him seething, breathing heavily; me, doing my best to ignore him, wiggling my feet and hands to keep them from falling asleep. The silence was suddenly interrupted by the doorbell ringing upstairs. Jinx let out a subdued woof and dashed out of the room. He always barked once when he heard the doorbell, but this time his bark sounded almost human; like the small, relieved noise a mother makes when her roving teenager comes home for the night. I heard Jinx trundle up the stairs to see who was at the door. It was probably Kendall. Good. She could put a stop to Coop's ridiculous game.

"I gotta deal with this," Coop said as he closed the door behind him. I heard him fiddling with the padlock outside door, his footsteps fading away.

"Unbelievable," I said aloud, working again at the tie on my wrists, the gravity of Coop's actions starting to sink in. He had truly lost it. He was so angry. The worst I'd ever seen him. What did he have to gain by tying me up, though? We could've had a civil conversation about everything sitting at our kitchen table.

I felt the tie give way a little, but the burn was excruciating, and I had to rest. Breaking the tie on my hands wouldn't have mattered much, anyway, since my right foot was still fastened to another post.

Suddenly I felt a thud above my head, like a piece of furniture falling over. The bookcase in the living room? Or Coop being his usual clumsy self, tripping on one of Jinx's toys? I strained to hear something, *anything*, but The Cave was as close to soundproof as it got. I'd known that for years.

A few uneventful minutes passed and then I heard Coop back at the door, fiddling with the lock. He must've sent the visitor away. The door swung open.

I gasped.

Coop stalked into the room with Kendall draped over his shoulder like a rag doll.

Chapter Seventeen

"What the..? Kendall? *Kendall!*"

"Your sister is a bit, ah, sleepy at the moment. It's amazing, the illicit substances you can get your hands on in my line of work. I would've given you a shot of it too, but I need you fully conscious."

I watched helplessly as he dumped Kendall on the floor at the other end of the shelving unit then pulled half a dozen zip-ties out of his pocket and set them on the top shelf out of my reach. When he took one from the pile and started towards Kendall, I threw my free leg out and tried to trip him but missed. He giggled fiendishly at my blunder as he fastened Kendall to the post. Satisfied with his handiwork, he righted the overturned camp chair and flumped down heavily, pulling his cell phone out of his shirt pocket and tapping at it for a few minutes before tucking it away. I couldn't help but think he was probably texting his girlfriend in Glenora, but I didn't bite.

"It was Brett, if you must know. Just giving him the scoop on your meltdown and that his helpful little wife has come to your rescue once again. He was only too happy to lend her services out. Nice guy, Brett. I've always liked him. Too bad he got stuck with that bitch."

I couldn't help but roll my eyes.

"Now, now, babe," Coop said. "You're in no position to get cheeky."

Who the hell was this guy? How had I never known about this side of the man I'd spent all these years with?

"Oh, so you're gonna give me the silent treatment now?" he said, leaning forward. His biceps bulged against his uniform sleeves, and I was instantly revolted by the pulsing in my crotch.

"You're scaring me, Coop."

"Aw."

"What's wrong with you?"

"*Sisters*," he said.

"Pardon me?"

"You heard me. You bitches ruined my life. Look what you made me do," he said, nodding his head in Kendall's direction. She was lying in a sorry heap on the floor, her head flopped to one side, her arms fixed upward, as in prayer, where they were strapped to the shelving unit.

"I did *not* make you do *that*," I said. "What did you do, anyway? Is she okay?"

"There you go, caring about that bitch more than me again."

Coop suddenly lurched out of his chair, pushing a case of Coke aside on the shelf opposite me, reaching toward the back. He produced a bottle of liquor—Caribou Ridge, according to the label—and tore into the stiff foil wrapper decorating its neck.

"Good thing you didn't know about my little bourbon stash. I'd damned near forgotten about it myself!" he said, popping the cap and taking a huge belt. "Whooo-eee, so that's what I've been missing all these years."

"Where'd that come from?" I said, stupidly, like it mattered.

"Jerry gave it to me last year for covering a shift. He didn't know I'm strictly a beer guy," he said. "Y'know, I don't even like beer. When you're a kid watching your bourbon-swilling asshole of a father destroying himself and everyone around him, you don't really develop a taste for liquor."

There it was again. A glimpse of his life before we met. How had he managed to keep his past from me for so long? Why had I neglected to ask him about it?

He dangled the bottle in front of my face. "Want a swig?"

What I really wanted was a can of Coke, but I decided to revisit his earlier line of questioning rather than asking him for a favor. "Do you really think I care about Kendall more than you?"

His face dropped. "Shut up. It doesn't matter."

"Yes. It does matter. I love you."

"Y'got a funny way of showing it, jumping into bed with that doctor."

I rolled my eyes. "Look, Morley was just…a friend."

"See? Right there. You hesitated. You might as well have said, *Yes, Coop, I was fucking that doctor!*"

He took five or six huge gulps from the bottle, and as he pulled it away, three-quarters empty, it slipped from his grip. He fumbled to catch it, but it cartwheeled through the air and smashed on the floor halfway between us. He looked as though he might cry as the rest of the bourbon trickled toward the drain.

"Well, guess the party's over," he said, heading to the door. "Whatever. I got a shit-ton of stuff to do, anyway."

As he pushed the door shut behind him, I heard him say, "No funny stuff."

Chapter Eighteen

"Oh Kendall, I'm so sorry," I whispered a few minutes after the creature loosely resembling my husband left the room.

A "*shit-ton*" of stuff to do, in Coop-speak, meant he was going for a drive. It had always meant that, even if he didn't know it himself. Now was my chance to use the talisman to timeblink to any random date, it didn't matter when, and on my return, I would no longer be tied to the shelf.

I cast a sympathetic eye toward Kendall who was propped at a weird angle with her legs pointing to the back of The Cave and her torso twisted toward me. Her eyes were closed. Her head hung limply to one side. Long chestnut curls obscured half her face, and her mouth was set in a neutral line that wasn't quite a smile, not quite *anything*, reminding me of my mother the last time I'd seen her in her shiny white coffin the day we all said goodbye. I let out a weary breath.

I couldn't wallow in self-pity, not when I had to complete my next timeblink before Kendall woke up. I leaned my neck over to my bound wrists to grab the chain from my neck.

It wasn't there.

"No!" I said, clumsily pawing at my neckline. Why did

everything have to be so difficult? It'd been there earlier, hadn't it? I'd almost used it. It had to be inside my shirt or hung up in my bra again. I shimmied closer to my hand and hooked my collar with my finger, pulling it away from my neck, peering inside to see if the talisman had become snagged. It hadn't, at least not that I could see.

Giving up wasn't an option. There had to be a way of breaking through the tie on my wrists. I scanned the room and laughed self-righteously when I saw the puddle of booze evaporating before my eyes. Typical, Coop had left the broken bottle in a pile on the floor, its jagged pieces twinkling in the low light. The biggest section curved upward like a miniature machete.

A machete!

I swung my left leg up to my hands to pull my sock off which promptly dropped on my nose. I shook it off then stretched my bare foot toward the pile of glass, splaying my big and second toes out, wrapping them around the shard. Reminding myself that battles were seldom won without bloodshed, I raised my foot off the ground. The glass was heavier than I'd expected. With my body angled alongside the shelving, I drew my weapon toward my hands in a type of modified heron pose with the shard suspended dangerously above my face like my sock had been moments ago.

"Easy, Syd. Easy," I kept repeating, as if speaking the words aloud would prevent the piece from slipping from my toes and possibly puncturing an eyeball. No sooner had this thought come to me than the shard shifted. My toes cramped. I clenched tighter. Blood trickled along the edge of the glass and dripped on my cheek. I couldn't stop now. With every ounce of remaining strength in my body, I jerked my foot still closer to my hands. The glass shifted again, its point dangling directly over my forehead. As it broke loose, I braced myself. This would not end well.

Instinct took over. I watched, detached, as my hands thrust

out far as they would go to catch the falling missile. I clamped my eyes shut, braced for impact. But it never came. When I opened my eyes, the shard was nestled between the pinky and ring finger of my left hand. It had been a tenuous catch, but it hadn't fallen on my face.

I carefully removed the shard with my other hand and savored the sweet release pulsing through my aching muscles. The glass was hefty in my grip, even sharper than I'd imagined, and I'd been lucky to sustain only a few minor cuts. I immediately began sawing at the plastic around my wrists, slowly, cautiously, focused on not dropping the glass or slicing my wrist open. It would be over in moments. The only obstacle between me and freedom was the possibility of Coop coming back unexpectedly. That, and the padlock on The Cave's door, but how hard could it be to knock down a door made of scrap wood salvaged from shipping pallets?

A rush of adrenaline zipped through my veins when the tie broke apart less than a minute later, and by the time the tie at my ankle snapped off, I knew exactly what my next steps would be. There was no doubt in my mind that Coop had gone to Glenora, and I couldn't wait to get out there—to catch him in his mammoth lie. But that was somewhere around Step Six.

First things first.

I pulled my sock back on, bloody foot and all, then rushed over to Kendall and cut her hands free. She didn't even stir. It seemed that she'd be out for a while longer.

Next, I grabbed one of Coop's golf clubs and started hacking at the door, which turned out to be stronger than I'd expected. My dad must've been preparing for an alien invasion when he'd constructed it, and after another ten minutes of fruitless hammering, I was sweaty and exhausted and on the verge of passing out. With no food or water all day—what time was it anyway? Three in the afternoon? Midnight?—my tank was dry. That's when I remembered the Coke. I grabbed a can and finished it in five gulps.

My muscles thanked me as I melted into the camping chair in the middle of the room. It felt like getting a hug from a big teddy bear after all the time I'd spent on the floor. I didn't dare fall asleep though. Coop could be back any minute. He had the annoying habit of changing his mind midstream, so even with his "shit-ton of stuff" to do, he could've been perched outside the door, lying in wait.

Maybe it was the exhaustion or lack of food, but I was starting to fabricate all sorts of crazy outcomes to the day. Did Coop intend to keep me captive in this room indefinitely? Was he going to kill me? *And* Kendall? I'd seen his venom. Crimes of passion happened every day, and it always seemed the victims lucky enough to survive said they hadn't seen it coming.

The thought of it gave me a fresh boost of energy, and I remembered the talisman. I'd been so focussed on the door I'd forgotten about it. It had to be in this room. I pulled myself out of the chair to start searching for it. As I stood, something slithered down my back and clinked at my feet. Small mercies, it was the talisman. I picked it up and settled myself back on the chair.

While I turned the dragonfly pendant over and over in my fingers, imploring it to give me an answer, Morley swam into my thoughts. I missed him, even though only two days had gone by since I'd last seen him. So much had happened since then. Maybe I would go see him, and he could help me figure out what to do.

But as quickly as the thought formed in my mind, I abandoned it. What if…what if I didn't make it out of here alive after all? It was crazy to think Coop could do such a thing, but people had been murdered for far less than scorned love, and as much as I wanted to see Morley, I could not squander my next timeblink on a rendezvous with him. However, I could still honour him indirectly.

He'd written three dates on his note, and I had traveled to all but the final one. Purposely. I couldn't imagine revisiting a time in my life more painful than that. I didn't need the piece of paper to remind me of the date, either. It had been imprinted on my brain like a tattoo twenty years ago: September 27, 1999, the day Isla went missing, and Morley wanted me to find out what happened. Before our intimate trysts at his cabin, I would've been suspicious about his motives in sending me there, but as we'd gotten to know each other and, yes, fall in love, I'd learned that he understood me on a level that no one else ever had. He wouldn't send me to that day if he didn't think I couldn't handle it.

I fastened the chain around my neck, double-checking the clasp, and took the talisman between my fingers. I made sure Kendall was still knocked out, then conjured up an image of a place I hadn't seen in two decades.

"Pembina Park, 4:30 p.m., September 27, 1999."

By good fortune, I landed in a small grouping of rhododendron bushes on the inside of the fence running along Birch Avenue. I didn't want to be seen if Isla's abductor was already busy scoping out the area, and the greenery provided the perfect cover. About ninety percent of the shrubs' leathery leaves had remained intact but they did little to provide protection from the biting wind. I hadn't expected to be tromping around in the chilly fall weather when I'd gotten dressed this morning and was without shoes or a coat to stave off the cold.

My eyes narrowed in the direction of the Maroon Mansion. It was what had gotten us into this mess to begin with.

Right on cue, Isla and Syd came racing down the sidewalk on their bikes, pushed along by punishing gusts of north wind. I wanted to yell, "Turn around! Go home now!" but instead hugged my arms close, keeping my mouth shut and steeling myself against the cold.

"You be the interviewer," I heard Syd say as they dumped their bikes in the grass about twenty feet from where I hid. I took a deep breath. This wasn't going to be easy.

"Interviewer of who?" Isla said. At least I think that's what she said. Their voices were competing with the howling wind, barely carrying over the distance between us. I would have to rely on my memory to fill in the blanks.

"Me, of course. I'll pretend to be a scared kid, and you can ask me questions about the house."

"Won't work," Isla said. "We can't both be in the scene together."

Isla had always been the pragmatic one, and I remembered how her quest for perfection had exhausted me at times. Syd just wanted to get on with the video but stared Isla down until she explained.

"Oh my God, Syd, really? Think about it. How believable will it be with me interviewing you, *my identical twin*, when I'm supposed to be the reporter and you're just some random kid?"

"You're going to be off screen. With your voice in the background."

Isla bristled. "Forget that! I want to be on camera too."

I recalled her assertion surprising me a little. Isla normally hated being in the limelight. Maybe she'd felt she wouldn't be given as much credit for the project if she didn't appear in the video. Whatever the reason, she folded her arms across her chest and dug in.

"Okay, fine then. But you'll need to go grab a disguise. Mom's raincoat and Kendall's glasses should do the trick,"

Syd said, pulling the video camera and tripod out of Isla's backpack.

"No way, bossy pants. You go," Isla said. "I'll stay here and set up the shots."

And with that decision, right then, right there, our lives veered off in two entirely different directions.

I watched helplessly as Syd hopped on her bike. "Uggh! You are so annoying!" she shouted over her shoulder as she pedalled away.

"Love you, too!" Isla yelled back, affixing the video camera to the tripod.

A few moments later, I saw it. A junky, beat-up wreck of a car—was that a Firewing?—creeping along Birch Street. The longer I looked, the more certain I was of the make. I'd recognize it anywhere—it was just like Coop's two-door, cherry-red mistress, Lucy. Unlike Lucy, though, this Firewing was riddled with rust holes and covered in primer spots, giving it a sinister look made worse by the black tinted windows. It rolled to a stop. The engine revved once, as if it was about to drag race another car, then quieted to a throaty idle near the opening in the fence. From my vantage point, the back half of the car was obscured by some low shrubs lining the fence, but there was no mistaking the model.

Isla picked up her backpack and hugged it to her chest when she saw the car stop. She shot a worried look in the direction Syd had gone, and it looked as though she might take off after her, but instead she stayed put, bringing her focus back to the chugging car. After a few seconds, the driver's door popped open and a middle-aged man with small, closely spaced eyes and a salt-and-pepper beard climbed out of the car. He positioned himself on the sidewalk near the opening in the fence and scanned the park dramatically, pretending not to see Isla. What a joke. How could anyone miss the pretty blonde girl in the neon pink hoodie? He shook his head in defeat. I held my breath. Maybe he would go away and change the course of history. But he just stood there, scratching his greasy head like a silent film actor who couldn't figure out where he'd left his umbrella. After a few moments of trying to look helpless and confused, he finally pretended to notice Isla and gave her a friendly wave. When she didn't return the wave, he leaned inside the car and brought out a cardboard box, like an apple box you'd find at the grocery store.

"Excuse me!" he yelled.

Isla whipped her head left and right, making sure he was talking to her. Realizing he was, she pressed her lips together as if suddenly remembering the adage *"Don't talk to strangers."*

The man seemed familiar, but I couldn't place from where. Maybe he was someone my parents had known? Statistics showed that if you're going to be abducted, there's a pretty good chance you know your kidnapper.

When Isla took a couple of steps toward him, my heart began thumping hard in my chest as if it wanted out, right fucking now.

"*No!*" I yelled, clapping my hand over my mouth. The man didn't flinch, but Isla stopped as if she'd heard me. I knew better.

The man shouted, "Sorry to bother you, but do you know where the nearest veterinarian is?"

Isla took another couple of steps, probably thinking, "Yes! Yes, I do!" Probably couldn't wait to give the man directions to our family's vet clinic over on Aster Street. Isla loved helping people. Isla loved animals. This wasn't looking good for a people-loving animal buff.

The man held up the box. "I found some newborn puppies down the road a ways, maybe you know who they belong to?"

That was it for my dear sister. She sprinted off toward the man with the Firewing, her blonde ponytail bouncing gaily in the wind. She dropped her backpack near the break in the fence and stepped onto the sidewalk like she'd known the man forever.

"*No, Isla! Damn you!*" I screamed into the wind, inadvertently inhaling a lock of my hair. I coughed it out, doubling over to catch my breath, and when I looked up, Isla had disappeared behind the shrubs along the fence. The man either hadn't heard me over the howling wind or was too involved in his actions to care. I watched helplessly as he bent over and began bobbing up and down, in a struggle it seemed, near the back of the car. I screamed again when I saw him lift his hand in a fist and punch it down with such force that I nearly vomited. After a few more seconds, the man chucked the apple box over the fence, took a sweeping glance at the park, then slid behind the wheel and drove away unhurriedly.

I ran over to the fence to see if Isla was on the sidewalk behind the shrubs, knowing the futility in it, not caring if I was spotted by this horrible man, but the car kept its pace. When I came to Isla's abandoned backpack and the empty apple box, I collapsed to the ground and bawled. A stiff gust caught the box. I watched it tumble across the field and out of sight along with my hope.

My attention went back to the Firewing, which was making a left onto Fowl Bay Road at the end of Birch, and I was paralyzed. What could I do? Run after it? Go to the cops and tell them what had happened? But I was in a timeblink, and there were limitations. Fuck it, I had to do something. Anything.

I got up, brushed dried grass off my jeans, and as I set off in the direction of my sister and her abductor, I caught sight of something across the street that stopped me in my tracks.

The baby blue Bug.

Chapter Nineteen

Coop/Viktor

The wind in my hair and the power of the Firewing boosted my mood to new and momentous levels. I was so excited that I hadn't even turned my stereo on. Finally! The dark cloud of uncertainty that had hung over me so long was parting, and my plan—Plan B as of today—was shining through as bright as the fucking sun. Soon the waiting and the worrying and the obsessing would end. My beautiful Princess would only be too happy to comply once I outlined the consequences of non-compliance. For our son's sake. She was a good gal who knew damned well what would happen if she didn't listen.

"Oh, Princess. It's too bad, but soon I'm going to have to have to start calling you Syd. You don't deserve that, but what can I do?"

Princess might have been Syd's identical twin, but she was *leagues* smarter, braver, sexier, and definitely mentally stronger than her sister. They were about the same in the sack—ah, twins—but I figured my Princess's skills might get even better once she started watching TV and movies and talking about sex with her friends. Yeah. She was gonna have a *giant* circle of friends, I could just tell. She'd be a social fucking butterfly. I already knew she was up for a couple of beers every once in a while, which is more than I could say for her water-chugging twin. The tricky part of my plan lay with Finn. While Princess would be easy enough to pass off as Syd, having a little boy suddenly appear in my life would be a different thing altogether.

First things first, though: Get rid of the two bitches back in town, move Princess and Finn into the house, and I don't know, maybe announce to our small circle of friends that we'd adopted a five-year-old boy? I'd cross that bridge later. The important thing was that Princess was a dead-ringer for her sister, so that part would be easy. I'd have to fatten her up a bit first, but that shouldn't be a problem. The only wild card before today had been that bitch Kendall, but with her out of the picture, it'd be smooth fucking sailing.

"Shit!" I said, eyeing my rear-view mirror. Red and blue flashing lights. "Shit, shit, *shit*."

I pulled over to the side of the road. There was no need to flee. I couldn't attract attention, not when I was so close to the finish line. As I sat waiting for the officer to get out of his cruiser, I rifled through my glovebox for my registration papers. Thankfully they were up to date. Even with two families to run and a full-time job to boot, I was still taking care of business. I glanced around me in the waning daylight. A few intermittent streetlights had come on. There was no sign of life in the sole house in the distance. No other cars on the road. What was this asshole doing way out here?

"Goddammit," I muttered under my breath, suddenly wondering if Syd had something to do with this. Had she escaped? Impossible. It was just my nerves getting the better of me. I kept my hands visible, resting them on my steering wheel while I tapped my thumbs anxiously. I willed them to stop. Couldn't appear nervous.

As the officer approached, I was surprised to see *he* was a *she*. Perfect! I had a way with ladies.

"Good evening, officer. Is there a problem?" I said as she appeared at my window.

"Evening," she said pleasantly enough. "May I see your license and registration?"

I handed her the registration and lifted my butt to grab my wallet. I'd forgotten she would need to see the license too.

She shone her flashlight on the papers, and as I handed her my license, she said, "Where're you off to?"

"Just out for a drive. Lucy likes to have her lines cleaned out every once in a while."

"Nice car," she said, stepping back, sweeping her flashlight front to back.

"Thanks. She's…she's a '70 Firewing 426." I patted the dashboard lovingly, hoping the cop hadn't noticed the minor slur in my voice.

"Have you been drinking, sir?"

"No ma'am. I work at Fire Hall No. 7. I've seen the devas…tation that drinking and driving causes." *Shit, get it together, bro.*

"Oh, you're a firefighter. I *thought* I recognized you," she said, slightly more congenially. Thank God. She was going to give me a pass. A friendly exchange between two first responders and a parting, *Now be on your way, sir.*

"Please step out of the car, Mr. Levin."

Fuck. This bitch was going to ruin my plan. I could pop her one right now and stuff her in my trunk.

Or play it cool. She probably had a dash-cam running.

I emerged from the car reluctantly.

"Stand straight and lift your foot like this," she said, demonstrating. I complied. "Keep it there for thirty seconds."

I stood, unwavering, for close to forty seconds, maybe even

more. This would be a piece of cake. After completing the first test, she asked me to look at her outstretched finger as she passed it slowly in front of my eyes. Pretty sure I passed that one too. By the time it came to walking heel-to-toe in a straight line, turning and doing it again, I was certain she was convinced of my sobriety.

She handed back my paperwork and flipped a pad of tickets open. "I'm going to let you go for now, Levin, but I originally pulled you over for speeding. Here's your fine," she said ripping the ticket out of her book.

"Regarding the alcohol on your breath," she said, "you passed the sobriety test, and I'm not going to ask you to blow a breathalyzer, but you should go straight home and think about your actions. As a fellow first responder, you should know better."

Ooh, I felt like she'd just sent me to the principal's office.

"Yes ma'am. May I ask one favor though?"

She looked at me like I was crazy.

"My friend lives just up the road. You mind if I hang out there for a bit before going home? My wife and I had a bit of a tiff before I left, and I'm kinda afraid to go home. She needs to cool her jets, if you know what I mean."

She rolled her eyes and blew an irritated breath through her teeth. "Get going, then. But no drinking with your buddy. Got it, Mr. Firefighter with a job you can't afford to lose?"

I smiled and folded myself into Lucy's leather seat, "You bet. Thank you, officer, ah…"

"Noble." She pointed to the name badge on her bomber jacket.

"Thank you, Officer Noble. You won't be troubled by me again. I promise."

As she walked away, I fired up my car, trying to keep its obnoxious growl to a minimum. Holy shit. Dropping that bottle of bourbon on the basement floor had been the best thing to happen all day. Lord knows I'd been in a good enough mood to drink the whole thing if I'd had the chance.

My nerves were zinging by the time I reached the house three minutes later, and as the garage door rattled shut behind me, I sat thanking my lucky stars. But how long would that luck last? In a few moments I would find out whether or not my son had survived his anaphylactic episode. Shit. Who woulda thought a delicate little flower could kill someone?

A few minutes later I was at Princess's door, fumbling with the key in the lock, wondering what I might find. It had been almost a day since Finn had first came into contact with the lily, and he'd either be sitting up enjoying a game of checkers with his mother or he'd be…not playing checkers.

I inched the door open with caution. If Finn had expired, I couldn't be sure what state his mother would be in. Would she come at me with some kind of improvised weapon? Or would she be curled up in the corner, catatonic and unresponsive like her sister had been after her lover's accident at The Merryport?

A tsunami of smells hit me as I stepped inside the door. Lilies. Sweat. Vomit. The room was warm and close. The small bedside lamp revealed a juice glass tipped on its side on the nightstand. There was no sound. No movement. Isla was curled up on the bed, her back toward me. I couldn't see Finn.

"Hey sweetheart," I whispered, tiptoeing toward the bed.

When I reached the bed, my legs almost buckled. Not in fear, but relief. The two of them were nestled together, spoon-style, with Finn wrapped up in his mother's arms. *Thank you, God.*

I placed my hand on Isla's shoulder and gave her a wiggle. When she didn't respond, I shook a little harder. It was then that I noticed a brown pill bottle laying on the bed just above Finn's head. There were only a few pills inside.

"*No!*"

I shook Isla more vigorously.

"Wake up! Goddammit, you can't do this to me! Not now!"

Her slack body flopped toward me, almost in slow motion. Her fingertips brushed my thigh as her arm unfurled like a fiddlehead.

Her lips were blue.

Oh, dear God. What had I done?

Chapter Twenty

I dashed across the street as fast as my legs would take me and yanked the door to the baby blue Bug open. Under the floor mat, right where newspapers had reported it to be, was the key. I jumped into the car and fired it up.

My brain had gone into autopilot. I barely knew where I was. Or *when* I was. And I had found a way to follow the Firewing.

"What the *fuck* is going on?"

I bunny hopped the car a few times, finally discovering the right combination of clutch and gas. As I turned left at the end of the street, I glanced over my shoulder just in time to see 11-year-old Syd pedalling across the field toward Isla's abandoned bike with her right hand curled protectively to her chest. I winced. That broken wrist was the least of the problems she was about to face.

I forced my focus back to the road ahead and actually laughed at the absurdity of my situation. At the same time I was following the beat-up Firewing that held my abducted twin, Coop was speeding down North Glenora Road in his sexy red Firewing in a completely different realm. It almost didn't matter to me anymore that he was on the way to see his secret lover.

Up ahead the junky Firewing made another left onto Broadmoor Street and sped up a little, but the driver seemed oblivious to the blue Volkswagen following behind.

I breathed in the vaguely comforting old-lady smell inside the car and calmed down enough to focus on the task at hand, paying particular mind not to speed. I'd come too far to screw this up now. My sister was *right there*, and here I was, moments away from clarity and I felt more at peace than I had in twenty years.

The Firewing turned right onto Windsor Street then continued past the open field where the strip mall and Fulcart Foods would eventually be built, coming to an important intersection a few minutes later. The gas station at the corner of Seaview Street and North Glenora Road was still there in my present, the same bulbous orange sign rotating on the roof.

To my surprise, the Firewing didn't turn left at the gas station where the neighborhoods were more densely populated and therefore easier to blend into, but instead turned right on North Glenora Road.

My stomach flipped.

"Oh my God. That's Coop's father."

Chapter Twenty-one

Isla

Finn's knobby spine follows the curve of my ribcage precisely, a perfect mother-son fit. As we lie quietly together, humiliating vignettes of the past twenty years flash behind my eyes. The torture, the beatings, the mental abuse. The rape. I shudder. At least Anton had never gotten to me. Why he'd spared me that fate, I'll never know, but it's not worth thinking about too much.

The only bright spot in my whole disastrous life is Finn, my *raison d'être*, my tiny hero, whom I love infinitely, in spite of his father. As he lies next to me now feigning sleep, my heart swells with pride. We're about to embark on the most important mission of our lives, and he knows exactly what is required of him.

To my utter astonishment, sometime around noon, his eyes had flickered open. He'd peered at me through two puffy, pink slits like a newborn gerbil I'd once seen at a pet store. But they'd been the most exquisite puffy pink slits I'd ever seen. At that moment, I'd known Finn was going to make it, and as he emerged from his groggy haze, I began preparing him for the "play" I'd cooked up. The one we would perform for Viktor.

It had been an ambitious endeavor to ask of my little boy, still wobbly and swollen from the effects of his brush with death, but he'd drunk up my plan thirstily and recited my instructions back to me almost verbatim.

Mr. Smileyface, I had explained, was a funny sort of play in which he and I would pretend to be asleep on my bed, and when Viktor came through the door, he would magically transform into Mr. Smileyface, even if he wasn't smiling. At that point, I'd said, Mr. Smileyface and mama would probably have a little tussle, a little "play-fight" *for fun*. I couldn't emphasize that point enough. He had to think it was all a big game of make-believe.

"What do you do if Mr. Smileyface pretends to hold Mommy down?" I'd quizzed him after a number of trial runs.

"Up the stairs!"

"Even if Mommy looks hurt?"

"Up the stairs!" he'd said, jumping up and down in front of me as I guided him back to the edge of the bed. His full attention was necessary.

The stairs. Finn had no idea what it felt like to climb stairs, so I'd stacked up some books and a chair in front of the table and led him up to the top by his hand. After three tries, he was scrambling up without my help and was having so much fun showing off his new skill he hadn't wanted to stop. The moment he reached the top, he'd throw his hands in the air and fly into my arms to do it again. He must have scaled the makeshift stairs two dozen times before I'd panicked and dismantled them for fear of Viktor showing up unexpectedly. I purposely hadn't taught Finn how to navigate back *down* the stairs.

"And what if Mr. Smileyface yells at you to stop? Or tries to pull you down the stairs?"

"Up, up!"

"Very good, sweetie. Yes. Mr. Smileyface might *seem* angry, but remember, it's a game, and he'll only be pretending. Won't it be fun?"

"Yep! Yep!" he'd said, swinging his feet excitedly, his eyes bouncing around the room.

"Look at me, sweetie, this is important. Good. Now what do you do when you get to the top of the st—"

"Open the door!"

Oh, he was smart! But like stairs, doors were pretty much foreign objects to him.

In order to demonstrate how one worked, I'd had him practice on our room's doorknob, pretending to turn it and pull it open. We also worked on pulling the shower stall door open so he could get an idea what it would feel like when the door swung open. He seemed to understand the concept that a real door would be heavier than the shower door and that he should be careful not to get knocked down by its weight. I prayed for an unlocked door leading to the outside world up there. Our whole plan hinged on it, in fact, and the only thing preventing Finn from busting out of the house was an overly complicated lock or too many locks. Hopefully it wouldn't come to that—to Finn navigating his escape solo. If my plan went smoothly, the two of us would run through that door together.

With every possible scenario rehearsed and all the potential hiccups addressed, my next step was to design a set and costumes for the opening night of *Mr. Smileyface*. I'd used one of Finn's felt markers to color our lips and eyelids a subtle shade of blue. I'd shoved my finger down my throat and vomited on the bed. I'd laid three painkillers and the empty bottle out near the top of the bed; the rest were hidden away in the cupboard. A tipped over glass on the nightstand was the final touch to our credible tableau.

We're ready, asshole. Come and get us.

And now, with Finn snuggled up next to me, I hear Viktor

clomping down the stairs. Finn sniggers. I shush him gently and he becomes absolutely still and quiet, even when I adjust my grip on the scissors concealed under his right shoulder. "Okay, sweetie," I breathe into his ear. "Let's show Mr. Smileyface what good actors we are."

Not a muscle twitches. Good boy.

By the time the door swings open, my heart is pounding so hard I worry Finn can feel it and will get spooked, but he remains stock still.

"Hey sweetheart," I hear Viktor say.

God, please give me strength.

Viktor touches my shoulder. Gives it a gentle wiggle when I don't move. Vomit rises in my throat. I suppress it. A bead of sweat pops out on my brow. *Patience.*

Viktor suddenly blurts, "*No!*" shaking my shoulder again, but with much more force. He must've seen the pill bottle.

"Wake up! Goddammit, you can't do this to me! Not now!"

The anguish in his voice makes me feel sorry for him somehow, but I have to stay focused. I roll over limply while he continues to shake me. I keep my eyes shut. As far as I can tell, Finn still hasn't moved. I let my left arm flop to the bed to distract Viktor while I whip the scissors out from under Finn and stab Viktor in the thigh.

Viktor gasps. Staggers backward. Stunned. He sinks down into one of the plastic chairs at the table as a crimson stain spreads down the leg of his navy uniform.

Finn, my little soldier, remains curled up on the bed unflinching, just like we'd rehearsed, and I realize he's awaiting direction. "*Now, Finn!*" I scream.

He jumps up, giggling with pure glee, flying off the bed.

As he runs toward the door—which is miraculously ajar—Viktor jumps from his chair, snagging Finn's arm. My poor little boy spins and falls, screeching when his head glances off the table leg. I take advantage of Viktor's change of focus to fly at him again with my scissors, this time sinking them into his neck below his left ear. He screams and wheels around.

I pull my weapon from his neck meaning to stab him again, but he kicks me and I stumble back, crashing to the floor. The scissors, now slick with blood, fly out of my hand and slide across the floor. I scramble after them on my hands and knees, vaguely aware of Viktor at my heels. As his hand clamps down on my ankle, I snatch up the scissors, turn, and stab him in the chest just below his collarbone three, maybe four times.

"Bitch!" he yells, wrenching the scissors from my grasp, but he loses grip and they go spinning off under the bed. He scuttles after them.

I see Finn push himself up. He rubs at his head, confused. Frightened.

I turn my attention back to Viktor, who's given up on the scissors and is now facing me, propped up against the bed on the floor. His hand is pressed against the hole in his neck and a rivulet of blood streams onto his white t-shirt like hot wax. Deep maroon flowers bloom on his chest, getting bigger by the second. I'm horrified, elated and proud of myself all at the same time. He scrunches his eyebrows together in a beseeching look. "What the fuck, Princess?"

"Finn! Are you okay, sweetie?" I say, keeping my eyes on Viktor.

"There's a egg," Finn answers. "On my head."

Great. I hope he doesn't have a concussion. "Are you dizzy?"

"*Shut up, bitch!*" Viktor yells, suddenly lurching toward me, grabbing hold of my wrists with both hands. I try to yank them away, but he's shockingly robust for someone with so many wounds.

"Finn. It's time to go," I say, turning to my son, giving him an encouraging smile. He just has to make it out of here, whether I do or not.

"Where?" Finn says, getting to his feet.

"You remember. Go on, baby. Just like we practised."

"*Finn! Sit the fuck down!*" Viktor screams.

Finn stares at Viktor a moment before turning his focus to the stairs. Then he just stands there, transfixed, shifting from foot to foot.

"*If you set one foot on those stairs, I will kill your mother. And then you!*"

Finn turns around, wide-eyed, looking to me for reassurance. I give him the slightest nod.

Suddenly Viktor lunges off the floor toward Finn.

"*NOW, Finn! Get going!*" I yell, jumping on Viktor's back. He teeters under my weight. Tries to shake me off. Banks left, then stumbles. We crash onto the table and I roll off his back and onto the floor. I look up just as his fist—

Chapter Twenty-Two

"Oh my God. That's Coop's father," I said again, turning onto North Glenora Road a fair distance behind the Firewing. No wonder I'd recognized him at the park. He was the slimy jerk from the hardware store years ago—the man Coop had passed off as his old boss.

I shook my head. How had I not suspected the Firewing might be *the Firewing* until this minute?

Outside, farmhouses, long driveways and sprawling fields of green pumpkins sped past in a blur. I started to cry. Morley was the whole reason I was about to learn about Isla's fate, good, bad, or otherwise.

Wiping tears from my cheeks, I accelerated to keep pace with Coop's father who'd sped up when he'd reached the country road. It wouldn't have mattered if I lost sight of the Firewing; I knew exactly where it was headed.

"I wonder if Coop knows," I said to the empty car.

I sighed. There was no way. He'd have blown the whistle on that monster for sure, father or not. He was going to be devastated when he found out.

I felt nauseous all of a sudden and rolled the window down to get some air.

The wind rushed past my ears as voices—both my own and those of others—rang out in my mind. Coop's was the loudest, the closest. His words flew past me in disjointed bursts: *You've been up to no good. Why so sneaky? You bitches have ruined my life.*

I shook my head to quiet the voices and focus on the beat up hot-rod up ahead. Isla was *right there*, terrified and alone, traveling toward an uncertain fate. If she was even still alive. Maybe the nasty blow Coop's father delivered to her at the park had already killed her. Maybe his plan was to bury her body on the acreage somewhere.

By the time I pulled over thirty yards short of the old man's house, I was itching to bolt out of the car and rip his head off. If only this hadn't been a timeblink. If only the asshole hadn't deposited his disgusting skin cells all over me at the hardware store.

The wind roared outside the car, jostling it slightly, and I swore under my breath at my lack of shoes and a coat. I glanced over my shoulder to the back seat and actually laughed when I saw it: Kitty Salazar's neatly folded yellow cardigan that seemed to have been placed there expressly for my use. Realizing the significance of its presence made me laugh even harder. *I* had been the car thief. *I* had stolen Kitty's sweater. It had been *my* DNA, not Isla's.

After composing myself, I wriggled into the sweater and reached for the door handle, noticing my hand was trembling. I imagined Morley just then—not Coop—cheering me on from the sidelines.

"*Don't be scared,*" he said. "*Put one foot in front of the other and remember...I love you.*"

It felt like I'd been granted the courage of an army. I climbed out of the car into the dull, blustery evening.

By the time I got to the garage, my delicate pink socks were riddled with burrs, twigs and dead leaves, making me angrier by the minute. That old fuck was lucky I couldn't deck him. As I pulled the worst of the prickles out of my socks, I eyed the house. It had been in better shape back then, though it still carried the distinct air of neglect. The basement windows were boarded up just like they'd been the night I'd followed Coop here. I shivered and wrapped the cardigan tighter around me. Suddenly the side door to the garage banged open. A tiny, blindfolded wisp of a girl emerged, hands secured behind her back. I clapped a hand over my mouth to suppress a scream.

Isla.

It was torture, not being able to run over there, pick her up, and whisk her away from this awful place. Without warning, I bent over and vomited in a clump of weeds next to the garage. It provided no relief. I wiped my mouth on a dusty tissue I'd found in Kitty's sweater and edged closer to Isla and her captor.

The details of these moments, moments where I could easily picture me in her place, would haunt my thoughts forever. That could have been me. *Should* have been me.

Below the faded red handkerchief acting as a blindfold over Isla's eyes, a strip of duct tape spanned the lower half of her face so that only her little nose peeped out. The handkerchief was wet with tears and she was drawing clipped, panicked breaths through her nose. A green scrunchie held her hair in a loose ponytail, which was askew and artlessly pinned to her head under the blindfold. And then, the most obvious sign of Isla's terror: a dark spot spreading halfway down her leggings from where she'd wet herself in terror.

Tears pooled in my eyes as she shuffled clumsily along the path, trying to keep upright in the stiff gusts of wind. Right behind her came Coop's father, prodding her, telling her not to worry, everything was going to be okay.

"Asshole," I said.

By this time, I was so close I could hear the old man's raspy breath—surely the product of decades of smoking and hard drinking. I followed alongside Isla, foolishly imploring her to run away. She took a couple of unsteady steps on the cracked concrete sidewalk, lost her balance and toppled to the ground, letting out a muffled scream. Instinctively, I swooped down to help her up, but stopped when I remembered I couldn't.

"Viktor! Get your ass out here!" the old man yelled over his shoulder.

Seconds later, a lanky, long-haired teenaged boy dressed in jeans and a beat-up leather jacket stalked out of the garage.

"What?" the boy said, sounding both annoyed and terrified at the same time. His hair hung in long greasy ropes that covered his face. His gaze seemed to be fixed on the ground or his feet, anywhere but Isla.

"Help me get her into the goddamned house, you useless piece of shit!"

When the kid tossed his hair over his shoulder, exposing his face, I gasped and backed away, my knees buckling. I collapsed in a heap.

A young Coop.

The scene unfolded in front of me like a horror movie I didn't want to watch yet felt absolutely compelled to look at just the same. Isla's muffled cries. The old man barking orders. Viktor—*Coop*—scooping Isla off the walk and throwing her over his shoulder like he'd done with Kendall mere hours ago in present time.

When my senses came back, I realized I was bawling uncontrollably.

After the three of them disappeared into the house, I dragged myself off the ground and staggered out to the road, sobbing. I didn't even notice the truck speeding toward me. It swerved, missing me by inches, sliding sideways on some loose gravel.

"*Fucking asshole!*" I screamed back in the direction of the house.

"Whoa, lady, are you okay?" I heard a man's voice say behind me.

I spun around to face the man, who had pulled the truck to the side of the road and was rolling down his window to check on me.

"My sister's been kidnapped!" I shouted, pointing to the house behind me.

Long tendrils of my hair whirled around me in the wind as the man jumped out of his truck and approached me carefully. The man was short and thickset, like a bodybuilder, and looked as though he could've lifted his truck above his head without effort. "*Kidnapped?* Are you joking?" he said, looking curiously at my socked feet and then to the house.

"You have to help her! Please!"

"I'll go get the cops," he said, turning back to his truck. I briefly wondered why he didn't pull out his cell phone, remembering it was 1999, before everyone on the planet owned one.

"No, no! She's in danger! We have to help her!" I said, grabbing his thick arm, pulling him toward the house.

Over the maelstrom of the storm I heard him sigh, as though this wasn't the first time he'd had to rescue a damsel in distress. Considering my age, he probably didn't even realize that the damsel was a helpless child. "Okay, I'll go. But you're staying here."

My heart soared. Fresh tears streamed down my cheeks. The past *could* be changed after all. *That* was the reason Morley had sent me here.

The man ran back to his truck and produced a wooden baseball bat from behind the seat then hustled by me. At the bottom of the stairs he stopped and looked down at the bat as if he couldn't figure out how it had gotten there. A moment later he turned and stalked back to his truck.

"Where are you going?"

"You're fine, aren't you?" he said, tossing the bat through

the driver's side window into the cab. "And listen, you shouldn't run into the road like that, or next time you *will* get hit."

It was like he'd been asleep since he'd nearly run me over. "But my sister!"

He shot me a confused look then scrambled into his truck. The wind pushed the door shut with a bang.

"Can you call the police?" I said, running up to his window.

"Fuck that! I didn't even hit you!" He cranked up the window and sped away with gravel spewing from his back tires, and I watched until his tail lights disappeared into the darkness.

Absolutely baffled, I turned back to the house. Why would Morley send me here if it wasn't to help Isla escape? I reached for the talisman, but hesitated. This timeblink wasn't finished yet. Kitty Salazar's car had been returned that same night and I had been the one driving it. At least I knew that part of the puzzle.

It was everything else to follow that I had no idea about.

Chapter Twenty-three

My only thought when I got back to The Cave involved breaking the fuck out of there. Kendall was sprawled out spread-eagle on the floor, mumbling to herself. If ever I needed her help it was now.

"Kenny! Get up!" I yelled, crouching down next to her, patting her cheeks. "Come on, come on!"

Her eyes fluttered open. Squiggly red veins stood out against the whites of her eyes. She tried to speak but her tongue was thick and dry, so she slurred when she murmured my name.

"It's okay," I said, helping her into the chair. I grabbed a can of Coke off the shelf and gave her a few sips, finishing the rest myself.

With Kendall settled, I went to the door and banged on it with my fists, screaming at the top of my lungs. When my voice went hoarse and I couldn't scream anymore, I remembered the golf club and ran over to it, inadvertently slamming my foot down on some broken glass.

"*Shit, shit, shit!*" I screeched, tearing the bloodied sock off my foot.

"Syd?" I heard Kendall murmur. I limped over to her. She

was shaking. Her eyebrows seemed to form two sideways question marks.

"Oh, Kenny. Are you okay?"

She nodded, wincing. "Headache."

"Do you know where you are?"

"Cave?"

The one-word sentences would have to suffice. At least the words were coherent and she understood where she was.

As I was wrapping my foot with a flannel dust rag and pulling my sock back on, there was a light knock at the door. I sprang to my feet.

"Hello?" came a muffled voice.

A female voice.

I lunged for the door, plastering my ear against it, ignoring my sore foot. "*Help!*"

"Are you locked in?" Had this stranger—this angel—been walking by the house, heard my screams and let herself in? This was no time to postulate. She was here now.

"Yes! There should be a key hanging on a hook above the washing machine."

She didn't say anything for a full minute that felt more like ten. "There's no key, dear," she reported.

"Damnit!" I yelled, banging the door with my fist. Coop must've taken it with him.

"There *is* an axe, dear," came the mild-mannered voice a moment later. "Shall I use it?"

"*Yes! Please! Yes!*" I was almost laughing by this point.

"Stand back."

"I'm back. Way back. Go ahead!"

Where I had expected heavy, violent hacking, there were a series of soft, intermittent taps that wouldn't have knocked over a kitten. It went on for about two minutes before the woman said, "I'm just going to take a break. My shoulder. It's not good on the best of days."

"It's okay…" I said, approaching the door. "Who are you anyway?"

"It's Mrs. Vanderthorpe, dear. From across the street."

I slapped my hand over my mouth and shot a wide-eyed look at Kendall. "*The Nose!*" I mouthed. She gave me a goofy grin.

"You take all the time you need, Mrs. Vanderthorpe. We're not going anywhere," I said.

Kendall rubbed at her temples with her fingertips. She was still groggy but getting better. "What did Coop do to me?" She asked, her voice surprisingly clear.

"I'll tell you everything later. Promise."

"Dear?" I heard Mrs. Vanderthorpe say.

"Yes?"

"Are you Sydney?"

Kendall flashed me a surprised smile.

"Yes. I didn't honestly think you knew my name."

"Oh, the whole town knows your name, dear. Well, at least the whole neighborhood does. Your family went through some troubling times many years ago."

She said this as if I didn't know.

"Your mother was very distraught," she continued. "A lovely woman, that Maggie. I do miss our chats. She used to come for tea while you girls were at school. Before and after your sister went missing. Especially after. We were both grieving terrible losses, and we found strength in each other's company."

My lips curled into a frown. I hadn't known about a special friendship between my mother and Mrs. V. Maybe I'd just been too young to remember.

"I'm sure she appreciated you, too," I said to the door.

"Sydney?" she said.

"Yes?"

"Shall I call the police?"

"*No!*" Oh God, no. Kenny and I were going out to Glenora to deal with Coop ourselves.

"It seems to me this is just the kind of thing the police could help you with."

"Yes, Mrs. Vanderthorpe. I know. It's just something I would rather handle myself. You understand, right? Surely you and your husband used to have little tiffs every once in a while?"

Silence.

"I'm sorry, I didn't mean to remind you of—"

"Oh, it's okay, dear. I like it when people talk about George."

I smiled. This lady wasn't the horrible person we'd assumed she was. Nosy, yes. Misunderstood, perhaps. Horrible, no.

"Dear?"

"Yes?"

"I just noticed a key lying on the stairs. It's the kind that might fit this padlock. Shall I try it?"

I rolled my eyes at Kendall who was looking brighter by the moment.

"Yes, please, Mrs. Vanderthorpe. Please try the key."

I heard some scraping and fiddling and imagined thin, knobby fingers taking clumsy stabs at the lock. Thirty seconds later, the door swung open. I nearly knocked the frail little thing over when I threw my arms around her.

"Thank you! Thank you so much!" I repeated hoarsely.

"It's okay, Sydney. That's what neighbors are for. Are you sure you wouldn't like me to call the police?"

"Yes, I'm sure," I said. Kendall shuffled out of The Cave and gave our savior a quick hug.

"Thank you," Kendall said. "What made you come over? Did you hear Syd screaming?"

"No dear," she said. "I happened to glance at your living room window and saw Mr. Levin throwing you over his shoulder. At first I thought he was showing off one of his fancy fire-fighter moves to Sydney, but when he peeled out of here in that obnoxious car a little while later, with no sign of either of you girls, I thought I'd better come have a look-see."

"We can't thank you enough. It's nice to have neighbors that care. After you," I said, eager to get out of the basement before Coop or Viktor or whoever the hell that monster was came home.

When Mrs. V mounted the stairs, Kendall flashed me a smirk that seemed to say, *"See, she's pretty decent after all."* I swatted her butt and told her to get moving, then followed them both up the stairs.

"Do you girls have time for a nice cup of tea?" Mrs. V asked when we reached the top.

As comforting as that sounded, I was desperate to shuffle her on her way and get going. "We'll take a rain check on that, Mrs. V, er Vanderthorpe."

"You can call me Diane, dear." she said, looking around the living room tenderly, as if recalling a memory. I started toward the door and she moved with me reluctantly while Kendall flopped onto the sofa.

"Let's get together soon, Diane," I said as she stepped onto the porch. She ambled down the stairs and along the path, waving her hand in the air without looking back.

"God, I thought she'd never leave!" I blurted when the door clicked shut. "We gotta get the fuck outta here."

"What?" Kendall said from the sofa where she was hugging a cushion to her chest. "Where are we going?"

"It's a surprise," I said, jamming my bloodied foot into a boot. "Come on, get up."

"I'm tired. Can we go after a nap? I'm just so—"

"*What? No!* Shit, those must have been some strong drugs Coop gave you."

"I'm so *tired.*"

"Too bad. Get your ass up now! We're taking your car."

She hauled herself off the sofa and staggered over to her shoes and coat near the front door. As she struggled to put them on, I heard Jinx bark upstairs. "Meet you outside! I'm driving."

I opened the door to the spare bedroom a few seconds later to a very nervous but excited dog. Next to him lay the remains of two cell phones—mine and Kendall's—smashed to nearly unrecognizable bits, so even if I'd wanted to call the cops, Coop had taken the option away.

Jinx tried to jump up and lick my face, but he seemed sluggish and groggy, and I briefly wondered if Coop had given him some sort of sedative. I tried to coax him onto the sofa after carefully guiding him down to the living room. He was having none of it and practically wrapped his front legs around mine when I tried to close the front door on him. I relented and let him through. He lost his balance and tumbled down the last five stairs onto the sidewalk where he lay in a heap. By the time I reached him at the bottom of the stairs, he'd sprung to his feet and was shaking himself off. He relieved himself on the hydrangea bush next to the stairs as usual. I shook my head in disbelief.

"That dog is part cat," Kendall said from the sidewalk next to her car. It was a bright yellow sports coupe that I'd never seen before, an Audi, I think. Perfect. We'd be in Glenora in no time. As I loaded Jinx and Kendall into the sexy little speed machine, I cast a mildly guilty eye at my old rusted Civic before tearing away from the curb. Mrs. V waved at us from her living room window, teacup in hand. I waved back.

Chapter Twenty-four

"**W**hat?" Kendall yelled, her voice deadened by cramped interior of the car.

We were halfway to Glenora when Kendall finally started resembling her old chipper self. I slammed the car into fifth then checked myself; I didn't need the cops on my tail right now.

"I just found out today."

"He owns a house in Glenora? Is it on an acreage?"

"Isn't it enough that he owns an entire house that he's never told me about?"

Kendall considered this. "Not really. Brett's come across that kind of thing before. You should hear some of the stories…"

I barely heard her. I was too busy thinking about Isla, and as we neared the house under a starry sky fifteen minutes later, I began to weep.

"Squid? Are you okay?"

"Yeah. I think so," I said, brushing away a tear, sniffing. I'd waited more than half my life for this day. Runaway emotions were part of the package.

We were close now. I could see the pinpoint of the porch light shining up ahead.

"There it is," I said, glancing at Kendall.

"Look out!" She yelled, grabbing the wheel.

I slammed on the brakes. The car swerved to the left, fishtailed, and veered off the road into a shallow ditch with a bump. Everything went quiet but for the ticking of the stalled engine.

"What the hell, Kenny?"

"There was something on the road!"

"I didn't see anything." I re-started the car and began backing out of the ditch.

"Wait!" she yelled.

I hit the brakes. Kendall flung her door open and jumped out of the car without closing it. Jinx scrambled out after her.

"What's going on? I yelled. I couldn't see Kendall but heard Jinx barking.

A moment later, I heard screaming—screeching more like —but it wasn't Kendall.

"Syd! Quick!"

I turned off the engine and climbed out of the car. This was infuriating. We were so close.

As the screeching got louder, more panicked, I realized the voice belonged to a child, and when I got closer I saw a tiny fair-haired boy standing in some tall grass at the side of the road, crying and screaming and batting at Kendall's arms as she tried to reach out and console him. Jinx was barking now, too. I shooed him away and he dashed off into a nearby field.

"What on Earth?" I said.

The boy's head whipped around when he heard my voice and we locked eyes. At once he stopped screaming and bolted toward me. I stooped down and he jumped into my arms.

"It's okay, shhhh. You're safe," I said, casting Kendall a confused look which she returned.

I rocked the little boy gently back and forth, stroking his head like I'd done countless times with Devin and Connor when they'd been hurt or were scared. "What's your name, sweetie?" I asked.

He didn't answer.

Kendall's hand went up to her mouth, no doubt thinking about her own two boys, safe at home with their father. "It's like he knows you," she said though her fingers.

The little boy was surprisingly strong as he clung to me, snuggling his face into my neck. For reasons I didn't understand, I started crying again. The boy leaned back to look at me then returned his head to my neck, hugging me tighter still.

"We have to find his parents." Kendall said.

"Not yet. We have something to do first."

"Are you insane? His parents are probably freaking out!"

To appease her, I said to the boy, "Where do you live, sweetie?"

Without taking his head off my shoulder, he pointed up the road.

"Where?" I said. Three houses stood in the direction of his outstretched finger: Coop's neglected shack and two warmly lit heritage homes further along the road. I remembered seeing a little boy playing piano in one of them when I'd been here before and figured it had been him.

I brushed past Kendall and slid into the passenger seat with the boy in my arms. "You're driving now."

The boy's eyes nearly popped out of his head when he saw the flashy buttons and glowing lights on the dashboard. I understood his fascination immediately. The first time I'd ridden in one of Kendall's fancy cars it had felt like I'd been in an alien spaceship.

Moments later, to my surprise, Kendall pulled into Coop's driveway. I'd been sure she would skip his house given its run-down state, opting instead for one of the lovely houses up the road.

"Do you live here, sweetie?" I asked, playing along.

The boy, still marvelling over the dashboard lights, glanced up at the house and then at me. He giggled. "Silly mama."

A jolt of electricity went from the base of my neck through my spine.

Kendall gave the child a pitying look as she got out and came around to the passenger door and tried to take his hand, but I held him tight. Thoughts swirled around in my head. Fast, urgent thoughts that I struggled to piece together.

A little boy. Near Coop's house. Who'd mistaken *me* for his mother.

"Come on, honey, time to go." Kendall's voice echoed somewhere far off.

At once the puzzle pieces slammed together. I took the little boy's face in my hands as tears spilled onto my cheeks.

"Uh, Syd?" Kendall said.

The boy reached up and gently patted my hands.

I wrapped my arms around the little guy and squeezed him so tight I thought he might break. I pulled him away from me, laughing and crying at the same time. I said to the boy, "Tell the lady your name."

"Syd," Kendall interrupted. "What's going on?"

"It's okay, you can tell her," I said, rubbing the boy's back.

Looking at a spot near Kendall's feet, he said shyly, "Finn."

"Finn!" I shrieked. "Isla's teddy bear was named Finn!"

He giggled again, a little more nervously this time, and leaned into me. I crawled out of the car with him and faced Kendall.

"Kenny, meet Finn!"

Kendall put her hands on my shoulders searching my eyes for any trace of sanity. It was the sanest I'd felt in years.

I pulled away from her grip. "You're not going to believ—"

"Put him the fuck down!"

Our attention snapped to the voice coming from the front steps of the house.

Coop.

Finn tightened his arms around me. It seemed like he would climb right inside my body if it were possible, but I had to get him away from me. Get him to safety. The car door was still open. I peeled Finn off me and shoved him into the car, uttering reassurances as best as I could over his screaming. There was no time to be gentle.

I slammed the door shut. Turned and braced myself.

Coop came limping toward us. His face, his t-shirt, and his jeans were covered in blood. Something shiny in his hand glinted in the low evening light. A butcher's knife.

My heart dropped. We were too late. But the battle was far from over. We scattered, Kendall toward the road, me to the house. Coop's injuries were serious enough to slow him down, but not enough to stop him. He lunged at me as I passed but he lost his balance and fell. I used the distraction to run up the stairs. When I looked back, Coop was already on his feet, stumbling toward the car. At the end of the driveway, Kendall raised her hand. The car beeped twice.

Perfect. She'd locked Finn inside. He was terrified, no doubt. But safe.

"Bitches! You're gonna pay for this!" Coop yelled as he banged his fist on the roof of the car and started stabbing at the window with his knife. I could hear Finn screaming bloody murder inside.

Kendall threw a wild look to me at the top of the stairs that said, *"Where the hell are you going?"* But there was no time to explain. I had to trust that she could handle Coop by herself for a few minutes, which surely wouldn't be too difficult given his injuries…injuries I allowed myself to believe had been inflicted by Isla.

I rushed into the house.

Chapter Twenty-five

My heart thudded in my chest. *This is it*, I thought as I entered the house. It smelled of stale cigarettes and dirty linen. I passed through a dingy kitchen into a short hallway lined with stacks of old books and magazines. Between two small bedrooms was a staircase leading down to the basement.

I took a breath and went down.

At the bottom of the stairs stood a riveted metal door bearing an assortment of locks. I shuddered. It reminded me of a vault door at a bank, but unlike a vault, the locks were designed to keep something in rather than out. Above the doorknob were two deadbolts and two sliding locks. None of them were engaged. In fact, the door was slightly ajar.

I poked my head inside, overcome instantly with a medley of smells: puke, sweat, unwashed hair. Something floral. The scene suggested a fight had taken place. A bedside lamp with a crumpled shade lay on the floor, its bulb flickering. The floor was littered with toppled furniture, dishes, wilted lilies, and books. Smudges of blood adorned the floor and walls. I set a plastic chair upright, and it was when I crouched to pick up the lamp that I saw her. Spattered in blood, slumped on the floor against the wall at the end of a small bed. Her hair hung in tangled bloody clumps across her face. The one eye I could see was swollen shut.

I sprinted over and dropped down next to her, wrapping my arms around her shoulders, pulling her to my chest. She was limp. But warm.

"Isla!" I rocked her in my arms. Her head lolled onto my shoulder, bloodied hair stuck to my neck. *He'd* done this to her. My supposed soulmate, who was outside right now doing what? He was in pretty rough shape. Not as bad as Isla, but close. She'd obviously put up quite the fight down here.

Her body suddenly convulsed in my arms, and tears spilled down my face. "Come on, girl! You're so close!" I hugged her tighter, trying to make us whole again.

"I'm so sorry, Isla, I'm so, so sorry."

Finally I pulled her off my shoulder and laid her down. She shuddered again and moaned so softly I could barely hear it. Her head rolled to one side, and she moaned louder this time, like Kendall had earlier when she'd come to. My hand flew up to my mouth.

"Come on, Isla. Finn needs you. I need you," I said, stroking her bloodied cheek.

She stirred. Licked her cracked, bloodied lips. I jumped up and filled a glass with water. Dove back down to her.

"Here. Drink this," I said, cradling her head. She took a tiny sip. Coughed weakly. Her eyes flickered open.

I burst into tears when her eyes met mine, and I couldn't stop.

I had so many things to tell her! That I was sorry for leaving her at the park. That it should have been me. That I'd never given up on her. That I loved her. So much. I had questions too, some I would probably never ask.

I pushed hair out of her face and saw that she was crying, too. Through my sobs, I said, "It's okay, hon, shhh. It's okay. You're safe now. Finn's safe too."

I helped her sit up and gave her another sip of water. She slung an arm around my shoulder. We wept together. Neither of us spoke. We rocked back and forth, clinging to one another, quivering with sadness for all the lost years; with rage for the injustices inflicted upon her. With joy.

I could've lived in that moment forever. That moment where decades of speculation and torment came to an end, where order was restored to the world, where Isla was finally free to reclaim her life. She was beat up and bruised and exhausted, but she was free, and when we could cry no more, she pulled her head off my shoulder and asked me to help her up.

"We should wait for an ambulance," I said.

"No," she said, wincing when she moved. "I'm getting out of here *now*."

I couldn't argue with her, no matter how battered she was. I secured her arm around my shoulder and helped her take the first steps toward freedom. This was the way it was supposed to be. Not a team of police officers swooping in and scaring Isla and Finn half to death. I'd been destined to find her.

We climbed the stairs, step by unsteady step, to the main floor, stopping twice for Isla to balance herself. I didn't know if she was dizzy from a concussion or from the overwhelming knowledge that she was finally free.

"Where did you find Finn?" she asked when we mounted the top stair.

"Strolling down the road like he owned it."

"My brave boy."

We shuffled through the living room toward the front door and were just about to go outside when Isla said, "I can't wait for Mom and Dad to meet him. And Kendall."

I smiled at her, knowing that now wasn't the time for explanations that would upset her. "Let's do this."

When the door swung open, the cool night air whooshed

over us. Isla looked radiant in the moonlight despite her gangly frame, despite all she'd endured. I surveyed the driveway where I'd left Coop, Kendall and Finn, and I could see Finn's little blonde head in the passenger seat of the Audi where it was still parked in the driveway, but there was no sign of Coop or Kendall. *Great. Now what?*

Oblivious to my concern and the possibility that Coop might come at her again, Isla closed her eyes and drew in a big breath through her nose, savoring the sweet smell of freedom.

"Why don't you sit here a minute," I said, lowering her to the porch landing.

"Where's Finn?" she asked, her eyes darting about the yard.

"He's in the car. See? Just sit tight. I have to find Kendall."

I jumped off the last stair and went to investigate.

When I came around the other side of the car, I took a small, panicked breath. Kendall was pinned to the ground with Coop on her back. He was facing me, grimacing, maybe in pain, maybe with glee. Probably both, I decided. And he was holding the knife to Kendall's throat.

"We've been waiting for you," Coop said through clenched teeth. I didn't recognize him anymore. He'd fully become Viktor, the abductor. There was nothing left of my sweet, loving Coop. If things turned ugly and I had to use force, it would be helpful to remember that.

"Coop," I said pleadingly.

"I called the cops. They're on their way," Kendall managed to say with her cheek squished against the gravel. I wasn't about to point out that her phone was lying in a hundred pieces on the floor back at my house. Coop was in such a state that seemed to have forgotten this fact.

"You're gonna regret that, bitch!" he said, lifting Kendall's head by the hair, slamming it down.

"Let her go, Coop. We can all walk away from this right now."

"Ha! Like I'd let *you* walk away."

"Look, you're scaring Finn." The little boy, I noticed, was tucked inside the car, in the passenger seat, staring out the window blankly. He appeared to be in shock.

"*Shut up!* Do not talk about *my son*. I suppose you found his mother, your pathetic little long-lost twin. Too bad she attacked me…even worse that I had to fight back. Oh well. One less problem to deal with."

Kendall's eye, the one not pressed into the ground, grew wide.

"Here's how things are gonna go, *wifey*," Coop said as a drop of blood trickled down his face and onto Kendall's jacket. "I'm gonna slit this bitch's throat, then I'm gonna do the same thing to you."

Kendall squirmed. Coop adjusted his weight over her.

"If only the three of you hadn't been so *goddamned stubborn!* But now you've gone and made the old twin switcheroo impossible. And you're all to blame equally. *Every single one of you.*"

"Coop, pleas—"

"*Shut up!* You're gonna hear me out so you can die knowing you brought this on *yourselves!*"

If the knife hadn't been positioned so close to Kendall's jugular vein, I would've jumped on him right there.

"Then I'm gonna bury you bitches in the meadow, take my fucking son, and start a new life somewhere far away from this *hell hole*. He deserves a better childhood than the one I was dealt."

He'd truly lost his mind to seriously think he could kill the three of us and toddle off into the sunset with Finn tucked under his arm? I just had to hang on long enough to—

Out of the darkness, a blur of chocolate-colored fur blew past me, launching into the air and straight at Coop's face, knocking him over. The knife went flying. Kendall scurried to her feet as I lunged and snatched the knife off the ground. Coop scrambled, trying to stand, but the gash in his leg held him back.

By this time, Jinx had circled around and was crouched in front of Coop, snarling and barking, daring him to get up.

"Don't move!" I said, pointing the knife in Coop's direction. He stopped in his tracks, but not because I'd told him to. He was looking past me in a sort of stunned awe—like he'd seen a ghost—and I followed his gaze over my shoulder. Isla had come around the car, and she was brandishing a rather menacing-looking knife of her own. God love her, she must've grabbed it from the kitchen.

"What the—? *Isla?!*" Kendall screeched, her eyes darting back and forth between me and Isla, as if trying to make sure she wasn't seeing double. She dissolved into tears, probably wishing she could come over and hug her little sister, but she held her ground.

Isla lowered her knife, a little embarrassed it seemed, and gave Kendall a timid wave.

We had Coop trapped—Isla, Kendall and Jinx and I—the four of us braced for any sudden movement. As I toyed with different ideas about what to do next, I heard a car traveling up the road.

"The cops!" I yelled, for Coop's benefit. I knew, of course, that it wasn't the police, but maybe the people in the car could help.

As if reading my mind, Kendall stepped into the road just far enough to flag the car down. Someone in it was bound to have a cell phone at least. As the car slowed, bright flashes of red and blue suddenly filled the darkness, bouncing off the house, the Audi, all of us gathered there. Kendall, who had bits of gravel imbedded in her right cheek, looked the most surprised out of everyone.

The police car rolled to a stop, engine still running, and

after a few moments, the driver's side door opened. Shielded by the car, the female police officer climbed out and yelled, "Everything okay here?"

Clearly everything was not okay, not with a dog barking incessantly at a bloodied, injured man on his knees surrounded by a circle of women, two of whom were identical twins holding kitchen knives, but the officer was giving us an opportunity to volunteer the information.

As Kendall opened her mouth to answer, the cop yelled, "Hold that thought." She pulled out her CB and spoke into it. I couldn't hear what she was saying, but I imagined she was describing the scene to a colleague back at the station, calling for backup at the same time, no doubt.

"Does anybody need medical help?" she shouted.

Nobody spoke.

"An ambulance is on the way regardless, more officers too. Anybody care to fill me in on what's going on? How about you, firefighter Levin? Looks like you've been busy since I last saw you."

Epilogue

SEPTEMBER 6, 2019

Morley

Sydney lowered herself to the chair, her eyes wide as she took in the elegant table for two I'd laid out. A jewel-pink sunset glinted off the polished silverware and gold-rimmed china I'd inherited from my mother when I was sixteen, and my late grandmother's crystal goblets held sparkling apple juice, its lively bubbles whisking upward and popping like tiny amber fireworks at the surface. The French linen tablecloth Collette had bought on our trip to Nice the year before she died was spread out under the tableware. Delicate treasures, like the women who'd once cherished them.

Starting with the blink to Chapman Falls, Syd had been to Sandalwood ninety-seven times and to my apartment in the city eighteen, for a total of 115 blinks since I'd given her the talisman. We'd made every single moment count.

"Everything okay?" I said to her across the table.

"Are you kidding? It's magical." She drew her napkin out from under the silverware and laid it across her lap. She looked magical herself in her black sleeveless cocktail dress and upswept hair, her face lit from the side by the pink evening sun.

I slipped into my seat and gestured toward the board of meats and cheeses. Syd partook, placing a triangle of mortadella on a cracker with ruffled edges.

"Ah, mortadella," I said, picking up a slice, studying it like one of my lab specimens. "The fanciest bologna you'll ever eat."

Syd giggled, her mouth full. When she finished the morsel, I picked up my glass and raised it to make a toast.

"To your precious Isla," I said. She lifted her glass, tipping it to mine with a delicate *ting*. It sounded like an ending.

"To the beautiful Collette."

We both took sips to honour our loved ones like we'd done at The Merryport so many times before.

"And to Finn," I added, raising my glass a little higher before taking another sip.

"Of course. How could we forget my sweet little nephew?"

"How's he doing, anyway?"

"Still good. Much better than any of us expected. He's like a little sponge, soaking up everything this big, crazy world has to offer, good and bad."

"And Isla? Any improvement?"

"Not really. She still shakes when people get too close unless it's one of us. She's still mourning our mother's death. It took her no time to figure it out, you know, the reason for the suicide."

"She'll be okay. She's strong."

"I know. It's just...I still can't believe what he did to her."

"And to you. At least he won't be doing it to anyone else, not from his prison cell. Unless he has a dragonfly talisman we don't know about."

Syd shook her head, ignoring my quip. "I missed it, all that time. Even Kendall sensed he was evil. I'd never understood her stickiness toward him, why they'd gotten on each other's nerves so much, but just yesterday she admitted that even *she* couldn't explain it…only that she'd always felt something was off. What does that say about me as a judge of character?"

"He was a chameleon, Syd. A master of disguise. His own father probably hadn't even seen it coming."

"What, the murder? Pff. The old prick deserved it. That's the one courtesy Coop, *Viktor*, performed the whole time Isla was in captivity."

"Yep. If he'd been alive when Isla turned nineteen…" I couldn't say the words out loud, it was too horrendous. "Well, things could have been a lot worse for her."

Syd shuddered. "So much worse. And as much as it stings me to say it, even now, I'm glad Viktor loved her. It probably saved her life."

"At the very least, it prevented Anton from violating her."

Syd sighed. "I'll never understand why he went along with his father's plan, though, right from the beginning. He was old enough to know better. Why didn't he just play the hero and let her go the first chance he got?"

"The defense lawyer painted Viktor as a victim, someone who'd been emotionally and physically abused his whole life by his father. You'd be surprised at the effects that has on a child. They grow up feeling powerless, and it often doesn't stop in the teen or adult years."

"He said as much at the trial. Apparently he had to go along with whatever Anton told him to do or he'd 'chop him up and feed him to the neighbor's pigs'." Syd put the piece of cheese she was eating down on her plate like she'd lost her appetite.

I shook my head. Anton had definitely ruined his son's life, but the law doesn't care about an offender's pitiable past. Not when he's been a party to kidnapping, forcible confinement, torture. Serial rape.

"At least the old fuck never got his hands on her. Sexually, anyway."

I noticed she didn't bring up that while Anton hadn't raped Isla, Viktor most certainly had.

We sat in silence for a long moment, watching the final sliver of sun dip behind the hills.

"So, what's the occasion anyway? Hoping to lure me into bed?" she said, giving me a mischievous smile, lightening the mood.

"Come on, you know it takes way less effort than that. No, this spread is for much nobler purposes. I'm calling it a formal celebration of Isla and Finn's new life."

She swept her eyes over the glamorous table and sighed. "I wish Isla could see all of this."

"What? You mean like bring her here, on a timeblink?" I winced. Hadn't planned on telling her tandem blinking was possible. Not yet. I'd just learned about it yesterday myself.

She appeared not to catch the slip. "No. God, no. I would never tell Isla about timeblinking. She's anxious enough. Besides, you told me not to tell anyone."

"You told Kendall," I reminded her as I leapt up to check on the prime rib.

"Yes, but I didn't tell her how it was done." She smiled and took another sip of her drink.

"Have you told your family about this place yet? That you own it outright?"

She shook her head, a little sheepishly I thought.

I closed the oven door and walked back to the table, oven mitts on my hips, "Really? What about the penthouse? The Bayliner? The chalet at Whistler? You haven't told them about those, either?"

"I'm working on it."

"Have you thought about letting Isla and Finn move into the penthouse? There's plenty of room for both of them. Three bedrooms. View of the harbor. Gym. Rooftop deck."

"The condo is spectacular, Morley, it really is. But I wouldn't count on Isla to get too excited about it. She's so afraid to go anywhere. Feels safest in our childhood home."

"That's understandable. So why don't *you* move into it?"

"Isla doesn't want to be alone." Syd stuck out her bottom lip and shrugged. "And maybe I don't want to, either."

An hour later, we pushed back from the table to retreat to the living room with full bellies. Syd curled up in front of me on the sofa and we watched the fire as it crackled and spat. For a few minutes, it was the only sound within the muffled quiet of the log walls. Any other day I would've described the room as cozy, but where the sun from earlier had brightened everything with a warm promise of the future, a dullness had settled in around us. I closed my eyes, drawing her closer.

"You've been visiting me for what, four months now, your time?" I said.

"Has it been that long?"

"It *is* February in your world right now."

"Hmm. Time flies when…I mean, time *blinks* when you're having fun," she said, chuckling to herself. She wasn't making this easy.

"It has been a wonderful journey. Did you know you've visited me over a hundred times now?"

"That's a silly question. You're well aware I've recorded every visit in my journal, right down to the minute. Double-booking be damned," she laughed.

'Double booking' had been a prickly little thorn in our sides, especially lately, with dwindling dates available on the calendar where Syd wasn't already here. A few weeks ago, while I stood in a hot shower at my penthouse in the city, future-Syd entered my bathroom, dropped her clothing piece by piece, and had her way with me for the next twenty minutes. We'd run out of hot water.

Then another Syd dropped in unannounced.

Luckily, *that* Syd had been able to see her counterpart already busy with me and backed out of the bathroom immediately. She'd told me later how jealous she'd been, especially since the shower sex hadn't yet occurred in her timeline. It had been a lesson well learned, though, prompting Syd to start keeping track in a journal for fear of already being there. The whole arrangement was getting complicated.

"It's especially interesting when you refer to something you've mentioned on a visit that hasn't happened for me yet. Those twisty little puzzles are always fun to piece together."

"Sorry about that. I really should've been following a more chronological pattern with my timeblinks from the beginning."

"Regardless, love, I'm glad you're here tonight. I wanted it to be extra special."

She looked up at me from my chest. "You have *not* disappointed."

Syd nestled her head back down, and we snuggled in silence, watching the fire. I couldn't put this off any longer.

"Why do you think I chose you as my timeblinking protégé?"

She didn't even pause. "Because you said I had the most to gain from everyone you knew."

"You certainly did. And I've not regretted giving you that talisman once throughout this whole thing. Best decision of my life."

Syd fell silent. She picked up my hand and held the back of it to her lips.

"I have a confession, my dear," I said tenderly to ease the heaviness of heart we both felt.

"Uh oh," Syd said. "I get nervous when you say that."

The wind picked up outside, brushing a tree branch against a window. I pressed on.

"The minute we met, my heart nearly jumped out of my chest. I was drawn to you, like a bee to a flower, even before I'd discovered the power of the talisman."

"Pretty sure you already told me that," she said.

"You have to stop, love."

She didn't respond, as if pretending not to hear me.

I took a nervous breath. "You have to stop visiting me."

As expected, she pushed off my chest to face me, the space between her brows forming a tight knot. I grasped both of her hands in mine.

"We knew it would have to end at some point. It's September sixth, sweetheart."

"No," she said, shaking her head, tears brimming. "No. I need you, Morley. You need *me*."

"Syd. I love you more than anyone I've ever loved before. Even Collette, *sorry Collette*," I said, looking at the ceiling. "But we know how this story ends."

She shook her head, squeezing my hands tighter as though she was trying to protect the only thing that had ever made sense in her life, and I instantly hated myself for doing this.

"It doesn't have to end," she said, but I could hear the doubt in her voice.

We rested our foreheads together while the fire cracked and hissed in the background. My groin stirred. Goddammit, I couldn't help it. Thankfully, she felt it too.

Suddenly we were peeling clothes off each other, frantically, ferociously, as if it meant the difference between life and death. We didn't even bother going upstairs. Someone—me? Syd?—shoved the coffee table aside. I laid Syd down on the rug and entered her hungrily. We screamed. We cried. We held each other so tight I felt we might break bones, and afterwards, we stayed next to each other looking up at the ceiling while our heart rates came back to normal. I pulled the blanket from the sofa down over us.

"You can't stop me from coming back," she said defiantly.

I sighed. Propped my head up with my hand to study her profile in the flickering light. I hadn't noticed the slight upturn of her nose before, and my stomach churned with despair. There was so much I would never know about her. "Syd. I love you, but we're running out of dates. It's awful when something like simple math gets in the way of love, but we can't ignore the numbers. At some point you would have to start visiting me *before* I knew about the power of the talisman, and we both know that's not an option."

She turned her head and looked at me dolefully. Her eyes shone with tears and understanding; she couldn't appear to me before I'd discovered the power because in my natural time, that hadn't occurred. We also had no idea how attempting such a feat would affect our ability to timeblink at all. It's why I'd expressly forbade her to visit before January fifteenth of this year, the day of my first timeblink.

"Surely we can find some dates that work. Early mornings? Late nights? I could stay a few hours at a time. Not weeks. I'll stop being such a time hoarder."

She was digging in. Regretfully, I would have to resort to a different plan.

"You need to be healthy for *him*," I said, placing my hand gently over her belly.

"Him?"

I took a long breath. "I didn't want to spoil it, but you've left me with no choice. Nine months from now, in your present time—November 2020—you're going to visit me here and place our newest family member in my arms. Christopher. My middle name. I met him yesterday afternoon. He's adorable."

She pushed herself upright to face me, her eyes huge and probing, sparkling.

"Do you understand why I don't want you taking any

chances? And before you strain yourself too much with the math, Christopher is one hundred percent my son."

"Are you serious?" she said, barely audibly. "How?"

I flashed her a wide smile. "Well, you see, the man puts his—"

"Stop it! I mean, how did this happen? Like, logistically? I've thought about it a lot, and—"

"You have?"

She blushed and, perhaps unconsciously, rubbed a hand over her belly. "Of course."

"I've thought about it too. And while I *had* been worried about the impact of all of this jumping around in time on the reproductive process, any doubt was quelled when I met our son. He's perfect. At least for now. Hopefully he doesn't start speed-aging or contract some weird timeblinker's lurgy."

"Oh my God, Morley! I love you!" She threw her arms around me, and we kissed urgently. After a few moments she pulled away, dropped her head into her hands and began sobbing. I got up to fetch the tissue box from the kitchen.

"I understand now. I'm such an idiot for ruining it," she said, blowing her nose gracelessly.

"You didn't ruin it. You got lucky. Not every expectant mom knows for sure she's going to give birth to a healthy baby."

"I won't let you down," she said with tears brimming in her eyes. "I'll give Christopher enough love for the both of us."

I drew her toward me. "I won't tell you much about yesterday's visit, apart from the fact that I was angry you took such a huge risk blinking here with baby Christopher, but as I said, I checked him out, and his vitals and general health were right on target."

"How was it even possible? Him coming with me?"

"Apparently there are things we don't know about the

talisman yet. Who knows? Maybe you'll discover how to blink to dates beyond our own lifetimes."

She shook her head rigorously, as if I'd just told her to jump off Chapman Falls again. "No way. I'm leaving things as they are. How could I be so selfish, dragging our son into this mess? I promise, I'll never do that again."

"It's for the best. As much as I would love you to drop in with him as he grows up, it's not safe."

She patted her belly. "My need to introduce him to you obviously trumped any common sense in my brain."

"Truth be told, I'm glad you did it. Now I can die fulfilled."

I briefly wondered if I should share the disturbing news she brought when she visited with Christopher. About the simmering pandemic that was about to rock the world. But I decided it wouldn't be fair to upset her, especially since there's nothing she can do about it anyway. Besides, she gave me a full rundown of the measures she'd been taking to keep herself and her family—*our* family—healthy, and I'm confident they'll get through it just fine.

I reached over and took a folded piece of paper out of my pocket and slipped it into her palm. Her final prescription. No dates or locations. Just a note to the woman I love. A tear raced down her cheek as she stood and picked up her clothes.

A few moments later, I joined her at the window and helped her zip up her dress. While she fixed her hair into a knot at the back of her head, I kissed each vertebra on her long, elegant neck then wrapped my arms around her middle, fastening my fingers over her belly. We stood for a few quiet moments watching stars come to life, glittering over the glassy lake.

"I think you're going to make a kick-ass mother, Ms. Brixton," I said into her ear.

She suddenly pulled away and twirled around to face me, her eyes glistening with tears. She tugged my hands to her chest. "It makes perfect sense now! The peace in your eyes when you took your last breath. You knew about Christopher. You knew you had a son!"

I smiled and pulled her close. Didn't want to let her go. Ever. But after gathering myself, I stepped back, wiping a tear from my cheek. "We shouldn't prolong this."

She took the talisman between her fingers and smiled a big, joyful smile that went right through me. It was true what they say about pregnant women. They do glow.

"I love you, Sydney Brixton," I said.

"I love you, Morley Scott. *Return!*"

<u>Buckle Up...</u>

Fast forward five years where Syd finds herself trapped on a crashing plane with her estranged half-sister, Lainie. As the ground rushes toward them, Syd uses the power of the talisman to timeblink them both to safety.

But when they arrive at Morley's cabin in 2019, Syd discovers three additional passengers have tagged along for the ride, one of them harboring a dark and deadly secret—and intentions that could leave the entire group stuck in the 2019 timeline for the rest of their lives.

Can Morley help Syd and her entourage return to their present, or will they be stranded five years in the past, invisible to their loved ones forever?

Prepare to board **_FLIGHT 444_**, the nail-biting second book in the TimeBlink series by visiting mjmumford.com or by scanning this QR code:

Acknowledgments

I'm deeply indebted to all the people who took time away from their busy lives to read the earliest version of *TimeBlink*, a manuscript so heavy I could barely lift it.

Much of that gratitude goes to Lee Gabel, fellow indie author, writing mentor, and self-publishing guru who extended his virtual hand to help me more times than I can count.

Also to author, Nick Tooke, whose forthright advice to "trim the fat" resulted in a second draft with just enough bulk to flatten a spider rather than a cat.

To all my beta readers who weren't shy about pointing out typos, plot holes and timeline inconsistencies. For informing me that my characters invariably ran up the stairs "two at a time" and who thought Syd was being too harsh on her mother. And for all the positive comments, too; without those little nuggets of sunshine, I might've abandoned the project altogether.

To my family for supporting me along this journey, especially my husband, Alistair, who never got jealous about my cozy relationship with a certain handsome pediatrician. To my sister, Erin, who devoured that first draft in two days when she should have been visiting with me. Much love.

To my mom, dad, and Auntie Momo who all left this Earth shortly before *TimeBlink*'s debut—I feel their presence in every milestone, silently encouraging me from beyond.

To my talented editor, Amanda Peters, who threw that unruly beast of a manuscript onto the operating table, excised the noxious bits, and handed it back to me in pieces. It was my job to put the story back together—stronger, leaner, and better than it was before. Surely Amanda will recognize her voice amongst these pages.

And of course, to you, my dear reader. I appreciate you hunkering down for a few hours and getting to know Syd and Morley and the rest of the gang on such an intimate level. If they've entertained you, please consider leaving a quick review on your favorite book platform. Even three words (*"A thrilling ride!"*) helps other readers find their way to The Syd Brixton TimeBlink series.

Finally, a heartfelt thank you to everyone engaging with me on social media, sharing thoughts via my **Cabin Crew** newsletter, and championing my books in the vast literary cosmos. You are the superstars in my universe. Keep shining!

About the Author

MJ Mumford is a huge fan of domestic thrillers, suspense stories, and anything to do with time travel. Her debut novel, *TimeBlink*, is a unique blend of all three genres under one cover.

When she's not dreaming up devious ways in which to torment her characters, MJ enjoys tap dancing, practicing yoga, and traveling to faraway places with her husband. Curiously, MJ never leaves home without her own trusty dragonfly talisman—an object rumored to be more than just decorative.

Join **MJ's Cabin Crew** for updates on new releases, book deals, exclusive contests, and a dash of time-traveling fun that'll brighten your inbox.

Scan the code below or visit mjmumford.com to subscribe.

Follow MJ Mumford

facebook.com/mjmumfordwrites
instagram.com/mjmumfordwrites
tiktok.com/@mjmumfordwrites

www.ingramcontent.com/pod-product-compliance
Lightning Source LLC
Chambersburg PA
CBHW021109110726
47900CB00007B/2108